Praise for **MR. WR...**

"The most sidesplittingly funny, s... tension–filled book I've read in a ... not to fall in love with Olivia and Colin, but most of all I dare you not to fall in love with Lynn Painter's writing!"

—Ali Hazelwood, author of *Loathe to Love You*

"Smart, sexy, and downright hilarious. *Mr. Wrong Number* is an absolutely pitch-perfect romantic comedy."

—Christina Lauren, international bestselling
author of *Something Wilder*

"One of my favorite rom-coms, heavy on the 'com' and steamy on the 'rom'!"

—Jesse Q. Sutanto, author of *Four Aunties and a Wedding*

"This book is an absolute blast, a classic rom-com setup with a modern twist. Lynn Painter's clever, charming voice sparkles on every page."

—Rachel Lynn Solomon, author of *Weather Girl*

"Filled with laugh-out-loud situations and moments of heart-fluttering swooniness, *Mr. Wrong Number* is a true romantic comedy. . . . I'll read anything Lynn Painter writes and I'm already impatiently waiting for her next book."

—Kerry Winfrey, author of *Just Another Love Song*

"Painter's mastery of sexy slow-burn tension and whip-sharp banter will have readers smiling from ear to ear. Perfect for fans of Christina Lauren, this deeply relatable romance proves that love may be closer than you expect."

—Amy Lea, author of *Exes and O's*

"A delightfully messy heroine and world-class banter make this oh-so-sweet story of hidden identities and mixed (text) messages impossible to put down. *Mr. Wrong Number* is a sexy, hilarious, compulsively readable rom-com."

—Emily Wibberley and Austin Siegemund-Broka,
authors of *Do I Know You?*

"*Mr. Wrong Number* by Lynn Painter is the perfect rom-com. Charming, laugh-out-loud, and full of heart, it is a sheer delight of a reading experience. . . . Gorgeous, glimmering, and guaranteed to make you laugh!"

—India Holton, author of *The Wisteria Society of Lady Scoundrels*

"Olivia's . . . chemistry with Colin sings. This is sure to charm." —*Publishers Weekly*

"If you like your romances steamy, then *Mr. Wrong Number* by Lynn Painter is sure to leave you hot and bothered in a good way." —PopSugar

"Olivia's journey will keep you eagerly turning pages."

—*USA Today*

"A laugh-out-loud, sexy rom-com . . . Painter's hilarious voice and vibrant characters are a breath of fresh air in this highly enjoyable romance." —BuzzFeed

"Readers have a rom-com sure to please—an especially good fit for fans of *The Hating Game* or television's *New Girl*."

—Shelf Awareness

Berkley titles by Lynn Painter

MR. WRONG NUMBER

THE LOVE WAGER

HAPPILY NEVER AFTER

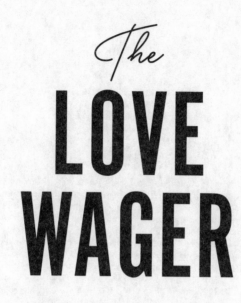

The

LOVE
WAGER

LYNN PAINTER

BERKLEY ROMANCE

New York

BERKLEY ROMANCE
Published by Berkley
An imprint of Penguin Random House LLC
penguinrandomhouse.com

Library of Congress Cataloging-in-Publication Data

Names: Painter, Lynn, author.
Title: The love wager / Lynn Painter.
Description: First Edition. | New York: Berkley Romance, 2023.
Identifiers: LCCN 2022032815 (print) | LCCN 2022032816 (ebook) |
ISBN 9780593437285 (trade paperback) | ISBN 9780593437292 (ebook)
Subjects: LCGFT: Novels.
Classification: LCC PS3616.A337846 L68 2023 (print) |
LCC PS3616.A337846 (ebook) | DDC 813/.6—dc23/eng/20220708
LC record available at https://lccn.loc.gov/2022032815
LC ebook record available at https://lccn.loc.gov/2022032816

First Edition: March 2023

Printed in the United States of America
6th Printing

Book design by George Towne

for Kevin

~~I love the way you always have a camping bag~~
~~fully packed & ready~~

~~Thank you for never overcooking my steak~~

~~Remember that time we brought vodka~~
~~on the train to New York~~

~~Because you can pick things up with your toes~~

~~2 words: Pam Anderson's car repairs~~

~~Your hands are big like Romance Man~~

~~Because I know that you would somehow know what~~
~~to do in a zombie apocalypse~~

~~Because you continue to choose me over a dog~~

~~You are the wind beneath my wings~~

~~I miss the newsie hats you wore~~
~~when we lived in Chicago~~

You are my happy place. ♥

Chapter ONE

Hallie

"Can I get a Manhattan and a chardonnay, please?"

"Sure thing." Hallie glanced over her shoulder as she handed one of the bridesmaids a Crown and Coke, and—wow—the dude shouting his order over the way-too-loud version of "Electric Slide" was *very* attractive. He was obviously in the bridal party, all tuxxed-up and looking fancy, and even though she'd sworn off dating, Hallie couldn't help but appreciate the dimples and the Hollywood bone structure. "You want that with bourbon?"

He leaned on his forearms and stretched a little closer to the bar as the hotel's ballroom hit peak noise level. "Rye, please."

"Nice." She reached into the gray plastic bucket and pulled a California bottle out of the ice. "Interested in trying it with orange bitters?"

His dimples popped and he raised his eyebrows, his blue(?)—yes, blue—eyes squinting. "Is that a thing?"

"It is." She poured the chardonnay and set the glass in front of him. "If you're not a moron, you'll love it."

He coughed a laugh and said, "I consider myself to be generally non-moronic, so hook me up."

Hallie started making his drink, and she kind of felt like she knew the guy. He seemed familiar. Not his face, necessarily, but his voice and super-tall height and twinkly eyes that made him look like he was down for any wild adventure.

She glanced at him as the dance floor's disco lights lit up his dark hair. Shaking the mixer and straining the Manhattan into a glass, she struggled to come up with it; *think, think, think*. He was looking back in the direction of the head table when it finally hit her.

"I know how I know you!"

He turned back around. "What?"

It was so loud that Hallie had to lean a little closer to him. She smiled and said, "You're Jack, right? I'm Hallie. I was the one who sold you the—"

"Hey!" he said, smiling, but then he set his hand on hers and gave her hard-core eye contact as he leaned closer and said, "Hallie. Listen. Let's not mention—"

"Oh. My. God." A blonde appeared beside him—*where did she come from?*—and her eyes narrowed as she looked at Hallie and said, "Seriously, Jack? The *waitress*?"

"Bartender," Hallie corrected, having no idea why she felt the need or what was up Superblonde's ass.

"You leave me alone for ten minutes—at your sister's wedding, for God's sake—to canoodle with the *waitress*?"

"Um, I can assure you there was no canoodling," Hallie said, painfully aware that the woman's loud voice was drawing a lot of attention. "And I'm a bartender, not a waitr—"

"Can you just shut *up*?" Superblonde said it through her nose and with the last word pitched an octave higher, like she was a Kardashian.

"Would you relax, Vanessa?" Jack said through his teeth, glancing over his lady friend's head as he tried to get her to quiet down. "I don't even know her—"

"I saw you!" She was near-yelling as the DJ switched to "Endless Love," which did zero to mute the outburst. *Where is the damn "Macarena" when you need it?* Superblonde—Vanessa, apparently—said, "You were leaning in and holding her hand. How long has this—"

"Come on, Van, it's not—"

"How long?" she shrieked.

The guy's jaw flexed, like he was clenching and unclenching his teeth, and then he said, "Since this morning."

Vanessa's mouth dropped open. "You were with her *this morning?*"

"Not *with me* with me," Hallie said, looking around, horrified by the implication. She worked part-time at Borsheim's on the weekends. The guy, Jack, had come into the store that morning, and she'd helped him find a ring.

And not just any ring.

The ring.

The *will-you-be-a-jealous-hag-for-the-rest-of-my-life?* ring.

"She sold me this." Jack pulled the ring box out of his pocket and practically shoved it in the girl's face as he spoke through his teeth. "I bought this for you, Vanessa. Christ."

The box was closed, but Hallie knew a stunning square-cut diamond engagement ring was nestled inside. He'd seemed like a funny, charming guy when she helped him shop for the perfect ring, but if he thought Vanessa was soul-mate material, he clearly only thought with his penis.

Or he really was a moron.

"Oh, my God," Vanessa squealed, her face transforming into sunlight as she beamed at Jack and put her hands over her heart. "You're proposing?"

He stared at her with his eyes squinted for a solid five seconds before saying, "I'm not *now*."

Her smile slipped. "You're not?"

"Fuck, no."

Hallie snorted.

Which made Vanessa swing her narrowed, long-lashed—wow, those had to be extensions—eyes in Hallie's direction. She hissed, "Is something funny?"

Hallie shook her head, but for some reason, she couldn't make her lips straighten. She kept hearing the dude's *fuck, no* and it was just so *chef's kiss*.

Before she had a second to realize what was happening, Vanessa grabbed the full glass of chardonnay from where it was sitting on the bar, turned her wrist, and threw its contents in Hallie's face.

"Gahh!" Cold wine splashed over her face and burned her eyes. Thankfully, as a bartender, she was surrounded by towels and happened to have one on her shoulder that very second. Hallie snatched it and wiped her face. "Hey. *Van*. What is your *problem*?"

"*You* are my prob—"

"I am *so* sorry," Jack said, looking pathetically apologetic. He grabbed Hallie's towel and started patting her dripping neck, which made Vanessa's eyes grow huge.

"Oh, my God, she's fine," Vanessa said.

"Yeah, I'm fine," Hallie said, giving him a weird look as she snatched back the towel. "She seems great, by the way."

He leaned in closer, so all Hallie could see was his worried face and blue eyes. "You're good?"

"Yeah." Hallie blinked and felt like she needed to take a step back. He was too attractive for human eyes, especially when giving that sort of eye contact. She ran her tongue over her freshly chardonnayed lips. "Well, actually, no, if I'm being honest. See, I recommend this chardonnay all the time because it's supposed to be oaky with a rich, buttery finish, but it's actually dry as hell with a bitter, stale aftertaste."

He pursed his lips.

"I've been perpetrating a lie this entire time."

His eyes crinkled around the edges and his mouth twitched. He looked like he was about to smile, but Vanessa grabbed his arm, and his face changed to straight-up pissed. Hallie watched his throat move as he swallowed, and then he turned around and said, "We need to go."

Her perfect eyebrows went up. "We're leaving?"

"Something like that. Come on."

He led his pretty monster away from the bar, and Hallie mopped up before getting back to making drinks. The entire dustup had happened over the course of a mere three minutes, but it'd felt like an eternity.

The other bartender, Julio, asked out of the side of his mouth as he poured vodka into five shot glasses, "What the hell was that?"

"Just a batshit jealous girlfriend." She moved to the other end of the bar and took an order for two whiskey sours. "I don't even know them."

"Oh, my God, Hallie Piper, I thought that was you!"

Hallie looked up and did a double take. *Seriously, universe?* "Allison Scott?"

Ugh. Allison. They'd gone to high school together, and she was one of those girls who was technically super nice but always managed to word things in ways that made people feel like shit. Hallie hadn't seen her since graduation eight years ago, and she definitely hadn't missed her.

"Oh, my God, you are the most adorable bartender I've ever seen." Allison beamed and gestured toward Hallie's damp black tank top and black jeans. "Seriously you're, like, a cutesy-cute drink-maker in a movie."

Allison was giving total Alexis Rose vibes, and Hallie pasted a smile on her face. "Can I make you something?"

"My boyfriend is one of the groomsmen," she said, apparently not in want of a beverage. "And when he ran over and said there was a catfight at the bar, I never in a million years would've guessed it'd be my super-anal, buttoned-up friend Hallie."

Did she just call me super-anal? Dear God. Hallie explained, "It wasn't a catfight, it was more like a misunderstanding between a couple, with me as collateral damage."

"I caught the end of it." She smiled, and there was something kind of Grinch-like in the slow, satisfied climb of it. "So what're you doing these days? Besides tending bar at wedding receptions. Are you still with Ben?"

A man behind Allison held up two empty Mich Ultra bottles, so Hallie grabbed two from under the bar, opened them, and set them down as she said, "Nope. I am living life Ben-free."

"Oh. Wow." Allison's eyes got big, like Hallie had just declared herself a serial killer because she'd had the audacity to break up with the guy who had once been considered their high school's star running back. She asked, "So what's your sister doing?"

Hallie wanted to scream when she heard the DJ announce the bride-and-groom dance, because it meant there would be no mad rush for drinks; people loved watching that sappy shit. Allison could loiter and make uncomfortable small talk for as long as she wanted, and that made Hallie daydream about chandeliers accidentally falling from the ceiling and crushing annoying ex-friends.

"Um, Lillie is engaged to Riley Harper—they're getting married next month. Do you remember him from—"

"Oh, my God—she's engaged to Riley Harper? He was our homecoming king, right?"

Hallie nodded and wondered if she was the only one who didn't think of their high school's homecoming royalty as *ours*. To her, the king was just some guy who wore the crown at a dance.

"Wow, good for her." Allison looked impressed. "Does she work?"

"Yeah, um, she's an engineer."

"You have *got* to be kidding!" She gave her chic, bobbed head a little shake. "You guys are like *Freaky Friday* chicks now."

"What?"

"You know. You were always the responsible, together one, and Lillie was the hot mess shit show. Now she's an engineer with a fiancé, and you're single and waiting tables and getting into bar fights." She smiled like it was hilarious. "Crazy."

Allison finally ordered a drink and stopped torturing

Hallie, but as soon as she walked away, her words played on a continuous loop in Hallie's mind. *Hot mess shit show. Hot mess shit show.*

God, *had* they *Freaky Friday*ed?

Hallie spent the next half-hour freaking out in her head while she continued slinging drinks on autopilot. *Hot mess shit show.* It wasn't until "Single Ladies" came on that she embraced her inner Beyoncé and remembered that everything was going to be okay.

Because she wasn't a hot mess shit show at all. Rather, it was just her "winter."

After she and Ben split up (aka after he realized he didn't love her at all), Hallie had decided to treat it as "the winter of her twenties." A cold, dormant season that would lead to a bountiful spring. She'd moved out of Ben's place and gotten a cheap apartment—with a roommate. She'd taken two part-time jobs, in addition to her career, to pay down her student loans in half the time.

The way she saw it, she was going to take advantage of her man-free time. She was going to live like a peasant and hustle her ass off. They were dark days, her winter season, but soon they would all pay off.

"YOU."

Hallie looked up, and the guy—Jack—was charging straight toward the bar. He looked intense—serious face, tie hanging untied around his neck—and his eyes were fixed on her.

"Me?" She looked behind her.

"Yes." He stopped when he reached the bar and said, "I need you."

"I beg your pardon?" Hallie tilted her head and said,

"And what happened to that sweetheart of a girlfriend of yours? Van, was it?"

"We need a bartender in the back." Jack ignored her remark, looking at Julio and saying, "Do you think you can spare her for a bit?"

Julio glanced at Hallie, trying to gauge her reaction, before saying, "Yes, but I believe the bride scheduled—"

"She's the one who sent me over. I'm her brother."

"First of all, don't talk to *him* about *me* like I'm not here. Just because I have breasts doesn't mean I'm incapable of speaking for myself. Second of all," Hallie said, irritated by the hot guy's obvious sexism, "I don't strip or give lap dances, so if 'the back' is code for something creepy, count me out."

That made Jack smirk down at her, the kind of smirk that made him look both amused and irritated all at the same time. "First of all, I was told that Julio here is the banquet supervisor, so your breasts played no part whatsoever in my choice of conversation partner."

"Oh," Hallie said.

"And second of all," he added, "you give off a strong no-creepy-lap-dance vibe, so I can assure you 'the back' is not code for anything untoward."

Hallie pushed back the stray hairs that'd fallen out of her ponytail, feeling a bit like an idiot. "Well, good."

"Follow me?"

"Why not?" Hallie came around the bar and followed Jack as he walked through the throngs of wedding revelers—most of whom smiled at him like he was their favorite cousin, even though he appeared oblivious—and when they got to the kitchen door, he pushed it open and held it for her.

"Thanks." She walked through the door, only to see that the kitchen was absolutely deserted. "Um . . . ?"

She turned around, and Jack had dropped his jacket on top of a box of bananas and was rolling up his shirtsleeves. He raised an eyebrow and waited for her to speak.

"I thought you said you needed a bartender."

"I do." He casually hopped up onto the stainless-steel prep counter and sat so that his long legs were dangling in front of him. "You got me dumped, so now it's your job to get me drunk."

Seriously, dude?

"Yeah, um, you aren't the king," Hallie said, "and I'm not interested in being your personal serving wench. But thank you."

"Dear God, I don't want you to serve me." He pointed to the spot beside him on the counter. "I just thought since we both had drinks thrown in our faces by Vanessa Robbins to-night, it might be nice to drown our troubles and share a bottle."

Hallie tilted her head and looked at the bottle of Crown Royal next to him.

Why did that sound so damn appealing?

Jack

He could see it in her face the minute she decided. It was like her entire posture relaxed.

And then she smiled.

Not that it mattered, but she was cute. A short little redhead with a big smartass mouth. He actually *had* remem-bered her from the jewelry store, not because of how she looked but because she'd been funny as hell as she'd shown him a slew of engagement rings.

She came over and hopped up on the counter, crisscrossing her legs and reaching for the bottle. "First of all, please tell me *you* dumped *her* and not the other way around."

"Obviously," he said.

"Thank God." She rolled in her lips and said, "Second of all, I had nothing to do with the implosion of your relationship."

"Well, if you hadn't said anything . . ."

"Then you'd be engaged to a jealous psycho." She narrowed her green eyes and said, "I think you actually owe me a ginormous thank-you."

"Is that right?"

"For sure," she said, and then she raised the bottle to her mouth and took a big drink. After she finished, she wiped her lips with the back of her hand. "Are you intentionally forgoing mixers? Because I'm okay with that, but since I'm only five feet tall, I'm going to get there a *lot* quicker without Coke."

He actually felt like smiling when he said, "Fine by me."

"And are you paying for the Uber that I will surely need when we're finished?"

Jack took the bottle as she held it out to him and noticed his fingers looked gigantic next to hers. He said, "If it comes to that, then yes."

"Oh, it will definitely come to that." She gave him another sarcastic grin and turned her body so she was facing him. "I plan on getting floor-licking drunk tonight, buddy. Like, can't-remember-your-own-mother, vomiting-in-the-elevator-phone-box, is-she-okay-or-should-we-call-someone hammered. Care to join me on the thrill ride?"

Jack tipped the bottle into his mouth and let the liquor burn through him, warming a path all the way down to his belly. She watched him the whole time, and he wasn't sure if it was the buzz or not, but he was suddenly all-in on getting drunk with the funny bartender. He wiped his mouth and handed the bottle back to her.

"So . . . ," she asked, wrapping her slim fingers around the bottle, "you in, Best Man?"

Jack couldn't help but smile as he said, "I'm all yours, Tiny Bartender."

Chapter
TWO

Hallie

Hallie opened her eyes and groaned.

Dear God.

Her temples pounded as she reached up and tugged on the blanket that was covering her head. She welcomed the cool air on her face once she was out from under the heavy duvet, but then she saw her own terrifying reflection in the mirror directly in front of her.

Mirror?

Wait. What?

It was then that she realized not only was she lying sideways across the bed, but she was at the foot of the bed. And that it was not "the" bed, as in a bed familiar to her, but "a" bed, as in one she didn't know.

Oh, Gawd.

No, no, no, no.

Scenes from the night before came flying at her, and she tried her best not to move the mattress as she sat up and peered over her shoulder. There was a sea of white bedding between them, sheets and comforters that were twisted and resting in haphazard piles, but yes—there was definitely a body sleeping at the top of the bed.

His head, which appeared to be facedown on the pillow, was covered in thick, dark hair that she knew firsthand felt surprisingly soft when you grabbed it by the handful. Visions of the two of them up against the door of the hotel room flashed through her mind, her hands buried in his hair while he—

GAH.

Nope.

She had to get out of there. She saw her pants and one of her shoes next to the door. Her other shoe lay in the bathroom doorway as if kicked off . . . oh, yeah, she remembered kicking it off and sliding out of her pants before the door was even closed behind them.

Idiot, idiot, idiot.

She moved gingerly, because the last thing she wanted was to wake the guy. Really, how awkward would *that* be? *Hi, remember me? I'm the bartender who ripped all the buttons off your tuxedo shirt.* No, Hallie needed to stealthily get dressed and get the hell out.

She rolled off the end of the bed, landing on her hands and knees. She forced herself not to think of how dirty the hotel carpet was—*bodily fluids everywhere and the black light thing arrrgghhhh*—and she popped her head up to make sure he was still sleeping.

Yep. Still asleep, or possibly dead, so that was good.

She dropped back down and crawled toward her pants. She imagined she made quite a picture, high-speed crawling in a tank top and a pair of pink underwear that had tiny squirrels plastered all over them. She was pretty sure this was a low point, but she didn't have time to slow down and find decorum.

When she reached her pants, she jumped into them as fast as she could, pulling them up as quietly as possible while staring at the bed. *Please keep sleeping.* She jammed her feet into her flats as she looked around the room for her bra.

Where in the hell was that underwired nightmare?

She checked the bathroom, then leaned down and checked under the bed, but that thing was nowhere to be found. She tiptoed closer to the bed. It was probably tangled in the bedding, but at that moment Jack made a noise and flipped over onto his back, which made her drop down to her knees again.

Why, you dipshit? screamed her brain in a very high-pitched and hysterical voice. *What is the point of that? You're not invisible if you're crawling, you tool.*

Hallie got back to her feet and realized that any other time, she'd be stopping to gaze upon the man's body. His broad chest, tight stomach, and ropy biceps were downright lovely, and she kind of maybe thought she might've bitten his forearm last night, but she was too focused on escape to enjoy the view.

She squinted and tried to see her bra amongst the sheets, but Jack seemed to be breathing a little louder, so she couldn't risk it. She said, *"Fuck it,"* and gave up, grabbed her purse, and left, letting out her breath when the door finally shut softly behind her. She could feel her bralessness as she jogged down the corridor, and she crossed her arms when she had to stop and wait for the elevator. There were girls who looked good doing the whole braless-in-a-tank-top vibe—Kate Hudson, perhaps—but Hallie was not one of them.

She looked obscene.

A housekeeper walked by with her cart, and Hallie wished she hadn't seen her reflection in that hotel room mirror, because she knew just how awful she looked. As she waited for the elevator, she wondered if Jack would be mad that she left without saying goodbye. Like, what was the etiquette in that situation? She'd never been a one-nighter kind of girl, so she didn't know what sort of niceties were usually exchanged before parting. *Maybe I'll creep on social media and DM him. "Thanks for the brilliant bonk, bro—"*

But before she could even finish that thought, it hit her.

She didn't know his last name.

The elevator doors opened, and she was in the grips of a tiny freak-out as she went into the shiny car and hit the lobby button.

Holy shit, I don't know his last name!

It wouldn't be hard to figure out Jack's full name if she wanted to. His sister had been the bride, and he'd bought a ring at Borsheim's the day before. It'd be easy for Hallie to find out his last name, but that wasn't the point.

She took a deep breath as the elevator reached the ground floor with a ding.

The point, she thought as she took the walk of shame through the lobby with bed head and unsupported bouncy bits, was that she had just woken up in the hotel room of a guy whose full name she didn't know. Her undergarment was missing, her head was throbbing, and she had to walk by a front desk that was staffed with employees who all knew she'd worked the wedding the night before.

Hot mess shit show, indeed.

And when Robert, the sweet, grandfatherly bellman who usually showed her pics of his kids when she worked a wedding, gave her a friendly wave before dropping his eyes down to her chest and quickly looking away in extreme awkwardness, she realized that she'd definitely hit rock bottom.

Jack

Jack entered the hotel restaurant, his head throbbing as he walked toward the big table where his entire family was having post-wedding brunch. He was thirty minutes late, and there was approximately zero chance his mother wouldn't notice.

"Jackie boy," his uncle said, smiling and holding up a bagel in greeting.

"Morning, Uncle Gary," Jack said, trying to smile but finding it incredibly difficult. Did it have to be so goddamn bright in there?

"You're so fucking late," his older brother, Will, said, half smiling as he chewed what looked to be eggs. "Ever heard of an alarm?"

Jack ignored him and pulled out the empty chair next to Colin, his best friend and brand-new brother-in-law. He lowered himself into the seat and said, his throat dry as hell, "Where's Livvie?"

Colin's eyes narrowed. "You look like shit."

"Gee, thanks."

"She's at the buffet getting more pancakes," Colin said, gesturing with his head in the direction of the long line of tables.

Jack looked at the buffet, and sure enough, his sister was

filling her plate. "Dear God, if they have pancakes, you're missing your flight for sure."

Olivia and Colin were leaving for a two-week Italian honeymoon once brunch was over.

"She's bottomless, right?" Colin said, smiling, and Jack was too hungover—and suddenly too single—to sit there and listen to Colin get gooey about his sister. He was glad they were happy, but that didn't mean he wanted to soak that shit up when he had a throbbing temple and an apartment to move out of.

"Hotcake junkie for sure." Jack got up and went to the buffet, careful to keep his head down to avoid conversations with cousins and aunties. There were far too many family members milling about the restaurant for his comfort, so he grabbed a plate and headed straight for Olivia.

"I cannot believe," she said, somehow knowing it was him without turning her head, "that you're this late and Mom hasn't said a word yet. If I'd been thirty *seconds* late, every relative would've heard about it."

"True." It was a well-known fact that Jack was the favorite child of Nancy Marshall.

"You smell like whiskey," she said, narrowing her eyes and finally looking at him. "Wow—and you look like you slept in a dumpster. What the hell happened to you?"

Jack raised a hand to his hair; did he look that bad? "Nothing."

"Seriously, though," she said, tilting her head a little. "What *did* happen to you? After Vanessa lost her shit, you kind of disappeared. Where'd you go?"

He wouldn't have told anyone else, but he'd always been able to be completely honest with Livvie when he screwed up. "Got hammered and had a sleepover with the bartender."

Her mouth dropped open. "You did not."

He shrugged.

She looked at him like he'd just declared himself a cheeseburger, and then she took his plate and set it beside hers on the buffet table before grabbing his arm and pulling him toward the back of the restaurant.

"Livvie—"

"Just come on."

She led him to a spot right beside the kitchen door, and when they stopped, she blinked up at him and said, "Jack, you were ready to propose twelve hours ago. How in God's name were you able to sleep with a bartender?"

"Do you mean, like, the mechanics of the act?"

She growled and said, "No, I mean that I *know* you were upset about Vanessa last night. I saw your face after you came back in from the parking lot."

He didn't want to think about that, dammit. "So?"

"So a random hookup is a terrible idea that isn't going to help your loneliness."

"I'm not *lonely*, for fuck's sake."

"Really." She crossed her arms and gave him a *bullshit* look. "You didn't rush everything with Vanessa because you were sad and didn't want to be alone?"

"Shut up, you nosy little shit," he muttered, giving in to a smile when she rolled her eyes and pinched him.

"Listen, you tool," she said, dropping her hand and looking serious. "We both know you loved the idea of a relationship so much that you forced it; you admitted it to me when you were drunk at Billy's a couple weeks ago, remember?"

He wished he'd never shared that little morsel.

"Well, it sucks the way things went down, but I think this is a blessing," she said, taking her phone out of her jeans pocket and looking at the display. "Now you're free to find someone you actually have something in common with. Someone you have *fun* with."

Just to mess with her, Jack said, "Well, I had a lot of fun with the bartender last night."

"Spare me the details and let me give you the log-in for the dating app for which you're now a paid subscriber."

"What?" He groaned and glared at his sister. "What did you do?"

"Nothing, really." It was her turn to shrug and smile. "After you said what you said at Billy's, I might've set up an account for you and paid the fees, just in case."

"In case . . . ?"

"In case you and Vanessa crashed and burned."

Jack sighed.

"Instead of making a fuss and pretending to be mad," she said, looking pleased with herself, "just say 'Thank you, Liv.'"

"Butt out, Liv," he replied.

"I'll butt out," she said, "as soon as *you* log in."

Hallie

A week later

"You have to be kidding." Chuck stabbed one of the Swedish meatballs on his plate and gave Hallie a look. "This could not have actually happened."

"Which part don't you believe?" Hallie asked her best

friend as she dipped one of her french fries into ketchup. "The botched proposal or the drunken hotel sex?"

"More water?" The waiter looked down at her, and her cheeks got hot as her words hovered there. *Drunken hotel sex.*

"Um, no, thank you."

Chuck started laughing and squealed out the words *hotel sex,* which made the waiter laugh, too. Once the server left, Chuck said, "All of it. I mean, what are the odds that you go to work, and all of *that* happens to you?"

Hallie jammed a few fries into her mouth and said, "I'm having trouble believing it myself, and it happened a week ago."

"So the guy was attractive?" Chuck popped a meatball into his mouth. "Good under the covers?"

"He was hot for sure." Hallie pictured Jack's face and said, "Good under the covers, against the wall, in the elevator . . ."

"Remind me again why you're complaining . . . ?"

"I'm not complaining." Hallie took a sip of her Diet Pepsi and said, "I'm just disgusted with myself for being a hot mess shit show. Waking up at the foot of a stranger's bed was the impetus I needed to change, and now I'm going to turn over a new leaf."

"Your old leaf wasn't fine?" Chuck rolled his eyes and said, "Because it seemed totally fine to me."

"When Ben and I broke up, everything I started doing was supposed to be temporary. But I'm still living like a college student, Chuck. I need to get a real apartment without a roommate, a fresh haircut, some new clothes, perhaps a meaningful relationship—"

"Oh, my God," he interrupted, his eyes huge and his mouth full of meaty ball bites as it hung wide open, his beard and mustache framing that mouth with orange fuzz. "Does this mean you're finally gonna do it?"

Hallie inhaled through her nose, closed her eyes, and gave a nod of confirmation.

Chuck had been trying to get Hallie to go on Looking 4TheReal, the dating app where he'd met Jamie (his now fiancée), since Hallie and Ben had broken up. He was convinced the app was some sort of magical matchmaker, and he never shut up about it.

Ever.

Chuck had never had a serious relationship before Jamie (which Hallie knew because she'd known him his entire life—he was also her second cousin). He was hands down the most unique person she'd ever met, but his inability to fit into a conventional category had always worked against him in the dating world.

Chuck was funny, smart, and handsome. But instead of watching football, he liked Disney movies. Instead of listening to hot singles, he listened to Broadway cast recordings. The man liked anime more than most humans did, and Hallie and Chuck had been known to spend hours texting about Bravo reality TV.

But a mere month after joining that stupid app, he'd found his soul mate.

And anyone who'd ever seen them together had no doubt that Jamie and Chuck were soul mates. She, too, was gorgeous, and Jamie *loved* his quirks, adored anime, and quickly joined Chuck and Hallie's reality TV group chat.

Hallie had always said she "wasn't ready" when he brought it up, because the mere thought of dating after Ben made her mildly nauseous, but now she felt almost desperate. It had occurred to her in the shower that morning that in addition to all the other ways she wanted to jump-start her life, she wanted love.

She did.

Maybe that made her pathetic, but she suddenly didn't want to be alone anymore.

"Can I call Jamie?" Chuck pulled his phone out of his pocket. "She's going to lose it—"

"No." Hallie shook her head. Jamie was like an overcaffeinated version of Chuck, and there was no reining her in when she got excited. "No Jamie."

"You know I'm going to call her the second we're done, right?"

"Yes, but I can't handle both of you at once. You're too much."

His mouth slid into a big stupid grin. He said around a dreamy sigh, "We are, aren't we?"

"That wasn't necessarily a compliment."

"Quit being a grouchy twat." Another thing about Chuck—he watched a ton of British programming, so he threw out the t-word all the time. He stood and dragged his chair around the table, not stopping until he plopped down right next to her. "Let's create a profile while we're here, so all you have to do later is sip on a glass of wine and scroll through the available gents."

"You make it sound like shopping," she said, watching as he grabbed her phone, punched in the passcode (030122), and immediately went to work on creating an account.

"It's basically the same thing," he replied, his eyes on the phone. "Only instead of the perfect handbag, you're shopping for the one person in the universe who will make you blissfully happy for the rest of your life."

"Well," Hallie said, irrationally excited underneath her feigned cynicism, "that sounds impossibly simple."

"Shut up and let me do this for you."

By the time they'd finished dinner, Hallie had an actual dating profile on an actual dating app. Chuck had come up with kickass verbiage that made her sound fun and smart, and she was genuinely excited to go home and start "shopping."

Only when he pulled up in front of her dumpy apartment to drop her off, Chuck gasped loudly and said, "Holy shit."

"What?" Hallie looked out the window but couldn't see any reason for alarm.

He said, "I think there was a delay or something when you told me about your new leaf, because your words are just hitting me right now. Did you say you're going to get your own place—without Ruthie?"

"Yes."

He tilted his head. "Have you thought about how you're going to tell her?"

Hallie narrowed her eyes and said, "I'm just going to tell her. We're both adults—it'll be fine."

"Really?"

"Yes."

"Really?" His voice was higher in pitch.

"Yes."

"Really."

"Ohmigawd, Chuck, quit trying to freak me out. I will tell her, she will accept it with a smile, and all will be well."

He nodded and said, "Sure it will."

Chapter
THREE

"Oh, thank God you're home!" Ruthie, Hallie's roommate, stood in the doorway as if she'd been waiting for Hallie to return. She was wearing an apron that had a man's ripped chest and speedo-covered junk drawn on it, and the cartooned Speedo had the words *Got meat?* written across the crotch in cursive. "I just made banana bread, and I want to get your opinion. Butter or no butter?"

Hallie moved around her and went inside. "My opinion on butter or no butter?"

Ruthie cackled at that. "Your opinion on the bread. Do you want butter or no butter?"

Hallie was stuffed and didn't particularly care for banana bread at the moment, but she didn't want to disappoint Ruthie, either. Especially when she was about to disappoint her by telling her she wanted to move out. "No butter, please."

Ruthie literally ran over to the galley kitchen and threw open the refrigerator door. She yelled, "You know how *I* feel about butter, so I'm slathering this whole motherfucking loaf—aside from your slices—with all the Country Crock the law will allow."

Hallie dropped her purse on the floor and slid out of her shoes. "I never doubted that you would."

Ruthie Kimball was an absolutely ridiculous person. She was the sister of one of Hallie's coworkers at the jewelry store, which was how they came to be roommates, and Hallie had never met anyone in her entire life who was so shockingly unpredictable. She genuinely had no idea—ever—what Ruthie was going to do, say, or think.

Ruthie drove a motorcycle year-round, whether it was sunny or snowing. If the temps were subzero, Ruthie bundled up in her puffy coat before climbing on her "hog" and proceeding to ride around town as if it were normal to have icicles forming underneath your nose.

And yes, she actually referred to it as her hog.

Incessantly.

Ruthie loved baking but hated cooking. She had piercings everywhere, but cried like a baby if she needed to get a shot. She took care of Hallie like an older sister, baking for her and ironing her clothes if she left them in the dryer for too long, but she scream-fought with her actual sister on a regular basis, shouting things into the phone like "I'd love to run you over with my hog but your stupid fucking ass would probably fuck up my suspension."

Before throwing the phone off the balcony.

Somehow the phone was never broken when she retrieved it. Soft grass, Hallie supposed.

Ruthie was thin, of average height, and kept her head

completely shaved because she found hair to be "so damn dumb." She had huge blue eyes and a pixie face—like Ariel from *The Little Mermaid*—and she belonged to a super-secret fighting club that left her bruised more often than not.

Last year, Hallie had briefly worried that someone was hurting Ruthie and the club was an excuse, but when she finally got the nerve to broach the subject, Ruthie broke down in tears because she was so touched by Hallie's concern.

And then she showed Hallie about a hundred pics of bruised, bloody women teeing off on each other in what looked to be a basement.

"Here it is." Ruthie sprinted out of the kitchen and shoved a plate into Hallie's hands. "My grandma's recipe, but with a little Ruthie magic."

"You know I can't do edibles," Hallie said, staring down at the hunk of bread. "They do random testing at my day job."

"Drug-free, I promise. The magic is actually the addition of a drop of vinegar."

Hallie sniffed the bread before taking a bite. "Mmmm," she moaned, meaning it. "That is so good!"

"Yay!" Ruthie turned a cartwheel, knocking over the floor lamp. Once she had it back up, she said, "Listen, I gotta go take a nap. I met this girl named Bawnda who does synchronized swimming, and she said she'll teach me if I don't mind working overnights."

"So . . . this is a job?"

"Did you not listen to me?" Ruthie smiled and shook her head, like Hallie was the ridiculous one. "I will be *swimming* in a synchronized fashion overnight tonight—not working—so I must sleep now. Night-night, Hallie baba."

"G'night," Hallie said, glancing at the microwave in the kitchen that showed it was seven p.m.

So much for discussing moving.

Chuck: So? How goes it?

Hallie picked up her glass and finished the last swallow of Riesling and responded with *so far so good.* She'd been sitting in bed with her phone since eight, just scrolling through available men. She'd heard the jokes about dudes being terrible at making good profiles, and it was actually not a lie. If what she'd looked at so far was indicative of the male species as a whole, there was a strong belief amongst them that a picture of a man with a fish was the pinnacle of profile photos.

Chuck: Jamie wants to know how swipe-happy you are.

Hallie snorted and responded: I haven't swiped on anyone yet. I'm just window shopping.

Hallie was surprised by the eye candy. She simply hadn't expected there to be so many relatively attractive specimens. But she could already see the cross-referencing problems.

Hallie: One guy is cute, but he's wearing a backward hat and holding a beer in every single picture.

One guy has a nice face, but the fact that he thinks a picture of him holding up the head of a deer he killed by the antlers is a good profile photo tells me we wouldn't be soul mates.

Hallie rolled her eyes when Chuck responded with Just go for it, you pussy!

She was going to take her time, and maybe not even swipe on anyone for a few days. There was no hurry—

"Holy shit!" Hallie squinted and clicked on the profile. It sure looked a lot like the wedding dude . . .

Jack Marshall.

Yep.

Dear God, it was him.

The photo was from the wedding—she'd remember him in that tux forever—so it had to have been taken the night she ended up sheet-wrestling with him. He was smiling and holding up a glass of champagne—giving his toast—and man, he was a stunningly beautiful human.

Whoa, he was a landscape architect. That sounded . . . interesting.

For some reason, she was surprised to see a guy like him on the app. He'd seemed too confident and dashing to be single.

But then she remembered.

Holy God, the man had bought an engagement ring and planned to propose a *week* ago. A week ago he'd been in love enough to pop the question, and now he was already on the app looking for ladies?

Clearly there was something majorly wrong with him.

She didn't know what possessed her, but she wanted to mess with him. Hallie clicked on the message box and started typing.

Hey, Jack, it's Hallie, the bartender from your sister's wedding! Why haven't you called? I really thought we connected and you were going to call, but . . . did you lose my number?

She sucked in a breath when she saw the conversation bubbles. Holy crap, he was responding! He was probably freaking out at the thought of a throwaway one-nighter coming for him, and something about that idea made her cackle.

After a few minutes, a message popped up:

Jack: Hey there, Hallie. I had a lot of fun with you after the wedding, and you seem like a cool person.

Oh, dear God, he thought she was serious. She typed:

God, Jack, relax. I'm just messing with you. I DO NOT WANT TO DATE YOU.

Jack: Uh wow ok.

Hallie: I saw your profile when I was shopping for soul mates and thought it would be fun to give you a heart attack. I never gave you my number and I didn't expect you to call.

Conversation bubbles popped up and went away. Popped up and went away. Finally he messaged: So . . . you're on here legitimately looking for love?

Hallie: Pathetic, right? But don't worry, you're not on my list.

Jack: First of all, I'm doing the same thing, so I'm going to go with no, that's not pathetic. Second of all, I can't believe I'm not on your list after our amazing night together.

Hallie groaned and looked up from the phone; she couldn't believe he brought it up. But she also couldn't hold in the smile as she typed: We were just so hammered—it's all kind of a blur.

Jack: But . . . ?

She let out a little squeaking sound and kicked her feet against the mattress, unable to believe they were having this conversation.

Hallie: But what? All in all, it was a fine time.

The reality was that the night had been red-hot and so good, but she'd also been crazy drunk, so that meant nothing. Kermit the Frog might've been able to scratch her itch if enough whiskey had been involved.

Jack: Fine?? Come ON, Hal.

For some reason, his usage of her shortened name did something to her stomach as she messaged: Not talking about this. I remember nothing.

That was a bald-faced lie. She remembered absolutely every minute of that night, from the very first kiss in the kitchen, to her hand on the elevator stop button, right down to the feel of his callused palms as they gripped her hips in that king-sized hotel bed.

Jack: You don't want to hear about the adorable noise you make when you . . .

Hallie: PLEASE GOD NO

Jack: I was going to say *sneeze*. But I do have your bra if you ever want it back.

Hallie: Where was it??

Jack: Underneath me. It was there the whole time you were belly-crawling around the bed.

Hallie did scream then, but quietly enough so Ruthie didn't come running in with one of her fencing foils.

Hallie: You were fake sleeping?!

Jack: It was obvious you wanted the quick exit, so who was I to get in the way?

She was laughing when she responded with: Well, um, thank you, I guess . . . ?

Jack: You're welcome, it would seem . . . ?

Hallie readjusted her pillows and got comfortable. So tell me something, Jack Marshall. What is it you're looking for on this app? TRUTH ONLY.

She wasn't actually expecting the truth, so his answer shocked the hell out of her.

Jack: Okay, truth only. The truth is that I have a lot of friends and a good job, and I date often enough, but I want someone important in my life. {insert your laughing at this desperate guy here}

Hallie would've been touched by the sentiment if it weren't for the fact that he'd *had* someone important in his life last week. Talk about a desperate need to be in a relationship. Still . . .

Hallie: Truth only: I'm looking for pretty much the same thing. She didn't want him to misunderstand, so she added: Only not with you, so don't get all squirmy again.

Jack: Rest assured, I will not squirm.

Hallie: Well, good luck on finding your perfect woman.

Jack: Good luck to you, as well. Your bra is hanging from my rearview mirror if you change your mind and want it back.

Hallie: Sicko.

Jack: Or I could keep it as a trophy.

Hallie: Y'know, you seem to be a little obsessed with that night.

Jack: I'm a little obsessed with that elevator.

Hallie's stomach dropped and she managed to type Good night and good luck, Sicko before exiting the app and turning off her light. She needed sleep, and a lot of it.

Jack

Jack stared at the phone, wearing a stupid smile.

He shut down his computer—enough work for one night—and went into the kitchen. There were still boxes scattered here and there, but the new place was actually starting to look good. He opened the fridge and grabbed the milk, his mind still on Hallie as he poured a glass.

Yes, she was hot, and he still couldn't stop himself from replaying moments of that night over and over again in his head, but it also seemed like she was genuinely *fun*.

It'd been too long since he'd had actual fun.

He wasn't interested in dating someone he'd had a one-night stand with, and she'd made it abundantly clear she wasn't interested in *him*, but in a weird way, he was glad she'd decided to mess with him on the app.

She'd reminded him that fun was a thing.

He put the milk back in the fridge and shut the door, only to see Mr. Meowgi staring up at him with those annoyingly adorable kitten eyes. It was day three of Jack being a cat owner, and the jury was still out on whether he'd made a terrible mistake.

"This is for me, buddy," he said, picking up the cup. "Not you."

It—*he*—meowed, and that tiny little squeak made the cat seem even smaller and more helpless than he actually was. Jack rolled his eyes, shook his head, and set the glass of milk on the floor.

"Here, you little beggar," he said, crouching down to pet the irritating fluffball as he started drinking his milk. "But this is the last time."

Meowgi started purring, as if to say, *Sure it is.*

Chapter
FOUR

Hallie

"What do you think?"

"I love it." Hallie looked in the mirror and smiled. She'd had the stylist take off four inches and give her some color, so now she had a shoulder-length bob with some subtle highlights, and she'd also gotten her brows done. Between that and the clothes she'd bought online the day before, she really did feel like some sort of "new" Hallie Piper.

She was making it happen, dammit.

She'd taken the day off to fix her life, and she was so glad she had.

First, she'd put in her notice at both of her part-time jobs. It was mind-boggling, all the time she was going to have for . . . well, pretty much anything, now that she would only be working from nine to five.

After that, she'd spent the morning looking at apartments, and an hour ago, she'd put down a security deposit on a new place. She hadn't meant to—she hadn't even told

Ruthie she was moving yet, and it was only the first day of the hunt—but the last building she'd visited had been too perfect to pass up. It was downtown, a former-hospital-turned-modern-apartment-complex, and it was amazing. City views, rooftop patio, indoor pool, sports bar in the lobby; she was obsessed. It was a little north of her price point, and waaaaay smaller than the others she'd looked at, but she liked it enough to make it work.

It was just so grown-up.

And as she walked to her car after leaving the salon, she found that she couldn't stop smiling. Everything was falling into place, and it made her feel good. She wasn't a hot mess shit show any longer.

She even had a date that night.

She'd been messaging Kyle through the app for a couple of days, and she wasn't sure how she felt about their impending evening. He had a job and seemed like a nice person, so that was good. But their exchanges were pretty . . . matter-of-fact. Yes, he could be amusing, but they didn't have the kind of banter that made Hal want to lock herself in her bedroom and chat all night, either.

Yet.

She kept reminding herself of that fact—they didn't have it *yet*. Hopefully they would meet up for dinner, share a few laughs, have a great time, and proceed to banter the hell out of each other from that night forward.

A girl could dream, right?

When Hallie got home, she was relieved that Ruthie was out. Her roommate had left a note on the door—**WENT FLISPING IN GD. BE BACK TOMORROW**—so she was alone for the entire night.

Hallie rarely understood Ruthie's notes. She had no idea what *flisping* was, but it probably involved being upside down with strangers or something. And *GD*—that was anybody's guess.

She turned on some music, opened a bottle of Lucky Bucket, and started putting on makeup. She had two hours before she was meeting Kyle, which she considered to be the perfect amount of time to pick an outfit, do her makeup, and maybe catch a tiny buzz to ward off those first-date-in-eighty-five-years nerves.

She was in her closet, rummaging for the black pants that made her butt look amazing, when her phone buzzed. She looked down at it and saw she had a notification from Look ing4TheReal. She clicked on the app and realized she was actually hoping that it was Kyle canceling.

The notification stamp (a heart, of course) was on her inbox. Hallie clicked on it and immediately felt disappointment when she didn't see Kyle's name.

The message was from Jack, the wedding guy.

Jack: Hey, Tiny Bartender. How's the hunt going?

Hallie sat down on her shoe shelf. You sure know how to make it sound romantic.

Jack: Sorry. Let me start over. AHEM. Have you found a man via your Soulmate-Home-Shopping-Network app?

Hallie: It is exactly like that, isn't it?

Jack: Only instead of beautiful jewels for just 14.99, you're mulling over whether to proceed to checkout with Dude Who Caught Fish.

Hallie snorted. I kind of want to just sit here and mock our dating lives right now, but I actually have a date tonight.

Jack: The hell you say.

Hallie: I clicked on the first guy I could find without a dead creature in his profile pic (who didn't look like an ogre) and he seems nice.

Jack: Wow. He seems nice? Is that where the bar is set—at nice?

Hallie: What's wrong with nice?

Jack: Nothing. I mean, I'm sure you cannot LIVE without getting railed by a "nice" guy.

Hallie: Eww, can you explain the particulars of what getting "railed" entails? It sounds . . . torturous. Painful. I think you might be doing it wrong.

Jack: HAL.

She started giggling in her closet and texted: I'm mocking the terminology and THAT IS ALL.

Hallie saw the pants hanging at the end of the rack, so she grabbed them and went back into her room.

Jack: I will concede that getting railed is a shit phrase. May I toss out other options for your approval? I also have a date this evening and want to make sure I don't say something offensive.

Hallie: WAIT. YOU HAVE A DATE? Was it through the app? Tell me everything.

Jack: Settle your ass down. Yes, through the app. According to her profile, she's blond, works in marketing, and enjoys running and getting railed.

Hallie: Haha. Are you excited?

Jack: Honestly? Not at all. She seemed cool when we talked, but there's something nerve-racking about meeting up with someone for the first time when there's already a love/dating expectation. Chemistry is the thing that matters most on a first date, and it's so hard for it to be there naturally when everything feels formulaic.

He hit it on the head, why she felt like she was getting ready for a job interview. Hallie dropped her sweatpants and stepped into the good pants.

Hallie: HARD feel that. Hopefully we will both have delightful evenings.

Jack: Your lips to Ditka's ears. Also, what about "bonked"?

Hallie: First of all, Ditka is not God. And nope, that's not it.

Jack: Blasphemy. How about "getting hammered."

Hallie: Sounds like a home repair.

Jack: Getting my parts jostled?

Hallie: Are you going in for your annual checkup or having sex?

Jack: I've got it. "Playing a little in and out"?

Hallie: You are a child, a tiny little man boy who will not be getting bonked, hammered, jostled, or railed if you say any of those things.

Jack: What about "making love"?

Hallie: Vomited in my mouth a little.

Jack: FINE. I'm just taking her out for food and conversation now. You ruined everything.

Hallie: Well, good luck, Jack.

Jack: Good luck to you, Tiny Bartender.

Hallie: I'm not a bartender anymore, FYI.

Jack: You'll always be MY tiny bartender, but what happened? Did they fire you for getting railed by the best man at a wedding you worked?

Hallie: Ignoring your dipshittery to say that I quit both of my part-time jobs to be a full-time grown-up.

Jack: So if I want to return that engagement ring . . .

Hallie: You'll have to bother someone else.

Jack: Too bad. You're quickly becoming my favorite person to bother.

Hallie: Later, Jack.

Jack: Later, TB.

Hallie: You do see why that cannot be a thing, right?

Jack: My apologies for calling you an infectious disease.

Hallie: I hope you never have to say that to me again.

Jack: You should be so lucky.

Jack

"Why are you smiling like a jackass?" Colin asked.

Jack looked up from his phone, and Colin was watching him like he'd lost his damn mind. He replied, "Why are you staring at me like a creep?"

Colin flipped him off, and Jack set down his phone and said, "Your wedding bartender is fucking hilarious, if you must know."

"So you two are talking now?" Colin asked, picking up a wing and raising his eyes to the wall of TVs above the bar.

"Not like that." Jack finished off his wings while he told Colin about the app and his conversations with Hallie. "And don't mention it to Liv. I don't want her to think it's a thing when it isn't."

Colin grinned. "Your sister doesn't have a lot going on right now, so this really *would* get her mind firing."

"Poor Livvie," Jack said, laughing.

The morning after their wedding, the Uber driver who was supposed to take Colin and Olivia to the airport accidentally ran over her foot. Thankfully, he just got her toes, so no surgery was required, but they had to reschedule the honeymoon because she couldn't even wear a shoe over her swollen, broken toes.

"She's okay," Colin said, still wearing the dumb smile he always wore when he talked about Liv. "I took her to Barnes & Noble, so she's in bookish heaven at the moment."

"She probably doesn't even care about the foot anymore."

"Right?" Colin wiped his fingers on a napkin and reached for his beer. "Is there anything you *do* want me to report to her about the dating app, by the way?"

"Oh, shit, what time is it?" Jack looked down at his watch and muttered, "Yeah, you can report to her that I have a date tonight."

He raised his hand and gestured to the waitress that he was ready to settle his tab.

"You just inhaled twelve wings and now you're going to *dinner?*" Colin looked equal parts impressed and disgusted. "Seriously?"

"Yup." Jack picked up his glass and finished the last of his iced tea. If he were being totally honest, he wasn't looking forward to the date. At all. He still felt like shit about Vanessa, but not because he was heartbroken about the breakup or hesitant to move on.

No, Jack felt like a goddamn fool.

If he was sad about Vanessa, it was because he was sad to learn he was wholly lacking in self-awareness and good judgment. He was sad to discover he was too desperate to see things clearly.

Because how had he ever thought he and Van were a good idea?

She was beautiful, and a decent person (when she wasn't being jealous), but they were wildly different. He liked eating wings and watching football, whereas she liked pointing out how disgusting wings were and how pointless football was. He'd grown up with three dogs and was an animal lover, but Vanessa thought dogs had revolting breath and had repeatedly told him that she would never, ever get one.

She'd even said *ewwww* when his dad's dog licked her hand.

Which, honestly, should've been the world's biggest red flag, right? *What kind of a monster says "ewwww" in regard to Maury the Pug?*

Yet instead of parting ways with Miss Dog Hater, he'd purchased a diamond ring for her. He'd ignored everything that should've been obvious to him in his rush for . . . hell, he didn't even know *what* he'd been rushing toward, exactly.

But what if he made that sort of mistake again? Was he so pathetic that he'd blindly latch onto anything pretty and interested?

He forced his neuroses out of his mind and said, "This way I can order something healthy and look responsible."

"You have *got* to be kidding."

"Nope." Jack pulled out his wallet and tossed a twenty on the table. "I'm a genius."

"I think you mean moron." Colin picked up another wing and gave him a look. "Have fun on your date, moron."

Chapter
FIVE

Hallie

Hallie walked into Charlie's, and once her eyes adjusted to the darkness of the restaurant, she looked around for Kyle. It was tough, since she'd only seen the pictures on his profile, but maybe since she was ten minutes early, he wasn't there—

"Hallie."

She turned around at the sound of the voice, and there he was.

Thankfully, his face looked the same as his photo and he was a little taller than her. Overall, her first impression was that he was handsome and had a nice smile. He was wearing a button-down and jeans, and she had no complaints.

"Hey, Kyle." She smiled and put her handbag under her arm. "Nice to finally meet you. You know, um, in person."

"Same, same," he said, gesturing with his arm toward the dining area. "I already have a table over there."

"Perfect," she said, and followed him over to the spot.

Maybe it wouldn't be so bad, she thought. It was just two

people eating food together and talking; she liked both of those things, right? And she felt pretty confident that night, with her new hair, cute cashmere sweater, and full-on makeup, so she was going to throw herself into the magic and see what transpired.

She sat down across from him and picked up a menu, trying to remember what two strangers talked about on a first date.

"I've never eaten here, so you can't blame me if it's shit," Kyle said, giving her a half smile. "Smells good, though."

Hallie nodded. "It does."

She opened her menu and started reading, trying to think of something to say. "Wow, everything looks so good."

"Holy shit, twenty bucks for a burger?" Kyle shook his head in disgust and said, "That better be a gold-plated patty, am I right?"

She smiled and nodded, suddenly nervous about what she should order. If twenty was too much for a burger, would he think twelve was too much for a salad? "Right," she said.

"It's a first date, though, so you order whatever you want, Hal," he said, smiling.

"Okay." She laughed, feeling very uncomfortable all of a sudden, both with his attention to pricing and his comfort in dropping the second syllable of her name. She wanted to tell him that she'd happily pay for her meal, because she totally would, but she felt like he might be the kind of guy who would take that as an insult.

"No lobster, though," he teased, and she'd never been so stressed out by the decision of what to order at a restaurant in all her life.

"Got it."

When the waiter came over, Hallie ended up ordering a side salad and french fries, just to be doubly sure it wasn't too expensive.

After they handed off their menus to the waiter before he walked away, Hallie took a sip of the wine Kyle had ordered before she arrived. When she glanced at Kyle, he was giving her a funny grin.

"What?" she asked, smiling.

He shook his head and said, "That's all you're going to eat? I swear, you women and your diets."

Yes, because the french fry diet is all the rage, Kyle. She just said, "It just sounded really good to me."

"Okay, hon," he replied teasingly, and she reached for her wine yet again.

He started telling her about his job, and it was pretty interesting. He was a diesel mechanic who worked on big Caterpillar machines, and it sounded really cool. There was something super attractive about him as he talked about tools and mechanical things.

Made him seem incredibly capable.

"So what do you do, Hal?" He grabbed a roll from the basket at the center of the table, tore it open, and dipped his knife in the silver bowl of butter. "Something in finance, right?"

She nodded, grabbed a roll, and said, "I'm a tax accountant for—"

"Holy crap, this is fate!" Kyle smeared butter on his bun. "I've been looking for a new tax guy—mine moved to Frisco—and boom, here you are."

I am tax guy? she thought.

He took a bite of his roll, smiled, and said, "How much do you charge?"

Hallie tore off a piece of her roll. "I don't actually do people's taxes; I'm a corporate tax accountant at HCC Corporation."

His eyebrows went down. "But you know how to do them, right?"

"Well, yeah—" she started, but he interrupted her.

"So it'll be some nice side money for you."

She didn't want to seem like a jerk, but she had no interest in doing anyone's taxes. "Yeah, but I don't really need any side money right now."

He snorted and said, "What are you, rich?"

Okay, that condescending tone was not necessary, and she was over it.

"Rich enough to not have to do my blind date's taxes," she blurted out, regretting it immediately when, instead of laughing, his face got really, really red.

Needless to say, Hallie was unlocking her front door at nine thirty p.m. Which, to be fair, didn't bother her all that much. She'd become quite the homebody since she and Ben had broken up, so Netflix and flannel pants were kind of her jam.

An hour later, when she was knuckle-deep in a bowl of popcorn, she got a message notification from the app. *Please don't let it be Kyle*, she thought, imagining him reaching out to see if she'd reconsidered her aggressive opinions. She clicked into her messages and was happy to see it was Jack, not Kyle.

Jack: So . . . ? Did you find a love connection?

Hallie: Hardly. I found a man who got mad when I said I wouldn't do his taxes.

Jack: Oof. Sorry, TB.

Hallie: Didn't I tell you not to call me that?

Jack: Yeah, but I can't help myself.

Hallie: So what about you? How was your date?

Jack: It wasn't a date, it was an interview.

Hallie: She asked a lot of questions?

Jack: NOPE. I asked her questions—so what do you do, did you grow up here, etc. etc.—and she answered each question. Then . . . she didn't say another word but just stared at me or her food.

Hallie: So it was like you were interviewing her and she was . . . ?

Jack: Absolutely uninterested in getting to know me.

Hallie: You didn't say anything about getting your parts jiggled, did you?

Jack: It was jostled, and no. Maybe I should have.

Hallie: Did she seem like soul mate material if she HAD felt like engaging with your junk-jostled self?

Jack: Not at all.

Hallie took a sip of her soda and set it on the coffee table. I guess I'm making an assumption. Maybe you aren't looking for a soul mate.

Jack: No, I am.

Hallie thought of his ex—what was her stupid name? *Cam? Stran?*

Van! *Vanessa.* Okay, so it wasn't really a stupid name, but Hal still couldn't get over the fact that he'd chosen *her.* To propose to. He clearly had I-can't-be-single issues. She didn't really *know* him, other than the fact that he was just as sarcastic as she was, but she still had to ask.

Hallie: Okay, don't be pissed, because I'm not judging, but, like, you JUST broke up with your very serious girlfriend. How can you already be looking for a soul mate?

Jack: It's a fair question, so I'll allow it.

Hallie: Gee, thanks.

Jack: I know it sounds weird, but I think Vanessa and I were just going through the motions. Like, it felt serious on the outside, but it kind of wasn't at all when it came down to what matters. Does that make any sense at all?

She was surprised that it sort of did.

Jack: We made all the big moves—living together, near-engagement—but we weren't especially close in our day-to-day lives.

Hallie put her feet up on the coffee table and wondered if Ben would say that about *their* former relationship. She texted: Were you like roommates who slept together?

Sadly, that was something Ben had said to *her* during his break-up speech.

Jack: That is depressingly accurate.

Yes—totally depressing.

Jack: But regardless of the Vanessa mistake, I'm surprisingly serious about wanting to find someone.

Hallie realized as she read his text that her opinion on Jack had already changed. She still thought he was moving a little quickly, but the way he'd explained the situation with his ex made her think that perhaps he just knew himself well enough to know what he was looking for now.

She texted: For more than just a jostling?

Jack: For jostling 'n' forever. I want to find the person who makes me complete.

Hallie: People really don't use the country 'n' enough anymore.

Jack: We should give it a renaissance.

Hallie: We really should. Hallie 'n' Jack should bring it back.

Jack: What about your soul mate goals? If a Looking4The Real genie appeared and granted your dating wish, what exactly would you want to find?

Hallie: Someone who likes me more than everyone else in the world.

Jack: Likes? Isn't that bar a little low?

Hallie: Well, of course love, but I want to spend forever with my favorite human. The person who cracks me up and gets me and likes the way I think. Romance is nice, but I want to be with the one person where if something happens to me—funny, awful, wonderful—I'm dying to tell them.

Jack: It sounds like you want to marry your best friend.

Hallie: I literally do.

Jack: Good luck. That's a tall order.

Hallie: No taller than your "you complete me" dream lady.

Jack: Somehow, mine seems more possible.

Hallie: Agree to disagree.

Jack: Care to make a wager?

Hallie set down the now-empty bowl of popcorn and reached for the throw on the couch's arm. On what?

Jack: Who finds it first.

Hallie: Doesn't that seem rather cavalier, to make a wager on something we've both agreed is important to us?

Jack: I don't think so, because it's not like a bet is going to make me behave differently to win. I still want the same thing. I just win a prize if I find it first.

Hallie: Ooh—I DO like prizes.

Jack: Right? I already hate this app and blind dates and I really don't feel like continuing. But if there's a fun incentive, and I'm in it with someone else, it might not feel like an endless, depressing chore.

Well, Hallie absolutely understood that. She was already tired of dating, and she'd only been on one date so far. Hallie: It has to be something really good, then.

Jack: Duh.

Hallie started thinking about what she wanted that he might be able to provide for her. Well, what services can you offer?

Jack: (Ahem—elevator) What exactly do you mean?

Hallie rolled her eyes but laughed. He had a way of teasing her about the hotel night that was funny but didn't feel like he was trying to get her back into bed.

Hallie: Example: I'm a tax accountant. I can do your taxes if I lose. And my sister is engaged to a guy who owns a Toyota dealership, so if you're looking for a new Corolla, I can get you the friends and family price. What can you do for me?

Jack: Please shoot me in the face if I'm ever looking for a Corolla, and taxes are for suckers. Regarding what I can provide, I'm a landscape architect, so I can design a backyard oasis that will make you never want to leave the house.

Hallie: Sounds wonderful, but I live in an apartment.

Jack: I have a Parisian honeymoon that I've already paid for.

Hallie could see by the bubbles that he was still typing, but she didn't care.

Hallie: That's it. I want it. I get Paris if I win.

Man, she hadn't been on a vacation since she lived at home and her family went on a trip to Milwaukee. Nothing in the world sounded better to her than traveling abroad.

Jack: Okay, um, I wasn't done (did you not see the text bubbles, Piper?). I was saying that I have a Parisian honeymoon that I bought for Vanessa, but now that I'm not going, I will give you my airline points.

Hallie: After thinking the win would get me a trip to Paris, airline points sounds like winning a coupon. Keep thinking.

Jack: I have a LOT of points. More than enough for you to fly wherever you want for free.

Hallie: Still feels like a loss, but I will take it. Them. I will take your points.

Jack: So what can you give me? We don't have a deal until you give me something good.

Hallie started thinking, racking her brain for something she had that might be valuable to him. She looked around her crappy living room—maybe he wanted an Ansel Adams coffee table book?—and just saw crap.

Hallie: Do you like baseball?

Jack: Yes.

Hallie: When my ex and I broke up (he was very awful so don't judge me) I took an autographed baseball of his just to make him sad.

Jack: You fiend. I don't really get into signed memorabilia, but who signed it?

Hallie: The Cubs.

Jack: As in, Chicago? And which Cubs players?

Hallie: All of them that were on the World Series team.

Jack: Hold please. I need a minute.

Hallie took her bowl and can into the kitchen, set them in the sink, and went into her room. For some reason, she always felt more alone when she was sitting in the living room at night than when she was in the bedroom.

Hallie: WTF are you doing?

Jack: Trying to remember to breathe. Are you telling me that you have an MLB baseball that is signed by the entire 2016 World Series team?

Hallie: Yup.

Jack: I went to Game 7 with my brother, my dad, and my uncle Mack. It was amazing.

Hallie: So the ball works to incentivize your love?

Jack: Absolutely it does. Holy shit, my father will cry like a baby and deem me the favorite child if I give that to him for Christmas.

Hallie: So you have daddy issues. Got it.

Jack: Very funny. This wager is brilliant. I literally will not give up and will date my ass off, just because I need that ball before Christmas.

Hallie: It's September, dumbass. You really think you'll find love by then?

Jack: I will die trying. Doesn't the free airfare put you in the same frame of mind?

Hallie: I mean, I guess. I AM dying for a vacation, but since I'll still have to pay for lodging and daily spending, it feels like something that I'll put off forever.

Jack: This is only fun if you're trying, Hal.

Hallie: I will try, I promise.

Jack: What if I throw in 5 nights at the hotel of your choice?

Hallie: Ooh, I think you've got a deal.

Jack: I'm only agreeing because I know I won't lose, btw.

Hallie pulled back her comforter and climbed into bed. Sure you won't.

Jack: Hey—here's my number so we can text instead of going through the app.

Hallie snorted as she added him to her contacts. You're so obsessed with me it's disgusting. Here's my number.

Jack: Pretty quick with those digits, Piper.

Hallie: Pretty lame with those comebacks, Marshall.

Hallie's phone started ringing, which startled her for a quick second before it made her laugh.

"Why are you calling me?" she asked.

"I had to test the number and make sure it wasn't a fake," he said, and her brain immediately recalled that deep voice from the wedding night.

"So now you know."

"I do." Hallie heard him clear his throat, like he was about to launch into a business presentation, and he said, "So, Hal. Listen. My sister told me about this speed dating event tomorrow night for young professionals. I wasn't going to go, but the whole setup kind of makes sense for our situation, and since we're both on the hunt . . ."

"Are you kidding me right now?" She'd never done speed dating, but she was fairly certain she would fail spectacularly at it. "I didn't think speed dating was a thing anymore."

"I have a flyer," he said.

"That sounds culty," she replied.

"Just come, you chickenshit."

Hallie shook her head and said, "Text me a pic of the flyer and where we should meet. I'll go, but only because I have a roommate issue I don't want to deal with."

"What's her deal? Does she party all night? Eat all your food? Get too loud when she's entertaining visitors?"

"No," Hallie said. "I'm moving into my own place, and I'm scared to tell her because I don't want her to feel sad."

"Oh, my God, Hallie, are you a tender little sweetheart of a girl? I did *not* get that vibe from you. Although, to be fair, you bit my shoulder so hard it left a bruise, so it might've left a bad—and literal—impression on me."

Her mouth dropped open. Hallie was torn between

wanting to tell him to shut up and wanting him to confirm whether she'd actually left a mark, so she just said, "I'm hanging up now. Send the info if you want me to go."

He let out a quiet, deep laugh and said, "Coming your way, TB."

Chapter
SIX

Hallie pushed the door and exited Starbucks, glad she'd decided to show up a little early. She felt ridiculously nervous about talking to so many people, all in a row, and she needed a big old cup of caffeine to soothe her nerves.

Surely that couldn't backfire, right?

She was meeting Jack outside the coffee shop at 7:40 p.m., and then they were going to walk two blocks down to the bar where the speed dating event was occurring. But before she could give the night another fleeting thought, there he was.

He walked down the sidewalk with long strides, and she realized as she watched him approach that he was even more attractive than she'd remembered.

He was tall, dark-haired, and handsome; she'd remembered that. But there was something about his face that screamed mischief. His eyes positively crackled as he looked around the entrance, presumably for her, and then they crinkled at the corners when he saw her and smiled.

Hot damn—it was ridiculous how gorgeous he was.

Wrong, actually. Positively unfair to the rest of the human race.

Thank God he was just her partner in crime, because he had the kind of face that left piles of broken hearts and the occasional bra behind.

"Wow. You look incredible, Tiny Bartender." His eyes dipped down to her fuzzy black sweater and jeans, and she didn't feel like he was checking her out but rather genuinely just saying she looked good that night.

Hallie rolled her eyes and said, "You only think I'm hot because we bonked."

He cocked an eyebrow. "Is that a thing?"

She shrugged and wondered what kind of workout made a chest that broad. A lot of guys had pecs, but he looked like a professional athlete in his black V-neck sweater with the oxford underneath. Like he'd just showered and was ready for a post-game presser.

She got distracted for the briefest of seconds by his prominent Adam's apple and a flashback from the hotel of her tongue on his neck.

"I think it's a cavemannish, biological thing," Hallie said, taking a sip of her coffee and righting her mind. "Your brain knows you copulated with a particular female, so now your ego ensures that you see said female as attractive."

That made his dimples pop. "Is this what you tell yourself so you feel better about finding me wickedly attractive? That you only think I'm hot because we bonked?"

"First of all, I find you painfully *un*attractive. It hurts my eyes to look at you, if I'm being honest."

"Ouch," he said, putting his hands into the pockets of his pants.

"Yeah, *suuuuper* disgusting."

"I get that a lot."

"I'm not surprised. Second of all, it's very unappealing for a man to say 'bonk.' Very ungentlemanlike. Let the ladies use their power words, and you stick to being charming."

"I'll do better. Shall we walk?"

Hallie nodded and they started their way down the street. She caught a whiff of cologne—or soap or something manly—and she was trying to identify the scent when he interrupted her thoughts.

"So. Have you practiced your lines?"

"What lines?"

"Your speed dating lines." He nudged her arm with his elbow and said, "You're going to get a lot of questions thrown at you fast, so you have to be ready."

"Crap, I totally didn't study. Let's practice."

He cleared his throat, changed his voice, and said, "So, Hallie. What do you do for fun?"

Hallie looked at his face and drew a blank. "I, um, I read a lot . . . ?"

He scrunched up his nose. "Said the most boring girl in history. Try again."

"I watch TV," she tried again, and realized that she absolutely was the most boring girl. "I like to run, and nothing thrills me quite like a *New Girl* marathon."

"Come on, TB—strive for interesting. At least throw on an accent. That makes anything sound exciting."

"Okay." Hallie racked her brain before saying in a deplorable Southern accent, "I sew tiny articles of clothing for baby chipmunks, y'all."

"Do you actually do that?"

"Of course not, y'all."

"People from the South don't say 'y'all' in every sentence."

"You sure, y'all?"

"You must stop that at once."

"Fine." She cleared her throat before whispering, *Y'all.*

"On a side note, even if you did sew tiny chipmunk attire, it's only interesting if it involves short-shorts."

"On me or the chipmunks?"

He rolled his eyes. "Obviously the chipmunks."

"Obviously."

He said, "Okay, well, let's hope you don't get asked that question. How about this—what do you do for a living?"

They reached the corner and stopped, waiting for the light to change. She said, "I am a tax accountant. What about you?"

"Amateur taxidermist."

Hallie turned and looked up at him. Something about the teasing glint in his eye made her think of Chris Evans; they both had that "I would prank you so hard" vibe. She attempted a British accent and replied, "That sounds bloody fascinating. How long have you been doing that?"

"Since they told me being an amateur mortician is a felony."

"Well, that is certainly alarming, you frigging bloke, but—"

"No." Jack put his large hand over her mouth, leaned a little closer, and said, "No more accents."

Hallie just blinked up at him.

"Okay?" he asked, not removing his hand as he smiled wickedly, like a dark-haired, blue-eyed villain.

She nodded, and he dropped his palm from her face and said, "I didn't think it was possible for someone to be so bad at accents. I look at the world differently now that I've heard those voices."

"I do a stellar Irish lilt, so your loss by cutting me off."

"I'm comfortable with that."

When they finally reached the bar, Hallie's nerves returned. She reached up and straightened her hair as he grabbed the door and pulled it open. He gave her a relaxed, confident smile as he held the door for her and said, "You ready to date at a ridiculously high rate of speed, Piper?"

"I guess," she said, her stomach dipping as the noise of the bar suddenly engulfed her. "But don't ditch me if you connect with someone, okay?"

His eyes narrowed and his smile softened into something she couldn't put her finger on. He said, "Okay."

They were barely inside the bar when a woman with a microphone started going over the event. She explained it was "typical" speed dating, which meant five minutes per date with a bell notifying participants of when it was time to advance to the next person. Everyone was given a tiny notepad (with the words *Love Happens* on the front—gag) and pencil so they could jot down the names of dates they connected with so they could communicate with them after the event.

"The ladies will be seated at the tables over there," the woman said, pointing toward the side of the room where tables were lined up side by side, "and our gentlemen will rotate."

"Why?" Hallie asked, not really meaning to interrupt. "I read an article last night in which researchers discovered that whichever gender is seated at these events tends to be pickier about their selections, whereas the person approaching is more accepting."

The woman's smile stayed pinned on her mouth, but her eyes lost their perk. "Well, wouldn't that work in your favor, as someone who will be seated?"

Hallie rolled her eyes. "Respectfully, it seems incredibly sexist to have women lined up to receive suitors, don't you think? Aren't we more evolved than that?"

She heard Jack snort, and it was then that she realized she should have kept her big mouth shut.

Jack

Jack couldn't hold in his grin as the participants all looked at Hallie as if she were suggesting they play the game naked or something. They probably thought she was a militant feminist, but he kind of wanted to hear more about the study.

Also, she wasn't wrong.

"I see what you're saying," the lady said, "but this is just the way speed dating is usually done. I can take your ideas back to—"

Jack raised his hand and said, "The odd woman makes a good point. I'd like to sit. Maybe we should randomly draw numbers to decide who sits and who rotates, just to keep it 'modern.'"

He didn't really give a damn who sat and who stood, but he also didn't want Hallie to be ostracized for having an intelligent, independent thought.

"Um," the organizer said, sounding exasperated as she looked around the bar, "I guess we can try something new."

"Very progressive of you," Jack said, and the organizer grinned at him like he'd just given her a bouquet of long-stemmed roses.

"Yeah, thank you," Hallie said, which made the organizer's smile falter. The woman looked at her as if she wished an anvil would fall from the sky and crush her.

"But how will we match up guys and girls when the bell rings?" The woman was beginning to slowly lose her shit. Her eyes shifted around the room and she said, "It won't work."

A blonde said, "We can assign a number to each participant, and when the bell rings, each person moves on to the next number up from theirs."

"No, this is too confusing and we're scheduled to start in two minutes," the organizer said, raising the microphone to her mouth and almost shouting at this point. "We're sticking with our original plan. I'm sorry."

Hallie looked at Jack and he couldn't stop himself from grinning.

"Thank you for trying," she muttered.

"Fuck that," he whispered. "Now I have to stand the whole time."

That made her start laughing.

Which made the organizer glare even harder and say, "Maybe we can make the number thing work. Take five, everyone."

Hallie threw a closed-mouth smile at the girl to her left, who just rolled her eyes like Hallie was a moron, and she said "Hi" to the girl on her right, who gave her a very terse "Hello."

"This is going swimmingly," Jack heard her say to herself, under her breath.

Jack wondered if it was strange that he was having a great

time just watching Hallie be Hallie. "You little trouble-maker."

"I should've kept my mouth shut."

"No, this is funny shit right here," he said. "And what you said makes sense. Why should the ladies get to sit and choose? I want to sit and have them come before me like the king I am."

"That is *not* what I was requesting," she said with a laugh, rolling her eyes.

God, she has a really great laugh.

"Okay, everyone," the organizer yelled through the microphone, her voice tense. "We're running behind, but I think we have it figured out."

She quickly explained the numbering system and how it would work, then shouted out numbers that determined who would sit and who would stand.

In the end, Hallie was still sitting.

And so was Jack, who took the table right beside her. He watched as she stuck her purse under the small table, pushed back her hair, and straightened her posture. She looked nervous as she took a deep breath, and he had no idea why he felt like squeezing her hand in reassurance.

Hallie

"I dare you to use an accent," Jack said out of the corner of his mouth.

"You're not getting the baseball, so knock it off."

"We'll see," he said.

Before she was even ready, the bell rang. Hallie took a

deep breath, and a guy sat down in the chair in front of her. He had a nice face and curly blond hair, and as she smiled and tried to think of something to say, he said, "Hi, I'm Blayne."

"I'm Hallie."

"Oh my God, I used to love *The Parent Trap*."

She forced herself not to roll her eyes. "Same."

"So what's your thing, Hal?" The guy smiled and put his chin on his hand. "Tell me every little thing about Hallister McHalliegirl."

"Nope." She fake-laughed and tried thinking of an answer. "I'm a tax accountant, but you first. Tell me about Blayne."

"I'm a financial planner who lives out in Westfield. I like camping and hiking, anything outdoorsy, and I'm super into yoga right now. Do you like yoga?"

She tilted her head and tried to picture Blayne doing yoga. She could totally see it. "I've really only tried it a couple times."

That was apparently a green light for him to spend the entirety of their micro-date telling her the who/what/where/when of the yoga class he facilitated in a strip mall. He gave her the promo code to get a friends and family discount, and she realized as he expounded upon the benefits of yoga that this speed dating thing wasn't actually a bad promotional idea.

She glanced to her right, and wow, Jack's current date was stunning. She was smiling and talking, and he looked absolutely enthralled by her. Hallie wondered—feeling slightly panicked—if he'd already found his love connection.

The bell rang, and Hallie let out a breath. She wasn't sure

if she was relieved that the first one was over or terrified about the next one beginning.

"Your date looked awesome," Jack said quietly, and when she looked over at him, he was giving her a half smile. "I bet he wears a man bun on the weekends."

"Blayne was nice," she whispered.

"Blayne?" Jack rolled his eyes. "I thought Duckie already covered what a stupid name that is."

"Nice *Pretty in Pink* reference." Hallie straightened as a man began to approach her table. She said out of the side of her mouth, "It looked like you were having a good date, by the way."

"Yeah, no. That girl told me the reason why she's here tonight is because she's committed to the goal of getting married in the next year."

"She sounds perfect, then," she said, smiling at her next date and saying, "Hi, I'm Hallie."

"Nope," she heard Jack mutter before he started talking to his next candidate.

"I'm Thomas," said her new guy. "So how'd your first date go?"

That made her smile and relax a little. "It was fine, how about yours?"

Thomas had nice hair and good teeth, and he was wearing a Dolce & Gabbana shirt; she wasn't certain if that fashion choice worked as a pro or a con. She wasn't sure how she'd expected him to respond, but he leaned a little closer, lowered his voice, and proceeded to rip some poor girl to shreds.

Apparently his first candidate had crooked teeth, split ends, strong perfume, and the audacity to talk about TV shows she liked to watch. He said, "If you don't have anything better to share than your obsession with the *You* series on Netflix, maybe you should just stay home, right?"

Hallie squinted and waited for him to say *kidding.* Because no one could be that dickish, right?

When he didn't, she said, "I'm actually obsessed with Joe Goldberg, too. I can't believe you aren't, Thomas."

He laughed, but then he tilted his head. "You're kidding, right?"

"Not one bit. I wish I had *more* time to devote to TV watching. And more time to talk about it."

He blinked fast, scratched his head, and then said, "Y'know what? I'm going to go get a drink before the bell rings."

"Bye, Thomas."

Aaaaand . . . she'd already lost one. Hallie watched him get up and go to the bar, and she wondered if she would be part of his bad speed dating stories. She crossed her arms and glanced to her right, and was surprised to see Jack looking right at *her*. His date was scrolling on her phone, just leaning on her elbow like she was bored, and Hallie raised her eyebrows and mouthed, *"What did you do?"*

He leaned to his left, closer to her, and quietly said, "We have an agreement. She doesn't want to be here but is just trying to appease her married friend, so I told her we didn't even have to talk if she didn't want to."

That made Hallie bark out a laugh. "Seriously?"

"What did *you* do, to make your guy bolt pre-bell?"

"Why would you assume I was the one who did some-thing?"

"You can tell me, Hal," he crooned in a soothing voice. "What did you say?"

She rolled her eyes. "He just didn't like me."

"Impossible," he said, grinning sarcastically.

She flipped him off.

And then the bell rang.

She watched Jack's date thank him, and they shared a smile of commiseration.

"I don't want to do this anymore," Hallie said quietly.

"Me, neither," he agreed. "Should we bolt? There's a Taco Hut on the corner, and I need a burrito." He looked dead serious.

"Can we?" she asked. "Won't that throw off the numbers?"

"Nah," he said, turning his gaze to the woman sitting down across from him as he spoke to Hallie in a low voice. "There are two of us, so it'll still be even. If these two aren't love matches let's go when the bell rings."

Hallie met her next candidate while wearing a huge smile, eager to finish the date quickly and painlessly. "Hi, I'm Hallie."

"Nick," the guy said, giving her a very nice smile.

Nick looked good—as in, someone she might actually be interested in dating if appearances were all that mattered. He was wearing a Yankees hoodie and jeans, he had dark hair and light eyes, and his smile was easy, like he did it a lot.

"Nice to meet you, Nick," she said. "How's your night going so far?"

He gave her a look with his eyes, like *come on*, and they both laughed as she said, "Okay, I get that. So, um, what do you do for a living, Nick? I think that's what I'm supposed to ask you."

"That *is* the norm, isn't it?" He leaned back a little in his chair and said, "Well, I don't actually do the work thing at all."

Hallie laughed, but he didn't change his expression.

So she said, "You're, um, like, in between jobs right now?"

He shook his head. "I'm in between *no* jobs. I grew up with money and invested it well. I've got enough to live on, so why would I want to work?"

"Wow," she said, shocked and awed by his honesty. And wealth. "You're literally living the dream."

"Right?" He crossed his arms across his chest and said, "I just need a wife and a few kids now."

Hallie nodded but didn't really know what to say. She rubbed her lips together and came up with, "So what do you do all day, since you don't have to work?"

She didn't know what she'd expected, but it wasn't, "I play a *lot* of *COD* and *Madden*."

She laughed, but then his eyebrows went down like he didn't know what was funny. Like he'd meant it for real. She said, "When you're not, like, traveling the world, right?"

He shrugged. "I don't really like to travel. I'm a total homebody."

She nodded, even though she absolutely didn't relate. She knew she should move on, but she had to know more. "So tell me what you do on a normal day. Like . . . you wake up at nine, and then you . . . ?"

He went on to tell her that he never got up before noon; it was bad for his sciatica. After he was up, he pretty much just played video games all day until dinner. He usually went out to a restaurant, then hit the bars if they were "jumpin'."

"Don't you get a little bored?" Hallie rolled her eyes and said, "I mean, I'm sure you don't, but it just seems—"

"I have a lot of money, Hallie," he said. "If I get bored with my awesome life—which I won't—I'll just buy a new one."

"A new life?"

"Sure," he said, shrugging like he didn't care about anything, and she found him to be utterly fascinating.

"What do you usually eat for breakfast?" she asked.

He gave her a weird look. "Apple Jacks."

"Pour them yourself, or does the maid do it?"

"The cook," he replied.

"In a crystal goblet, or normal bowl?"

"Normal bowl."

The bell rang and the guy leisurely got up, like he was in no rush. Because, y'know, he wasn't—he had all the time in the world. *Fascinating*. Hallie said, "It was very nice meeting you, Nick."

He gave her a chin nod. "Same, Hallie."

"You ready?"

Hallie turned to her right, and Jack was there, looking down at her with his eyebrows raised. "We have to go now, before—"

She grabbed his arm and started for the door. "Let's get out of here."

Chapter
SEVEN

"The guy was lying."

"I don't think so." Hallie picked up her beer and said, "He didn't talk about cars or houses or anything braggy that would score him lady points; he literally just said he doesn't work because he doesn't have to."

"I bet we see him drive away in a Kia," Jack said. "With a taped-on bumper."

Hallie drained the rest of her beer and said, "I bet we see him drive away in a Kia with a taped-on bumper and a pile of diamonds in the trunk."

He gave her a look. "Diamonds, she says."

"Diamonds." Hallie grinned at Jack and was shocked that she was having a great time. She'd assumed the night would be an awkward bust, but since they'd left the date-a-thon and snagged an outdoor table at Taco Hut, she was actually having fun.

"Here you go." The waiter set down Hallie's taco basket

and said, "Two chicken tacos with cheese on the bottom for you."

Jack looked at her and gave his head a slow shake, like she was ridiculous.

"And four steak tacos with the works for you."

As soon as the waiter walked away, Jack said, "Seriously, Piper? Cheese on the bottom?"

Hallie shrugged and picked up one of her tacos. "If it's on top of the lettuce it doesn't melt, and what is the point of cold, hard cheese?"

He just looked at her for a long moment, and then he said, "I have no idea."

It was a gorgeous night, the downtown streets were buzzing with activity, and she herself was buzzing from the two quick beers. Jack had been wildly entertaining as he described in great detail the conversations he'd had with his candidates, and he'd thrown his head back and laughed his ass off when she told him about the TV-hater.

"So speed dating sucks." Jack drained the last of his tequila on the rocks and set the glass on the table dramatically. "Let's never do that again."

"Agreed."

"Want another one?" he asked.

She shook her head. "No, thanks. I'm going to have to go camp out at Starbucks for an hour as it is to get rid of this buzz."

"Pathetic. What happened to my Crown-guzzling buddy?"

"She hit rock bottom when she found herself in a stranger's hotel room."

"Whoa." Jack looked offended. "You consider me your rock bottom?"

"No," she said, laughing, "but I consider the *event* my rock bottom."

"Well," he said, looking amused, "I thought your rock bottom was an amazing fucking time."

Hallie laughed at the absurdity of the situation. Being with Jack was so different than being with Ben; it was so chill. Although it was ridiculous that she was even comparing the two, since she barely knew Jack Marshall.

"Okay. Jack." Hallie cleared her throat and looked straight into his devilish eyes. "I only know you in the context of rock-bottom night and the dating app. But we don't really *know* each other, do we? Are you from here? How many siblings do you have? What does a landscaping architect do?"

"You're obviously stuck in the speed dating line of questioning," he said. "Yes, I grew up here. I have a sister, Olivia—she was the bride on the rock-bottom night—and a brother, Will. I also have a sister-in-law, a brother-in-law who happens to be my best friend, and two nephews."

"And the job . . . ?" Hallie was picturing someone who did yard landscaping, which she knew wasn't correct.

"Um," he said, grabbing a straw from the center of the table and unwrapping it. "The easy definition is that I design outdoor spaces. What about you? Is being a tax accountant as exciting as it sounds?"

"I know—it's a job that's literally used in movies to show how boring a person is." Hallie laughed. "Want the viewer to know how bad your date was? Just say he was a tax accountant and that's all the characterization needed. But it's not boring to me. It's lame, but there's something very satisfying about numbers and reconciliation."

Hallie watched as Jack started winding up the clear straw

like she and her friends used to do in high school. He said, "I think that's really—"

"Don't say cool. It's not cool. I like my job, but in no way is it cool."

He gave a little laugh as he held out the straw and gestured for her to flick it. "Fine, it's lame as fuck."

"Easy"—she flicked the straw and smiled at the loud pop—"that's my career you're talking about."

"What do you want from me, Hal?" He dropped the cracked straw onto the table. "Tough to please much?"

She leaned back in her chair and kicked her legs all the way out in front of her. It was such a nice late-summer night, and she was glad she was out enjoying it instead of at home in her jammies.

"So how long have you been single, TB?"

Hallie glanced at Jack, and he looked ultra-relaxed, too, leaning back the exact same way as he looked at her with friendly curiosity and no judgment.

"Um . . ." She looked down at the date on her phone. "A year . . . ?"

"Holy shit." He looked at her like she'd just professed herself to be a llama. "You're kidding me, right?"

"Why is that so shocking?"

She knew why. That dude had had a ring in his pocket less than a month ago and he was already back out there—obviously he was all about relationships.

"It's not," he said, looking at her with a tiny crinkle between his eyebrows. "But when you said your whole winter-of-your-twenties thing, I assumed it was a fresh breakup."

"Oh." That made sense.

"So . . . you've dated during that time, haven't you?"

She cleared her throat. "Before joining the dating app?"

He just gave her a *duh* look.

"Um, that's a no, then."

"Oh my God, TB, you are blowing my mind," he said, and it was obvious he'd never considered someone could live their life without dating for that long of a stretch.

"That's not that long, you know," Hallie said. "I just didn't want to rush into something I wasn't ready for."

"That's smart, actually," he said, and looked like he meant it.

"And it *was* the winter of my twenties." She started explaining her thought processes and goals of the past year, feeling compelled to defend her actions even though he wasn't asking her to.

"So you figured since your douchebag ex had broken your heart, you were going to spend the next year being miserable . . . ?"

"Oh, my God, you're missing the point on purpose. I used that shitty time to save more money and improve myself so I'd be ready to take on the world when my spring arrived."

He quirked an eyebrow. "Is this your spring?"

She tilted her head and squinted. "I think it might be."

After that they decided to walk back to their cars. She told him about Ruthie and he didn't believe her that someone could be so unique, and then she told him about her new apartment. When she told him where it was, he suggested they walk to it so they could check it out at night and make sure the neighborhood wasn't shitty.

On the way there, he pointed at the Carson building and said, "That's my old building."

"For real?" Hallie looked up at the high rise that was like a historical monument in Omaha. "Fancy."

"My roommate made a shit ton of money and let me move into his condo and pay next to nothing on rent, so I was basically a mooch."

"I've always wanted to see the inside of the building. They used to light it up every Christmas, and I always wondered what it looked like up close."

"Wanna go in?"

"What?"

"Come on." He grabbed her hand and yanked her toward the entrance.

"Jack—"

"Just shut up and come on." He walked right up to the keypad beside the door and pressed a button.

A second later, a voice came out of the speaker and said, "Yes?"

"Olivia, it's Jack. Can I show Hallie your apartment?"

"Who's Hallie?" the woman—Olivia—asked.

"Jack, come on," Hallie whispered, feeling like an idiot all of a sudden.

"She's the wedding bartender," Jack said.

"Wait—your dating buddy?" Olivia asked, sounding surprised.

"Bingo."

"Come on up."

Hallie gave him side-eye as the door buzzed open. "Who is she and how does she know about me? Obsessed much?"

He gave her a tiny shove. "She's my sister, Olivia, the one who got me on the app—that's the only reason she knows."

"So your sister is—"

"Married to my former roommate and best friend. You were at their wedding."

"Ahh, she was the bride." Hallie followed him into the building, and the early-twentieth-century structure did not disappoint. Everything was meticulously designed and maintained, so it was almost like stepping into a fancy building from the past.

"I miss this building," Jack said, leaning against the wall after knocking on his sister's door. "So quiet."

After a few seconds, the door opened and his sister—whom Hallie remembered the minute she saw her—smiled warmly. "Well, hello. It's so nice to see you when my brother's date isn't throwing wine in your face."

Hallie smiled back. "Right?"

"Where's Col?" Jack asked, leading Hallie inside as Olivia held the door open.

"Colin," Olivia yelled, "your little play friend is here."

A door opened, revealing a room that looked like an office, and a guy walked out. She remembered him from the wedding because he was quite possibly the most attractive person she'd ever seen, and he grinned when he saw Jack.

"Did you come over for the game?" He walked over to the living room and picked up a remote. "Three minutes left in regulation."

"I missed the whole damn thing," Jack said.

"This is Hallie, by the way," Olivia said, hobbling into the room. "Hallie, this is my husband, Colin."

He smiled from across the room. "The wedding bartender. Nice to formally meet you."

She felt a little weird about the fact they both seemed aware of her existence, but then Jack said, "My entire family sees you as a hero because you broke up me and Vanessa."

"*I* didn't do anything," she said.

"Don't ruin it." Olivia laughed. "You're like a legend."

Before Jack had a chance to give her a tour of the condo, Olivia linked her arm through Hallie's and said, "We're going out on the balcony to chat. Don't bug us."

Jack

"Is she going to ask Hallie a hundred questions?" Jack asked, watching Olivia close the sliding door behind them.

"She's *your* sister—what do you think?"

Jack looked at the girls through the window. "Maybe I should go out there."

"Do you care, though?" Colin tipped back his bottle, drained the last of it, then said, "I mean, if she's just a friend, who cares if nosy Liv pokes around?"

"Y'know what?" Jack stared at Colin for a second. "You're right. It doesn't matter."

"She's cute, though."

"Huh?"

"Your bartender. Not too hard on the eyes, right?"

Jack looked at Hallie, chatting with Olivia out on the balcony.

No, she was not.

He'd barely noticed her looks the first time he'd met her at the jewelry store, probably because she'd been such a smartass while showing him rings, but now he found that fact pretty tough to believe.

Her green eyes, that lush mouth, the way she fell into easy laughter—TB was fucking hot. The image of her in those squirrel panties popped into his head, and he quickly pushed it away. That ridiculous undergarment shouldn't have been sexy, but it sure as fuck had been on her.

Dammit.

It felt important that he forget—or at least *try* to forget—their sexual details and history. He liked their partnership (friendship?), and he didn't want to get confused by attraction.

Again.

Hallie

"So." Olivia sat down on a deck chair, propped her foot on the small matching table, and said, "Jack told me you're, like, perma-wingmen to each other, is that right?"

"That's actually a perfect description." Hallie sat down on the other patio chair, relaxing a little since it was clear she wasn't trying to grill her or something. "We're both trying to find someone through the app, so we commiserate."

"But the two of you . . . aren't . . . like, interested in each other at all?"

"God, no." Hallie shook her head and said, "We're absolutely platonic."

"And you've actually discussed that you aren't into each other?"

"Wait, are you thinking he's into me or something?" Hallie asked. "Because he's totally not."

"No, no, not at all," she said. "Can I be honest with you?"

"Of course."

"Jack's kind of a hot mess right now. He's always breezed through life, enjoying flirty-fun relationships with women like an overgrown child. But last year—"

Olivia leaned her head toward the door, making sure no one was coming out.

"Last year, his life was kind of upended. First, Colin and I fell in love and moved in together, so he kind of lost his best friend. Then our uncle Mack, his favorite relative and totally his hero, passed away suddenly."

Hallie remembered Jack mentioning that his uncle Mack was with them at *the* baseball's corresponding game. "Oh, I'm so sorry."

"It's okay. But for Jack, it was like everything in his life changed overnight. And then when Mack died and the only people who came to his funeral were people in our family, it really screwed with Jack's head."

"No friends?"

"None." Olivia crossed her arms over her chest and said, "It was so unbelievable that this guy who was the life of every party and a total ladies' man would die alone. Not a single friend or girlfriend—and he'd had so many—was close enough to him to feel compelled to show up for his burial. Like, what the hell, right?"

"Oof," Hallie said.

"Total oof," Olivia agreed. "It was right about that time that Jack started dating Vanessa."

"Ah."

"I have a theory that he was having a mini-crisis and latched onto Van out of panic." Olivia gave her head a little shake and said, "He spent his whole life wanting to be like Mack, worshipping our fun party uncle, and then, just like that, he realized he had it all wrong."

"That makes sense," Hallie said quietly. It explained why someone like him would be with someone like his horrible ex. It also explained why he was already on a dating app, trying to make love happen.

"He went from single and loving it to moving in with his new girlfriend. Next thing I knew, he was buying a ring and talking about popping the question."

Hallie could still picture Vanessa's beautiful, bitchy face.

"Not gonna lie, I was thrilled about their inauspicious breakup. Sorry about the wine, by the way."

"It happens." Hallie shrugged and smiled at the memory.

"I put him on the app right away after that, hoping he'd meet someone nice, normal, and not in a race to the altar."

"The opposite of Vanessa."

"Bingo." Olivia crossed her arms and said, "So when he told me he was talking to the wedding bartender, I was terrified. Not that you're not awesome."

Hallie coughed out a laugh. "I get it."

"But I just worry about him jumping in too fast again," Olivia said. "He was so lonely that I was worried he'd start dating you simply because it's comfortable."

"Low-hanging fruit, right?"

"Exactly. Like, low-hanging fruit can be the *best* fruit, don't get me wrong, but you have to check the whole tree just to make sure."

Hallie nodded. "I'm not sure if that analogy is perfect or terrible."

"Perfectly terrible." Olivia snorted and said, "It was just so weird how fast he did things with Van. It didn't even seem like he really loved her, but more like he was forcing it, trying to make it fit."

I think I was in love with the idea of you, Hallie, instead of who you actually are.

Yeah—she was familiar with the concept. Ben and Jack were of like minds, it seemed.

"But now, I'm thrilled by how things are going. He's actually trying on the app, and he has you to encourage him. It's a win-win."

"For me, too," Hallie said, and then Olivia launched into a hilarious story about when she and Colin first got together and Jack tried to kick Colin's ass. After they went back inside, Hallie got the grand tour, and twenty minutes later she and Jack headed back out.

"I hope my sister didn't grill you," Jack said, giving her a questioning look.

"She didn't. She seems great. Although . . . I *do* have to ask you something, and I'm pretty scared of your answer."

"Uh-oh."

"Your Ditka comment, coupled with your reaction to the overtime finish we just witnessed, has me seriously terrified that you're a Bears fan. Say it isn't so, buddy."

They debated football as they walked toward her new apartment, and Hallie was disappointed to discover not only was he a Bears fan, but he also liked the Bulls. She could accept a lot of idiocy, but the Chicago Bulls?

Come on.

Thankfully they were both Liverpool fans, so she supposed they found some common ground. Outside her apartment, she pointed to where her balcony was and he pretended
he could see it amongst the myriad others in the darkness.

She knew he couldn't, but it was nice to have someone to
dream with.

Chapter
EIGHT

Jack: Good morning, my little number cruncher.

Hallie groaned as she read the text. The one that had woken her up because she'd forgotten to silence her notifications. It's 5:30 a.m. on a Sunday. Eat glass.

Jack: I just wanted to be the first to wish you a good day.

Hallie: Thanks, asshole.

Jack: Now, now. Also, make sure you visit the app today and search for your next date.

Hallie pictured her speed dating matchups and shook her head, turned on the beside lamp and texted: That sounds awful.

Jack: You go, I go. Let's do this together, Piper. Mr. Right, the guy who likes you more than anyone else in the world, is out there, just waiting for your little thumb to swipe him just right.

Hallie: Gross. The only way I'm going on another date already is if I can have Taco Hut afterward.

Jack: That is actually a great idea. Let's plan dates at the speed dating bar, and if they're a bust we'll get tacos after. Cheese on the bottom, of course.

Hallie: Of course. 😌 Okay—why does that sound like a good idea? I'm pretty sure there's a reason this is terrible and I'm just missing it.

Jack: No, it's genius. Make a connection today, and if a date is on the table, text me and we'll plan accordingly.

Hallie: Okay.

Jack: Atta girl.

Hallie: Why are you awake so early btw?

Jack: I like to get in a run before work.

Hallie: Same. But it's SUNDAY. Why are you working on a Sunday?

Jack: Because I have work to do.

Hallie: Also please tell me you don't wear those tiny little running shorts.

Jack: Stop tryna picture me and my luscious thighs, perv.

Hallie: Definitely not doing THAT.

Jack: Wait, were you asking for a pic? Was that what that was?

Hallie: Please don't make me block you.

Jack: Have a lovely day, TB.

Hallie rolled out of bed and went for a run since she was already awake, and the entire time, she practiced what she was going to say to Ruthie when she returned later that day. *I love living with you, but I really think it's time for me to get my own place like an adult. We can still hang out all the time.*

Only Ruthie never came home that day. She sent a text around ten a.m. that read, Having too much fun to come back to the States—will be back next week, and Hallie wasn't really surprised to discover that her roommate was out of the country.

After showering post-run and going on a quick Starbucks jaunt, she settled into the couch and started scrolling. It took a while, but she found a guy whose profile looked good enough to swipe and began messaging.

He seemed funny and nice, so when he asked if she wanted to meet up for dinner and drinks on Wednesday after work, she called Jack.

He answered after one ring, but she wondered if he was working, because he said, "This is Jack."

"Hey, it's Hallie. What's up?"

She heard the smile in his voice when he said, "I cannot believe you called me instead of texting, boomer."

"Do you have a sec?"

"Of course," he said, and she wondered if he was home or at the office.

"Are you still working?" she asked.

"Yeah, but I'm cutting out soon."

"Okay, well, I just had a guy ask me out on the app. Do you have any potential dates that you can do Wednesday night at six thirty-ish?"

"Who's the guy?"

"His name is Stephen, he doesn't hunt or fish, and he is a dentist. He's into running, bingeing Netflix, and getting railed."

"Whoa, dentist? That's a date with bonus points."

"Right? Although I'll probably be worried the whole time that he's checking out my plaque situation."

"'Plaques and racks'—I bet that's Stephen's motto."

"You're a pig."

"Chill. It's Stephen's motto, not mine."

Hallie said through her laugh, "So do you have any potential dates you can do Wednesday?"

"I actually have two."

"Shut your stupid mouth!" Hallie yelled into the phone. "Since last night, you have chatted up two girls with enough of a potential connection to facilitate a date?"

"For the record," he said, "I started talking to one of them yesterday before the speed dating thing."

That made Hallie pause. She had no reason to expect him to tell her everything, but she felt a little . . . weird . . . that he hadn't mentioned it. "So Wednesday . . . ?"

"That works."

She went back to the dating app after they hung up and set the date up with the dentist, and when they closed out the chat because he had to go coach his niece's little league soccer team, Hallie—ovaries imploding—was surprisingly excited about the date.

Stephen seemed promising, and if all else failed, there would be tacos.

Jack

Jack looked at the caller ID before raising the phone to his ear. "What's wrong?"

"Nothing," Olivia said, sounding confused. "Why?"

"Because we don't talk on the phone. This is weird."

"Yeah, but I'm super bored. Shoe full of broken toes, remember?"

"Oh, yes, that's right," he said, regretting the decision to answer the phone. He was trying to finish up work and go home, and he knew for a fact that Olivia's boredom was only going to slow him down. Still, he asked, "How are the little nubbins, by the way?"

"Less swollen," she said. "And marginally less purple."

"Gross."

"Right?"

"Listen, Liv, I'm trying to wrap things up here. Did you actually *need* something?"

"Rude," she said under her breath, before adding, "I just wanted to tell you that I really like Hallie. That's all."

"Okay . . . ?" He said, "Me, too. What's your point?"

"Nothing. I'm just really glad she's around to push you into finding a match."

"For fuck's sake, Liv, why are you so obsessed with my love life?"

"Because I worry about you being sad," she said. "Sue me for caring."

"I was hammered at Billy's that night. Will you please, for the love of God, just forget what I said?"

"You just sounded so sad and lonely, Jack."

"I was lit, not lonely."

He felt like a pathetic fuck whenever she brought it up, because he *had* been going through some weird emo phase over the past couple years. He had friends, coworkers, family—his life was full of people—yet he felt alone a lot.

Even when he was with them.

Shit—that is the literal definition of loneliness, isn't it?

"Fine, you weren't lonely." She sounded utterly unconvinced. "Just promise me you'll take the app seriously and keep trying, even when it sucks."

"I will if you'll promise to butt the hell out of my life."

"Deal," she said.

Hallie

Before she had a chance to get off the couch, her phone started ringing.

"Hello?"

"Hi, um, is this Hallie?"

"Yes . . . ?"

"Oh, good. Hey, it's Lydia from the leasing office at the Commons. There was a miscommunication within our office, and the apartment you'll be renting is all cleaned and ready if you wanted to move in early."

"Oh." Hallie had *not* expected that. "Um, how much more would it be?"

"That's the thing." The leasing agent lowered her voice and said, "I screwed up the paperwork, so basically if you want to move in now, it'll be the same. Rent will be due on the first, for the amount listed in your lease."

"So I can move in now and get a couple weeks for free?" She couldn't believe it. Hallie didn't have bad luck, per se, but she'd never had especially *good* luck, either.

"*If* you come in when I'm working."

Hallie was all of a sudden screamingly excited. "How much longer are you working today?"

"Until four."

"Ohmigod, I'm on my way."

Hallie ran to her car, cranked the radio, and flew downtown, beside herself with excitement over this surprising turn of events. She'd never lived alone before, especially not in a cool (though tiny) apartment, and she was pumped to move in early.

Maybe, she thought as she exited the interstate and followed the off-ramp, she could move all her stuff out before Ruthie came back (the living room furniture was all Ruthie's, so it wouldn't be a jerk move). Then she wouldn't have to worry about awkwardly trying to pack silently in her room, and if Ruthie responded badly to the news, Hallie could just leave and never return.

When she pulled into the apartment office, her phone buzzed.

Jack: I already lost one of my two women.

That made Hallie giggle. What'd you do?

Jack: I told her that I didn't like orangutans.

Hallie: First of all, is this true? Second of all, this upset her?

Jack: I know it's a character flaw, but I'm terrified of all monkey-like creatures; always have been. I saw a lady on Oprah who got her face ripped off by one and I was never the same. So when she started telling me about an orangutan preserve she wanted to visit, I may have said something similar to "I'd rather die than go there."

Hallie: You are a monster. I have a good friend who literally cries when she sees a cute orangutan because she loves them so much. BUT. Your comment torqued her off that much?

Jack: My comment big-time torqued her. She went on a rant about them, which I deserved, and then she went off about undatable men, which I felt was a low blow.

Hallie: Why is this story cracking me up?

Jack: Cuz you're a dick. What're you doing right now?

Hallie: Just pulled up to my new building. They're letting me move in early!!!

Jack: What about Ruthie?

Hallie laughed and looked out her windshield. Funny that he remembered Ruthie's name. She left me a msg that she's not coming back for another week.

Jack: So you're just going to be gone?

Hallie: No, but I can move my stuff out now. Everything in the living room is hers, so it's not like she'll even notice, because my bedroom door is always closed.

Jack: LMK if you want help moving.

Hallie: Seriously?

Jack: I'm a nice guy.

Hallie: But are you?

Jack: Sometimes. And I live nearby.

Hallie: Well then, yes. I want help. Please, please help.

Jack: When?

Hallie: I'm getting the keys now, and then I guess whenever you have time today would be great. You don't have a truck, do you?

Jack: I actually do.

Hallie: Shut up.

Jack: I will not.

Hallie: You don't seem like a truck guy.

Jack: Are you calling me a wuss?

Hallie: No. I think most guys who drive trucks do it to prove they're manly. You strike me as someone confident enough in his masculinity to drive a Prius.

Jack: So you ARE calling me a wuss.

Hallie: You're an idiot.

Jack: Better, thanks. Call me when you're done and we'll hatch a plan.

Well, the plan turned out to be something along the lines of "just do it." After getting the keys, running up to her new place, calling Jack, and dancing around like a maniac, she went home and threw her stuff together.

Jack showed up an hour later and got to work, hauling her bed, dresser, nightstand, and desk out the door like he was the Rock. She helped, but they both knew she was more like a spotter than an equal lifter.

On a side note, he looked very good in casual clothing. She'd only ever seen him in a tux, naked, and in nicer date-night clothes so far, but that day, he was wearing faded old jeans and a Cubs T-shirt that was so worn it looked baby soft. He looked like the kind of guy they'd cast in a commercial for grabbing beers with the guys or picking up two-by-fours at a home improvement store.

Once the bed of his truck was full and her room was cleared out, she followed him downtown in her car. She was a little shell-shocked that mere hours earlier she'd had no plans for the day and now she was moving into her new apartment, but it felt good.

This *was* her spring.

Chapter
NINE

"You're so wrong," Jack said, shaking his head. "It was the look on his face when she showed up at Pemberley with her relatives. The guy didn't even have to say a word. He beamed like a lovesick fool."

They were both lying on their stomachs on the floor of her new apartment (she didn't have a couch yet), watching the end of *Pride & Prejudice*. After moving everything in, they'd decided to order beer and a pizza and watch a movie since neither of them had anything else going on.

"I *do* love his face there," she agreed, picturing Matthew Macfadyen's sweet smile. "But the near-kiss in the rain is the best moment."

"Agree to disagree," Jack said, rolling onto his side to face her. "It's too devastating when they pull back."

"If I didn't know better—and I do, so don't worry—I'd think you're kind of a hopeless romantic." Hallie grinned and just looked at him; Jack Marshall was an absolute question mark of a guy. "So how many times have you seen this, not-romantic-person?"

"At least five, but it's only because Livvie loved it and she whined the loudest in the house. She usually won control of the TV."

"You're a very complex fellow, Marshall," she said as he smiled back at her.

"Oh, I know," he replied, and his blue eyes moved all over her face.

The moment held, and something passed between them. It was almost as if the memory of their past—the existence of their night together—suddenly reared its hot head, and Hallie was very aware of it.

"I need another beer," she said, climbing to her feet as she forced her mouth to stay in its smile, even though she felt unsettled all of a sudden. "Want something?"

"No, actually, I've got to get going," he said, clearing his throat while picking up his beer bottle and rising to his feet.

"Well, thank you for helping me move." Hallie walked into the kitchen, opened the pizza box, and grabbed a lukewarm slice. "Want a piece for the road?"

"Nah," he said, shoving his feet into his shoes and pulling on his jacket. "I'm good, but thanks."

After he left and she tossed the pizza box, Hallie started worrying. As she changed into her flannels, she wondered if that little second of weirdness was going to make things different for them. She didn't want it to, because she really liked having him as her partner in crime.

Her phone buzzed, and she was disappointed to see it was her mom.

Mom: Have you gone in for your final dress fitting?

Yes, her mother still thought she was ten years old.

Hallie: Yes.

Mom: What did you think?

Hallie: I can't remember. Fine, I think . . . ?

Mom: Very funny. Are you coming over this week?

Her mother made spaghetti and meatballs almost every Wednesday night, and Hallie usually tried to be there.

But she'd avoided it for the past month as the wedding planning amped up to a frenetic pace. It was all her mom and sister could talk about, which she totally understood, but it usually devolved into a discussion of how they would have an extra plus-one to work with because Hallie wasn't bringing anyone.

And how awkward it might be for her, since Ben was the best man.

Yes, her sister was marrying the best friend of the man who'd shredded Hallie's heart.

They usually lowered their voices when they discussed it, as if the entire scenario were the worst possible thing that could happen to her, and she'd decided it was better to miss out on meatballs than maim a family member.

Hallie: I have plans Wednesday, but I'll swing by on Thursday to watch Dancing Centerfolds with you.

Mom: I hope Darla gets eliminated. Her cha-cha was ass.

Hallie: But Delvin's samba was even worse.

Mom: His bum made it okay, though.

Hallie went out onto her balcony and took a deep breath of chilly September air, thrilled by her view. The city twinkled in front of her, below her, and she didn't think she'd ever want to move back to the suburbs.

She loved the bustle of downtown, and she also loved the utter adultness of living alone.

Her phone buzzed, but this time it was Jack.

Jack: Hey TB, are we cool?

Hallie: I am. The coolest.

Jack: For real—you didn't get freaked about that weird moment on your living room floor?

So it hadn't just been her. He'd felt it, too. She typed: Yeah, what WAS that?

Jack: I think it was just two young, healthy people having a split second of natural chemistry. Probably just happened because we already bonked, so our bodies know each other.

Hallie: Ew you did not just say that.

Jack: It's totally natural to get that bonking feeling. The important thing is that we immediately remembered we don't like each other that way, don't you think?

Hallie: Wasn't that a song? "You've Lost That Bonking Feeling"? That made her laugh as she leaned against the balcony railing. Well I am fine with it, whatever it was, as long as you are.

Jack: I am. It never happened.

Hallie: Good.

Jack: Great. So have you talked to the dentist today?

Hallie: Not since this morning, when he told me he had to go coach his niece's soccer team.

Jack: Wow, he opened with a total hormonal crusher, didn't he?

Hallie: Yeah, he did.

Jack: Did it work?

Hallie: It didn't hurt. She couldn't picture Stephen's face at the moment, but she could picture Jack's, so she texted: Tell me about your girl.

Jack: Her name is Carlie, she teaches eighth grade math, and she's a redhead. Likes sand volleyball and getting railed.

Hallie: Is she fun to talk to?

Jack: I'm not sure yet.

Hallie: I suppose that's what Wed is for, right?

Jack: I suppose so. I guess I'll see you Wednesday, then.

Hallie: I guess so.

Chapter
TEN

"Hi, um, I'm supposed to meet someone—"

"Hallie?" Stephen appeared beside the hostess, smiling and setting a hand on the hostess's arm in a way that told her he was who Hallie was looking for.

"Hey, Stephen." Wow. He looked nice; like, really, really nice. For starters, he was wearing khaki pants and a black cashmere sweater. His brown hair was thick and styled in that sweet spot that hit on well-coiffed without being high-maintenance, and he was wearing glasses that made him look like he needed a book in his hand.

"It's so nice to finally meet you," he said, giving Hallie just the kindest grin.

"You, too," she replied, unable to hold in her smitten smile.

He pointed to where their table was, and she followed him over. She almost tripped when she saw Jack, seated at the table right beside them. His eyes caught hers and widened just the tiniest amount, showing he was just as surprised as she was that they were sitting in such close proximity.

She recovered and took a seat, reminding herself to focus on Stephen.

"I used to eat here all the time, back when I was in college," he said, reaching out for his menu. "I'm so glad you suggested it."

"Me, too," she said, grabbing her menu and quickly muttering, "Not the dental school part, but the other. It's my first time here."

He gave a little laugh. "Noted."

"So what's good, then?" she asked, eyeballing the appetizers. "What was your favorite dish?"

"The lamb with mushroom risotto," he said, and Hallie realized that his college experience had been vastly different from her own Top Ramen version. "You have to try it."

Shit. Hallie was a picky eater. Picky as in most third graders had a broader palate than her own. She liked burgers and chicken strips and the occasional spaghetti, but lamb? With *mushrooms* in the risotto? No, no thank you. But since she'd asked his opinion, she kind of had to take his suggestion, right?

"I was kind of feeling like a burger, but maybe now . . ." She trailed off, hoping it would prompt him to say, *Get whatever sounds good.*

"Get the lamb." He smiled, snatched her menu out of her hand, and said, "You won't regret it. I ordered you a glass of chardonnay, by the way."

"Okay." Hallie reached for her glass. "Thank you. And I'm trusting you on the lamb."

"Good girl." He cleared his throat, picked up his wineglass, and said, "So how was work today? Did you make it through the marathon meeting?"

She'd told him about the quarterly business meetings that had been going on since Monday, and she was impressed he'd remembered. "I made it. It's amazing how challenging it is to look interested in very boring information."

"I bet."

She said, "I'm sure you have to listen to lots of rambling from your patients."

"Yeah, but I can stick my hands in their mouth and make it stop," he quipped, which made her laugh.

She glanced at Jack's table, where he and his date appeared to be deep in conversation. She was very pretty and wearing the cutest red dress, so unless she was a total bore, Jack was off to a great start.

She looked back at Stephen, the dentist, and felt pretty good about her start, as well.

They started talking about his job, and he was super interesting and funny as he told her dental horror stories. She interjected with her own stories, and she was surprisingly relaxed and comfortable.

She was actually having a good time on her date.

The food came, and she didn't want to eat lamb *or* risotto. But she started with the meat, which was tolerable if she didn't picture fluffy little baby lambs, and she pushed around the risotto so it looked like she'd eaten some.

While saying a lot of *Mmmm, this is so good.*

"So we should probably cover relationships, right? Isn't that a first-date thing?"

That made Hallie set down her fork and take a big ol' gulp of her chardonnay before saying, "Um, sure . . . ?"

"I just want to put it out there that I'm divorced."

"Oh." Hallie didn't really know what to say. She didn't have a problem with someone being divorced, but she also didn't want to squeal something inane like *I love divorce*. The way she saw it, divorce was no different from her breakup except for the fact that he'd had a party with formal wear and she hadn't.

"We got married young, I guess, and didn't realize until it was too late that we didn't have much in common."

Hallie gave a nod and said, "It happens."

"The worst part was telling the twins."

"Ohmigosh." Hallie set down her glass and cleared her throat. "I didn't know you had twins. How old are they?"

"Four years old," he said, his smile returning as he talked about the kids he clearly adored. "They're really incredible."

"That's such a fun age," she said, her mind a little blown that he hadn't included that on his profile. She'd never considered the possibility that she might find someone on the dating app who had children. She could potentially become a stepmom? God, she didn't even want to go there.

"It is. They've finally stopped putting everything in their mouths and falling asleep on top of me."

That made Hallie a little gooey inside, picturing this handsome man with sleeping munchkins draped all over him. He really was a hormonal destroyer, wasn't he?

"Wow, how do you tell someone so young about divorce?" she asked. Her own parents just lived by the you-irritate-me-but-till-death-do-us-part motto.

"My ex and I were super emotional when we sat them down," he said, getting choked up, "but we were just honest.

We said, 'Listen, when we bought you two and brought you home, we had every intention of staying together forever.'"

Hallie narrowed her eyes. Had he just said "bought"?

"'But sometimes forever isn't possible, and that's okay. We love both of you, but we're going to have to split you up.'"

Hallie still just kept hearing the word *bought* as he continued speaking. He was blinking back tears, clearly very emotional, but she was having a hard time empathizing, because she couldn't figure out what he'd said. *Bought?!*

"It's never ideal to split up your kids, to each take one and go your separate ways, but somehow that seems better than a lifetime of forced interactions that would surely end in fights, right?"

Hallie pursed her lips before saying, "So the twins were adopted . . . ?"

He smiled guiltily and said, "I wouldn't say adopted, per se, because we wanted to make sure we got the exact kind we wanted."

Hallie just stared at him, the gooey feeling gone. Dried up. Turned to dust.

"I know, I know—rescue is the thing to do." He sighed and steepled his fingers under his chin. "But we really wanted Labradoodles from the same mother."

Dogs? He was talking about his *dogs?* Surely he couldn't have thought that was obvious, could he? Hallie couldn't stop her eyebrows from bunching together as she said, "So they're not actually twins."

Now his eyebrows went down. "No, they are."

"Twin dogs are actually super rare." Hallie knew it was splitting hairs, but she was suddenly irritated as hell at the dentist. "One pregnancy with just two puppies in the litter."

"Oh." He cleared his throat and looked confused by her words. "Well, they're identical Labradoodles from the same litter, then."

Hallie rubbed her lips together and told herself it was no big deal. So the guy talked about his dogs like they were his children; that wasn't bad, right? At least he wasn't a dick who hated animals. She inhaled through her nose—*chill, Hal*—before saying, "So you each walked away with one of the dogs when you split up . . . ?"

He nodded, and his eyes filled with tears again. "One of the reasons we wanted Labradoodles was because they're very emotional animals, but that was what made telling them so tough, y'know?"

Hallie nodded her head in an understanding way, but she was struggling. "I can't even imagine."

She kept trying to find empathy, because she was a very empathetic person, but Dr. Stephen was literally crying at dinner because he was worried about the emotional scars he and his ex-wife might've left on their dogs.

Dogs she'd thought were human toddlers five minutes before.

Once he'd wiped his eyes and they'd moved onto a safe topic—the new movie theater out on the west side of town—she excused herself to go to the restroom. But as she crossed the restaurant and headed for the hallway that led to the facilities, she was filled with disappointment.

Because the dog conversation, or maybe the misunderstanding about kids, had brought on the ick. She'd lost that initial attraction for the dentist, and she could tell it was lost forever.

"How's it going with the doc, TB?"

She turned around, and there was Jack, also entering the bathroom hallway. He was giving her a grin, and she felt her face fall into a huge smile as she found comfort in her partner in crime. "Oh, my God, Jack, you won't even believe it."

She grabbed his sleeve and jerked him closer to the ladies' room so they were out of sight from the table. She looked up into those teasing blue eyes and quickly told the absurd story. "I mean, am I being a bitch? Is he a delightful dog lover and I'm just an ass?"

He narrowed his eyes, and as he looked down at her, she was struck again by how tall he was. "Did he literally call them his kids, or was that you paraphrasing?"

She squinted and recalled the conversation. "At first he called them the twins, but then yeah, he totally called them kids."

"You're not wrong here; that's bonkers."

"*Thank* you." Hallie felt a little better. "How's Carlie?"

"Great, except she told me she wants to be 'treated like a queen.'"

"So?" Jack seemed like he'd treat a significant other well. "Is it that hard to treat a woman well?"

"No, a fucking actual queen." He glanced over his shoulder, like he was worried about getting busted, and said, "She wants a man who will put her on a pedestal, shower her with gifts, defer to her wishes—her words, not mine—and never look at another woman again."

"You are lying," Hallie said, leaning her backside against the wall. "No one would say that on a first date."

"It was my fault." He put his hands in his pockets and said, "I made the mistake of saying, 'I would totally respect a woman who just straight up says what she's looking for.'"

"Well." Hallie rolled her eyes. "You asked for it."

"Right?"

"Stephen's going to come looking for me or think I have diarrhea—I have to go."

"Do you want out?" Jack asked, looking concerned, and she wasn't sure why the sweet expression on his face made her stomach flip.

"What?"

"Do you want out of your date early, or are you still feeling it out?"

That made her laugh. "He refers to his dogs as 'the twins,' so I definitely want out. But I don't want to be rude; Stephen's a nice guy."

Jack took a step toward the men's room door and said, "I've got you. Just blink three times when you want to ditch for tacos."

Hallie giggled and blinked three times with obnoxious obviousness.

He gave her a chin nod before they both went into their respective restrooms. When Hallie got back to the table, Stephen was scrolling through his phone.

"Sorry I took so long," she said, feeling guilty, "but my mom texted and it was a whole thing."

"Oh, is everything okay?"

He looked genuinely concerned, and she was a bit bummed that she'd gotten the ick. Because he was attractive, successful, and friendly—a perfect catch for so many people. He should've been the perfect catch for *her*, but no, he had to care too much about his dogs.

Which she didn't even know could happen.

Was she a monster?

"Oh, it's fine, my mother is just—"

The hostess showed up at the table and said, "Excuse me, are you Hallie Piper?"

"Yes . . . ?" Hallie glanced at Stephen, then back at the hostess.

"Your mother called, and she said to tell you that your 'Auntie Helen is at it again, and you need to meet them in ten minutes if there's any shot of stopping her from making the hugest mistake of her life.' "

Hallie swallowed. *"What?"*

"Is this what your mother was texting you about?" Stephen asked.

"Huh?" Hallie looked at Stephen.

"In the bathroom," Stephen said, as if he was waiting for her to catch up. "You said it was a whole thing . . . ?"

"Oh." She blinked and tried thinking through what was happening. She'd made up a lie about texting her mom, but now Jack's plan was . . . involving her mom . . . ? Hallie nodded and said, "Yeah, this is that. That whole thing. Um, I thought she was over it, but clearly she still thinks my aunt needs help."

Hallie rolled her eyes and shook her head as if she found the entire thing exhausting.

"Do you need to go meet them?" he asked.

"I probably should," Hallie said. "I mean, we're already finished with dinner, so we're almost done anyway, right?"

Stephen looked like he was trying to figure out if she was crapping out on the date or if she was legitimately in possession of a wacko aunt and overbearing mother. He nodded. "Yes. Yes, you should totally go."

She gathered her purse before they exchanged the little

I'll call you goodbye that almost never resulted in an actual call. She said, "Thank you so much for tonight, Stephen."

"Anytime," he said, and then she waved and was virtually running out the front door.

She ordered a margarita at the Taco Hut bar, then walked straight out to the back patio. Somehow she just knew Jack would be out there, and she was right. He was leaning back in a chair with a lowball of tequila in his hand, smirking as he watched her approach.

The way he was looking at her might've seemed like *something* at one time, but now she was convinced Jack was right, that it was just the normal chemistry that existed between two people who'd previously had sex.

"Well, that was the weirdest escape call in the history of dating," Hallie said.

"That's what makes it genius," Jack said, kicking out the chair across from him at the table so she could sit on it. "You make it so batshit confusing that the other person has no choice but to say, 'You should go.'"

"I don't know if I'd call it genius, but it's certainly entertaining," Hallie said as she plopped down in her seat and took a sip of her drink. "I know we just ate, but I kind of want a taco."

"Already ordered you one."

"You did?"

"Chicken taco with cheese on the bottom," he said.

She almost choked as she laughed and swallowed at the same time. "You remembered!"

"I mean, what's the point of cold, hard cheese?"

It was impossible not to grin at Jack as he sat there being

thoughtful, smug, and absolutely adorable. "You've never sounded smarter, Marshall."

He tipped his glass. "Why, thank you, Piper."

They just sat there for a minute, grinning at their ridiculous situation.

"So, want to hear something weird?" Hallie asked, stirring her drink with her straw.

"Always," he said.

"When I was walking over here, I realized that my non-match date tonight actually gave me hope for finding Mr. Soul Mate."

He tilted his head a little. "How so?"

"Because Stephen is a good guy. Not for me, but still a catch—he's successful, nice, and attractive. So even though it didn't work out, I have hope in the possibilities. The next Stephen *could* be the one."

Jack gave a nod. "I mean, I suppose that's what dating is. Finding the quality person who's more than just a good candidate."

"Right?" She crossed her arms and said, "I just feel like it could be close."

"Your words to Ditka's ears, Piper."

"You *have* to stop saying that."

They ended up closing down the Taco Hut after getting way too into bar trivia. Hallie was great at pop culture, while Jack was ridiculously good at history, so they had an impossible time walking away when they were in first place.

After the restaurant closed, they walked home, which Hallie tipsily decided was the best perk of living downtown.

"Seriously, I should sell my car," she said, loving the feel of the city at night. All the colorful lights, the car noises, the smells of delicious food and garbage—it was intoxicating. "I love this."

"Watch the mud," Jack said, pointing to the thick sludge on the sidewalk. "You don't want to ruin those boots."

Hallie smiled at him and bumped his arm with hers. "I *knew* you'd noticed my pretty suede boots."

"I only noticed because you looked a little wobbly after your beers." He grabbed her arm and stopped her forward motion. "Look."

They'd hit a spot that was apparently at the bottom of the hill, because the entire sidewalk was covered in thick mud.

"Gah—my boots are going to get ruined," she whined.

Jack shook his head with a sigh and said, "Get on."

"What?"

He bent a little at the waist and gestured to his back. "Piggyback ride."

Her mouth dropped open and she couldn't stop the giggle. "Are you for real, Jack?"

"Hop on and shut up, Hal."

She climbed onto his back, and he straightened and carried her to her building as if she were as light as a feather. She buried her cold nose in his warm neck, getting buzzed on the smell of soap and Jack, but he didn't complain *too* much.

"Your nose is so cold," he said.

"But your neck is so warm, I can't help myself," she replied, burying her nose a little deeper into his collar.

"Fine."

When they finally reached her building, she climbed off his back and pulled a dollar out of her purse.

"For you, sir," she teased, holding out the money. "Thank you for seeing me home."

"A dollar?" He made a face, snatched the dollar from her fingers, and said, "I'm worth more than that, for the record, but I'll take it."

"Whatever. Just walk carefully the rest of the way, okay?"

He raised his eyebrows. "Worried about me?"

"You wish." She raised her key fob and pulled open the door when it beeped. "More like I'm worried about you dying before I get my free vacation."

Chapter
ELEVEN

Hallie exited out of the spreadsheet and glanced at the time: four thirty.

She'd worn date clothes to work that day, because she was meeting Alex for drinks and appetizers as soon as she logged out. She and Jack had gone out on two more *meh* dates that ended with them at Taco Hut, but after the last one, she'd started talking to a guy named Alex, and he seemed surprisingly promising.

He was an adorable blond real estate agent who was actually fun to text; witty and quick, just like Jack.

And when he'd called her, there had been flirty chemistry over the phone.

"Hallie." Claire, the new receptionist, popped her head into Hallie's office and said, "There's a Ruthie Someone here to see you."

"Oh, shit."

The receptionist looked concerned. "I'm sorry, was I sup-posed to—"

"No, no, it's a me thing, Claire. Can you please send her back?"

"Sure thing."

Hallie breathed in deeply through her nose, and before she could even think, Ruthie ran into her office, closed the door behind her, and sat down in the guest chair. "What in the actual fuck, Hal?"

Ruthie didn't look mad, or even sad. She looked . . . con-fused, maybe? She was wearing a long black dress, paired with a captain's hat and red glasses—glasses through which she peered at Hallie.

Hallie tried to come up with good words. "Ruthie, I wanted to talk to you before you saw—"

"That all of your stuff is gone? Too late, bruh. I can't be-lieve you moved out."

"Okay, here's the thing—" Hallie started.

"It's because of my allergies, isn't it?"

"What?"

Ruthie said, "I know that you want a cat, Hallie."

Hallie's mouth snapped shut. She'd wanted a cat for a hot minute after splitting with Ben, but she'd literally never given it a thought since. "Oh, Ruthie, I don't—"

"I get it, but can I at least go with you to pick it out?"

Hallie didn't even know what to say. Except, "What?"

"Because I've always wanted a cat, too. If I were you, I would absolutely move out, too, if it meant that I could have one. But since I can't, can I at least take a shit ton of allergy meds and tag along?"

"Um—"

"Oh, God." Ruthie's eyes got huge. "Was it something else? Was there some other reason that you're moving out?"

"No, um, it's just the, uh, the cat thing."

"So you're seriously going to the shelter with her tomorrow?"

Hallie grinned and raised her glass. "To cowardice."

Alex raised his, as well, and said, "To cowardice. And cats."

Hallie giggled; she was having a great time. She and Alex had downed a plate of nachos and were starting on mozzarella sticks, and they were both still having fun. She couldn't believe it, but things felt kind of promising with him.

"I need to look up good cat names," Hallie said.

"What about Whiskers?" Alex asked.

"Cliché."

"Garfield?" he suggested.

"Tired."

"Ann-Margret?"

Hallie raised her eyebrows and tilted her head. "Now you're talking."

They spent the next ten minutes laughing as Alex googled terrible cat names. She excused herself to go to the restroom, and the minute she entered the hallway, she turned and waited for Jack.

Who did not disappoint.

He came around the corner, wearing his usual sarcastic smile. He looked *really* good in his black sweater vest, white button-down, and black pants, she thought.

He was a very well-dressed dater.

"So . . . ?" he asked, the scent of his expensive-but-subtle cologne finding her nose.

"So I'm actually having a great time."

"Shut your face." His eyebrows slammed together and his eyes moved all over her face, like he was searching for the answer. "For real?"

"I cannot believe it myself. Alex is cute, hilarious, and really, really fun. You would like him."

He rolled his eyes. "Doubt it."

"How about you? How are things with Kayla?" His date was a stunning PhD candidate who looked like she could be Zendaya's older sister. Hallie wanted to vomit when she'd seen them together—they looked like a celebrity couple—so she was guessing Jack was pleased. "No ick yet?"

He swallowed and just said, "Not yet."

Hallie leaned her face in a little closer, and she saw him sniff. She wondered if her perfume was too strong as she said, "I can't believe I'm saying this, Jack, but I want to scratch the escape plan."

"I mean," he said, his face unreadable as he shrugged, "it's still early. There's plenty of time—"

"No, I'm serious. I can tell. No need for tacos." Hallie knew she was beaming like a fool, but she couldn't help it. She was actually having a good date for once, so she felt like jumping up and down. "Like, I don't want dinner to end—it's that good."

Jack gave her a wink and said, "Someone's moving in on that vacation."

"Your lips to Ditka's ears," she said, winking back at him before going into the ladies' room.

Jack

"So then I was stuck in the lab for the entire weekend."

He smiled at his date as he reached for his water. "Not exactly what you'd planned, eh?"

"Not at all." Kayla grinned and launched back into the story, but Jack was distracted by the table behind her.

Hallie was laughing and smiling at her date like she wanted to eat him whole. *There is no way that guy can be that funny.* No *way.* But every time she laughed, it was like the noise found his ears; he couldn't *not* hear it. And the way her red lips turned up when she smiled—didn't she know the message she was sending? The guy was going to think he had her, for God's sake, just by the flirty grin she was giving him.

Jack genuinely wanted Hal to find someone, but this guy was not it. His hair had so much product in it he'd probably combust if he walked too close to an open flame, and there was something about the way he looked at Hallie that was creepy.

Just looking at the guy as he shit-grinned at her made him annoyed as hell.

And the dude was wearing Chuck Taylors with a blazer; did he think he was a fucking talk show host?

"So to make a long story short, they shut down the college and arrested the dude." Kayla tucked her hair behind her ears and said, "Can you even believe that?"

"No," he said, feeling like shit for zoning out. He wasn't an asshole, and Kayla deserved his full attention on their date, whether they had a connection or not.

"It was absolutely bonk—" Her phone started ringing, and when she looked down at the display she said, "I need to take this—it's my roommate. Will you excuse me for a second?"

"Of course," Jack said, wondering if it was a bailout call. He pretty much assumed everyone on a first date employed one, so he had no ill will if that's what it was.

But the minute she stepped away, he pulled out his phone.

He texted: You sure about no tacos, TB?

He hit send.

And . . . *wait*. He watched Hallie glance down at her phone, read the message, then put her phone back in her pocket without responding.

She ignored his text.

Seriously?

For reasons he couldn't explain, that bothered him. A lot. Where was his partner in crime? Was their alliance no longer a thing now that she'd landed a date she considered decent? He felt a little kicked to the side as she went about her date like she didn't even know him.

Kayla returned to the table, and Jack managed to have a nice dinner with her. She was sweet and smart and funny, and he couldn't find a single thing wrong with her.

So why was he in a hurry to finish the date?

He could tell she wanted him to kiss her when he walked her to her car, but he wasn't feeling it and didn't want to be fake. He told her he'd call her, and he went home.

Irritated as fuck and entirely unsettled by the blond creep.

He waited a few hours, and at midnight finally gave in to his urges.

Jack: Did you make it home okay?

Hallie: Ohmigod Jack I wanted to text you but I was afraid you were railing the PhD candidate or at home sleeping!

Jack: I'm doing both. What's up?

Hallie: So dinner was great, and then he walked me home. He was super chatty and there was zero awkwardness, and then HE KISSED ME.

Jack: And . . . ?

Hallie: AHHHMAZING!!! He did the little face hold thing and I was done for. Small amount of tongue but not too much. It was kiss perfection.

Jack: That seems kind of forward, doesn't it?

Hallie: What? Kissing on the first date? Are you a puritan now?

Jack: I just mean you don't even really know the guy.

Hallie: I do, too. He's in real estate, plays slow-pitch softball, his favorite color is salmon, and he likes getting railed.

His favorite color was fucking salmon?

Jack: Sounds like a dipshit.

Hallie: I KNOW WHAT YOU'RE DOING.

Jack didn't know why, but her words made him feel guilty of something. He texted: What do you mean?

Hallie: You want to win the bet, so you're trying to sabotage the first good match I've had.

Jack: What's his name again?

Hallie: Alex Anderson.

Jack: I'm looking him up.

Hallie: What? Don't. Don't do anything stupid.

Jack: I'm not. Just googling Mr. AA.

Hallie: Did you do any googling with Dr. Gorgeous?

Jack: I left her at her car and walked home all alone because you ditched me.

Hallie: We probably needed a break from Taco Hut anyway. I've gained a pound since we started our arrangement.

Jack: You look great—don't give up.

Hallie: Hey. Do you want to go with me and Ruthie to find a cat tomorrow?

Jack: First of all, what the fuck—a cat? Second, you still haven't told her?

Hallie: I'm calling you now.

His phone rang, and he raised it to his ear as he leaned back against the headboard and watched SportsCenter. "Hey, Piper."

"So Ruthie showed up at my office today, wondering where my stuff had gone."

"Oh, snap."

"Right?"

Jack listened as she launched into a rambling story about her weird roommate and pet adoption. Something about the way Hallie told the story reminded him of the way she'd been in the kitchen of the hotel the night of the wedding.

Bossy, self-deprecating, funny, and charming as fuck.

"So we're going right at eight before work to adopt a cat. Ruthie is a *lot*, so I was hoping you'd want to join us. Be the sane one in our cat-grabbing trio."

"Maybe you should ask Alex," he said, then immediately regretted it.

"I don't want my pet to be affiliated with a potential love interest," she said, and he thought she sounded sleepy. Her voice was just a little deeper, a smidge quieter, than usual. She said, "It could make things very complicated. I'd rather pick out my cat with my friends so there will be no ill cat will if I break his heart or vice versa."

He said, "I can't believe you're getting a cat to avoid upsetting her."

"Small price, really."

That made him laugh because it was so ridiculous. "A pet that you have to feed and clean up after, till death do you part, is a small price?"

"I always wanted a cat." He could almost hear her shrug when she said, "And if *you* can handle having a cat, I'm certain *I* can."

Jack looked down at Meowgi, asleep on his lap.

"Fine," he said, not hating the idea of hanging with Hallie before work. He always got up at five thirty to run, so he would've been up early, regardless. "I'll pick you up at seven. I need coffee before this whole thing."

"You delightful boy," she said, a smile in her voice. "I'll have Ruthie meet us at the shelter, because you don't want her riding in your car. It's impossible to get the smell out."

"Oh, God," he said, so curious about her former roommate. "What smell?"

"It's like a mix between patchouli, onions, and vanilla."

"Care to explain?"

"I can't." It sounded like she was moving around when she said, "She's smelled like that since the day I met her. And I know for a fact that she takes at least three showers a day, so it isn't body odor."

"I am terrified and thrilled to finally meet your Ruthie."

"I am thrilled and terrified, as well. Sweet dreams, Jack."

"Sweet dreams to you, TB."

Chapter
TWELVE

"Come on, Jack," Hallie said, grinning from where she was sitting on the floor with an enormous orange tabby on her lap. "Ruthie's right. You have to see if you two pass the friend compatibility test."

It was asinine. The entire visit had been absolutely asinine so far, and his abs hurt like he'd just left the gym because he'd been laughing so damn hard.

Ruthie, Hallie's beautiful bald friend who was wearing what looked to be a pirate's shirt and booty shorts (with her Docs, of course), had insisted that whatever cat Hallie selected had to elicit emotions from all three of them.

Hallie fell instantly in love with the fattest old cat she'd ever seen, and when she'd put him on her lap, it'd seemed like fate. The cat started purring and pushing his face into her hand and holy shit, it seemed like Hallie had found her animal.

Then batshit-crazy Ruthie made her statement about the

friend compatibility test, and she'd taken the cat from Hallie. The second she cradled him in her arms, he'd lifted one of his mammoth paws and delivered a three-punch smackdown right to her forehead.

Jack had laughed his ass off.

But Ruthie hadn't let the cat go. She'd professed that she loved his energy and was drawn to his passion, so she sat there while the thing smacked her two more times and then bolted for the door.

Then the girl started sneezing because she was allergic, and once Hallie got the cat back in her arms, he settled right down and went back to purring.

"Come sit down right next to little Hallie," Hallie crooned, patting the floor beside her. "I want to see if he kicks your ass or not."

There was something about her face when she was being a smartass. Hallie's eyes almost twinkled, and he imagined that's exactly what she'd looked like as a pain-in-the-ass little kid.

"He's not going to kick my ass," he proclaimed as he walked over and dropped to the floor beside her. "Because I won't let him."

"I'm going to go get some air," Ruthie said.

Jack looked up at her, and the girl was so scrawny and childlike in her weirdness that he felt somehow protective of her. "Do you want me to go with you?"

She rolled her eyes. "Look at you, Prince Charming, so scared of a cat ass-whooping that you're going to accompany me to the parking lot. Bugger off."

"You bugger off, Ruthie," he replied, which made her burst into her wildly out-of-control laughter as she exited the room.

"Oh, my God—she loves you, Jack," Hallie said with a grin as she petted the beast. "I've never seen Ruthie so sweet to a guy before."

He gave her side-eye and ran a hand over the cat's back. "The first thing she said to me was 'Your car is a symbol of everything that's wrong with our world.'"

Hallie laughed. "But *then* what did she say?"

"That at least it didn't have fuckwit vanity plates . . . ?"

"See? That little aside means she forgives your capitalistic nature."

"Oh, thank God." He laughed, and over the smell of animal, he could smell her perfume. He wasn't sure what she wore, but it always drifted into his awareness in the same way he could always sniff out barbecue when he walked into a restaurant.

"I can't believe you have an Audi *and* a truck, by the way," she said, her forehead crinkling. "You must be really good at landscraping."

"Did you just say land*scraping*?"

She rolled her eyes and nodded. "I swear I'm sober."

He reached out a hand and scratched the cat's huge head. "I should hope so—it's seven thirty in the morning."

"Wanna hold him?"

"After witnessing Ruthie's beatdown?" He looked at her upturned face and fought the urge to trace the line of freckles on her cheek. "No, thanks."

"Chicken."

"Listen," Jack said, watching the cat watch him. "This guy knows that you are his. He has found his person. He doesn't *want* to be handed off to someone else now that he's met you."

"Do you really think that?" she said, smiling like an over-excited toddler at Christmas.

"I do."

"You think I'm his person?" she asked, her eyes on his. "That's kind of beautiful, Marshall."

He shrugged. "I know, I'm a beautiful fucking genius."

That made her laugh and smack his arm. She said, "I suppose we should probably go to work now, huh?"

He stopped petting the cat and wondered if her building actually even allowed cats, or if she'd even thought to check. He said, "Probably."

"If I pay you," she said, climbing to her feet with ginormo-cat in her arms, "will you swing by here after work so I can take him home?"

He stood. "I guess, but only if you're paying me."

She gave him a look and said, "Add it to my tab."

After she returned the cat and filled out all the paperwork, Hallie got a text from Ruthie as they exited the building.

"O-kay." She read the message and shook her head as they walked toward the parking lot. "Ruthie says that she got bored and grabbed a ride home, and also that she's throwing an adoption party for me and Purr Anthony Hopkitten this weekend."

"You're not seriously naming him that, are you?"

She grinned and shrugged. "I have a hard time telling Ruthie no."

"You tell Ruthie that I already named him and you have a hard time telling *me* no."

She gave him a snort-laugh. "What's your name for him?"

He hit unlock and she pulled open the passenger door of his car. "Umm . . . Tigger."

She got in the car and said, "I might not hate that," before slamming the door closed.

When he got in and buckled his seat belt, she was grinning and looking at her phone. "Alex says he likes Ruthie's name."

Why did that make Jack want to steal her phone and toss it out the window?

"Sounds like Alex is a moron."

She rolled her eyes and laughed. "You're not getting the baseball, you jag."

She texted Alex back as Jack drove his car a little too fast, and the way she grinned and made tiny noises frustrated the shit out of him. It was annoying. When he finally pulled up in front of her office, she looked up and said, "Wow, I can't believe we're here already."

"Right?" he managed, irritated by how sucked into her phone she'd been.

"Well, thanks for this morning. I'm so excited to go back and get Tigger, if you're still down."

"Sure. What time do you get off?"

"Five, but whenever you can get here works. Also, would you mind if we swing by Target first, so I can buy things like cat litter and an adorable cat bed?"

"Let's at least be honest with ourselves here," he said, getting distracted by the curl of her eyelashes as she blinked and listened to him. "If we go to Target for cat stuff, you know we'll end up leaving with a million other things, like, ten hours later."

"I know," she said, sounding excited as she opened her door. "I promise it'll be fun. We'll try on outlandish clothing and put on a fitting room fashion show."

That was *so* her. He said, "That's fun?"

"It will be when we do it." She climbed out of the car, and

once she was out, she leaned on the door and said, "Thanks for being so cool, Jackie boy."

"See you at five, Piper."

He was smiling as he pulled away, but when he met his sister, Olivia, for lunch a few hours later, he was not.

"So she texts me to tell me that *Alex* is going to take her to get the cat instead."

"So?" Olivia looked at him like he wasn't making any sense as she squirted ketchup onto her burger.

"So the guy is a total douchebag, and the whole reason I went this morning was because she didn't want to take him."

"So she changed her mind." Livvie put the bun back on her burger. "Since when do you care about who your friends take with them when they get a cat?"

"I don't care," he said, annoyed that she didn't get it. "I just think she might be rushing things with this guy."

He explained to her their post-date Taco Hut routine, and how Hallie had ignored his text during their last one.

Olivia screwed up her face in that overdramatic *duh* expression she'd given him a thousand times when they were kids. "She's finally found someone decent, who has real boyfriend potential, and you're pissed?"

"I'm not pissed, Liv."

She raised an eyebrow. "Really."

"Really." Jack stabbed his fork through his side salad and said, "I just want her to find someone better."

Olivia leaned back in her chair. She crossed her arms over her chest, tilted her head, and said, "Holy shit, you have feelings for her."

"No, I don't." He dropped his fork and said, "Why in the hell would you say that?"

"So you only like her as a friend."

"That's right."

"You sure?"

"Yes." Jack wanted to growl at Olivia, but like he was in a cheesy rom-com, an image of Hallie saying *bartender* every time Vanessa had called her a waitress played in his mind, followed by the sound of her laughter as that stupid fucking cat burrowed into her black skirt and covered it with orange fur. His chest hurt and he felt a little light-headed. "Shit. I don't know."

Olivia's mouth dropped open and she gasped, but she quickly closed it and held up a hand. "It's not up to me to know anything about your feelings. But, Jack, if you don't want her to go out with this guy, why don't you just mess up their next date?"

"This is what the advice columnist has to offer? They should fucking fire you."

"No, listen. Just something stupid, like canceling their dinner reservation before they get there or showing up at the cat adoption place even though he's going because you just want to help your bestie."

"I have to go." Jack stood, banging his knee on the table in the process and growling through his teeth, "Dammit."

"I'm not done, you tool," Livvie said, staring at him with huge eyes like he'd lost his mind as she shoved a fry into her mouth. "And you literally haven't taken a bite of your lunch yet. Sit your ass down."

"Can't." Jack shook his head and headed for the door, needing air because he wasn't sure he could handle his epiphany. He wasn't sure he could handle how stupid he'd been. He needed to be alone and think, so he said to Olivia over his shoulder, "I have to bail, Liv."

A few hours later, he found himself walking into the animal shelter. The minute he went through the door, he could see Hallie and Alex, standing at the counter. Hallie was talking to the woman behind the desk, and Alex was saying something that was making her smile.

Jack was supposed to be the one making her smile.

He walked up to Hallie and said, "Where's our cat?"

"Jack," she said, looking surprised. "What are you doing here?"

He shrugged, feeling a little stupid but also happy about the way she was looking at him. "I just thought after we saw Tigger's propensity for rage this morning, you might need some help getting him home."

"Hi, I'm Alex," the blond clown said, smiling and extending his hand.

"Jack," he replied, shaking the guy's hand. "Nice to meet you."

"And I'm Carole," said the woman who was standing behind the counter in a light blue smock. "Let's go get your cat."

Jack followed Hallie as she tried to get her fat boy into a kennel that she and the clown had apparently just purchased at Target. *Dammit.* The cat did not want to go in, and it seemed as if Jack and Alex were in some sort of primitive contest to win Hal's favor by being the one to succeed.

Alex tried patience, holding out his hand and waiting in a crouch for Tigger to come over. Hallie, on the other hand, kept trying to pick him up, but the furball was not having it. In the end, Jack won, simply because he was quick and basically landed on top of the cat and pinned him down until Hallie could get him scooped into the carrier.

When they were finished at the shelter, Hallie said, "I'm

so glad you came, Jack. Obviously we couldn't have done this without you."

"Yeah," Alex added, smiling at Jack even as they both shared a knowing look about what was really going on.

"No problem," he said as she looked at her cat through the kennel door.

"We're going back to Hallie's for Chinese takeout," Alex said, stepping marginally closer to her. "Want to join us?"

Hallie looked up from the kennel and right at Jack, grinning and making a funny face. He wasn't sure if it was meant to convey *Please come and save me* or *Don't you dare; I want to be alone with my date.*

"I've got plans, but thanks," he said.

As Jack walked to his car, he cursed his sister and her stupid ideas, because there was no way his visit to the shelter did a damn thing to derail Alex's progress with Hallie, or to put Jack in some better position—not that he necessarily wanted to be in a better position.

But a few days later, when he wanted Hal to meet him at Taco Hut but she couldn't because she and Alex had fancy dinner reservations, he lost his damn mind. He heard Olivia's voice in his head, dialed the fancy seafood bistro, and said, "I need to cancel a dinner reservation."

Chapter
THIRTEEN

Hallie

Hallie closed her apartment door and hit the dead bolt. As she kicked off her shoes and dropped her jacket on the floor, she realized she was still smiling. Alex had left her at the door five minutes before, yet the smile was still on her face.

She didn't see Tigger—he'd been with her for a week now, and every time she came home he was asleep on her pillow—but that was easy to fix. She walked over to the kitchen, opened the utensil drawer, and took out the can opener. From the bedroom she heard the telltale *mrrreow* before heavy paws landed on the wood floor and he hightailed it in her direction.

Yes, Tigger's superpower was that he could literally hear the clicking sound of the can opener from anywhere on the planet.

"Hello, Tiggy," she said as she crouched down and petted his fuzzy orange head. She still couldn't believe she had a cat, but she was grateful to Ruthie for the whole weird moving-out debacle, because she was head over heels obsessed with Tigger. "Let's get you some tuna."

She opened the can and poured the contents into a saucer. Her phone buzzed in her pocket as she turned to toss the container. She expected it to be Alex, but it was Jack—who'd been weirdly quiet over the past few days. But perhaps he was as smitten with his PhD girl as she was with Alex and didn't have time to text.

Jack: How was dinner?

She took the phone into the bedroom and plopped down on her bed. OK, so listen to this. I told you Alex made reservations at the Aquarium, right?

Jack: Yep—so fancy.

Hallie: Well, we got there, and there was no reservation and no tables. Alex's face got all red and he looked pissed.

Jack: Did Jekyll become Hyde over expensive fish?

Hallie: No, Jekyll became fucking Romeo.

Jack: He poisoned you?

Hallie: He went outside and made a phone call, and then asked if I minded going on a walk for a bit.

Jack: So he called his mom to talk him off the rage ledge.

Hallie: Shut up and wait for it. We took a walk, and then after like thirty minutes he led me to an igloo in the park. We went inside and there was heat, twinkling lights, and a picnic blanket on the ground with to-go burgers and fries.

Jack: Shut the fuck up.

Hallie laughed and still couldn't believe it. Right?!

Her phone started ringing as she looked at it, and the second she raised it to her ear she heard Jack say, "Are you telling me that when your reservation fell through, the blond clown arranged a burger picnic in the park?"

"That is exactly what I'm telling you!" Hallie flopped back on her bed and closed her eyes. "Can you believe how charming that is?"

He made a noise that sounded like a snort. "It sounds to me like the guy knew he couldn't get a table and made up the whole reservation story just so he could look charming."

Hallie opened her eyes and stared up at the ceiling. "That is ridiculous."

"And you're home at ten, TB, so obviously there isn't a lot of sexual chemistry there."

"I know you want that stupid World Series ball, but don't ruin this for me." Things with Alex were amazing and perfect so far and were exactly what she'd been looking for. But Jack was a tiny bit right on that front. On paper, Alex was perfect. But she'd yet to feel any sort of burn for him.

She liked it when he kissed her—he didn't cram his tongue down her throat or lick her face off—but it definitely didn't have the these-clothes-must-come-off vibe she'd had with Jack during that drunken elevator ride.

But that would come.

And probably wasn't all that important to the overall relationship, anyway.

"Sorry, sorry." She heard him clear his throat before he said, "How's Tig?"

Hallie rolled over onto her side and grinned. "Everything I could ever want in a bestie."

His chuckle was deep and raspy, like he was tired. "I should bring him some catnip. I can't give it to Meowgi anymore because he gets too hyper."

She loved the way he sounded annoyed and in love all at the same time whenever he talked about his kitten.

"You should. He misses you." Hallie kind of felt like *she* did, too, because they hadn't hung out in a while. "He wants to show you his new place."

When she'd gone back to the shelter with Alex to officially adopt Tigger that day, she'd been shocked to see Jack after she'd told him he didn't have to come. He said that he was on his way home and just thought he'd swing by to see if she needed any help, and then he'd been surprisingly friendly to Alex as the three of them got her fluffy boy into his carrier.

It had been unexpectedly sweet, and she honestly hadn't known what to make of it.

He said, "I'll be in Minneapolis for the next two weeks on business, but I'm having dinner with Kayla the Friday I get back. Maybe I'll swing by afterward."

"Sounds good." She looked over at the window and at the darkened city beyond it. "How are things going with Miss PhD, by the way?"

"Good." He cleared his throat and said, "We're both so busy with work that we haven't talked a lot, but good."

"Dinner is promising, though, right?" she asked, wishing he'd share a little more about Kayla. He said things like *She seems great*, but he never really went into any detail.

"Yeah, it'll be great," he said. "I imagine I'll be over at your place around ten, if that works."

It'll be great. What did that mean? She said, "We can Door-Dash ice cream and watch a movie."

"It's a date," he said.

Hallie turned her eyes back to the ceiling. *It's a date.* She wondered, not for the first time, if she was being honest, what it would be like to actually date Jack. She didn't want to—she loved their friendship—but she'd be lying if she said she didn't think of their hot hotel sex and their *Pride & Prejudice* moment in her living room from time to time.

They ended the call not long after that, and then Alex called her.

She liked talking to him, really, but she couldn't help but notice their conversations lacked the *fun* that always accompanied a call with Jack. It was probably an unfair comparison, though, because no one had the easy banter she and Jack had. They were friends, which was what made it so comfortable and natural, and she and Alex were still *becoming* something.

It had nothing to do with Jack, and everything to do with their newness.

Easy explanation.

Jack

Jack was waiting for the hotel elevator when his phone buzzed. It was Hallie.

Hallie: Help! Going to dinner and can't choose.

The picture that followed was of two pairs of shoes—high-heeled black boots and a pair of black pumps.

The elevator doors opened, and Jack stepped inside before texting her back.

Jack: Depends on the outfit.

Hallie: Okay, one sec.

As he rode the elevator down to the lobby, he had a hard time not smiling, picturing Hal hopping on one foot as she tried putting on her shoes quickly.

She texted: Option #1.

It was a picture of the whole outfit, and he *did* smile then. Hallie looked gorgeous in a black dress, tall boots, and red lipstick, but her tongue was out and her eyes were crossed.

The doors opened and Jack started walking toward the lobby.

Jack: Boots are sexy, that face is not.

Hallie: How about this sexiness?

She included a close-up of her ridiculous face.

Jack: Hot. #2 please.

Jack exited out into the chilly fall evening and started in the direction of his favorite bar. He'd always loved downtown Minneapolis, and for some reason, it smelled and felt even better while he was texting Hallie.

He didn't know how it'd happened, but she'd completely taken over his brain.

Every morning when he went for a run, *she* was what he was thinking about.

And he spent way too much time every day trying to figure out what the hell to do about it. Because the bottom line was that even though he had feelings for her beyond friendship, it might not be worth it to do anything about it if that meant risking everything else they had.

Which explained why he was helping her get dressed for a date instead of asking her to go on one with him.

He was halfway to the pub before she texted back: Here's #2.

It was a photo of Hallie wearing heels, the outfit both elegant and smoking hot. Her eyes were half-closed, in an exaggerated sexy face and ridiculous pout.

Jack: #1 is my fave but #2 is classy if you're going for that. And also don't make that face.

Hallie: I will go with 1 because it's just dinner. And I thought I looked sexy AF.

Jack gritted his teeth as he remembered what this was for. *Duh.*

Jack: Going out with Alex?

Hallie: I really think you'd like him if you gave him a chance.

He dialed her number, and she was laughing when she answered. "You would, Jack."

God, it was pathetic, the way the sound of her voice shot through him like a buzz. "Doubtful. Where are you going?"

She said the name of a restaurant he'd never heard of, and he said, "No matter how good the food is, don't put out. The third-date rule is bullshit and you shouldn't cave to that pressure."

What in the fuck was that? He kind of wanted to punch himself in the face for that one.

"What are you, fifteen?" She was laughing and outraged all at the same time, he could tell. "I will *put out*—gross, by the way—if I feel like it, thank you very much."

He knew it was immature, but the thought of her kissing Alex made his gut hurt. Hell, the thought of her kissing *any* man made his gut hurt. He wasn't sure how he'd gone from zero to full-bore feelings for Hal, but it made him feel like a bit of a shit show. "I just meant that he seems a little slick to me and I want you to be careful."

"Awww," she said, her voice teasing and quiet. "It's so adorable when you make me want to hug you and throat-punch you all at the same time."

"That's my sweet spot," he said, trying to force himself to stop thinking about her and Alex.

"What are you doing tonight?" she asked.

"Walking to a bar to eat in solitude."

"Maybe you'll meet someone," she said, sounding ridiculously cheery.

"Nah," he said.

"Why not? You don't like Minnesota girls?"

"I don't like meeting strangers in bars."

"I'm sorry—what?"

"Seriously."

"The judges need clarification. Jack Marshall, man known to get freaky in hotel elevators with red-hot bartenders he doesn't know, doesn't like picking up chicks in bars?"

"I've always thought it was creepy."

She sounded amused when she said, "Please explain."

"It just seems idiotic to see someone and decide you like their appearance enough to start a conversation. It feels so . . . ?"

"Superficial?"

"Bingo."

"I have to go put on makeup, but I'm intrigued by this side of you. So you're saying it seems wrong to select a possible mate by their looks without considering their brain first?"

"You have a way with words, and yes."

"Wow, I might be a little turned on by this feministic outlook on the bar scene," she teased. "Text me later if you're bored, okay?"

"Okay." He cleared his throat and said, "Have fun."

"But not too much fun, right? Not *putting out* fun?"

"You're such a little shit," he said with a laugh.

He ended the call as he walked into McKenna's. He bellied up to the bar, where he'd always sat with his uncle Mack, and ordered a burger and a beer.

He looked around—it was starting to get busy for happy

hour—and thought how weird it was being there without him.

In the past, Jack had loved it when work sent him to the Twin Cities, because it'd been an excuse to stay with his favorite uncle and hang out. Mack lived in the building above the bar, so McKenna's had felt like his own personal kitchen. Every time Jack crashed there, he and Mack hit the bar for nearly every meal.

Everyone who walked through the door seemed to know Mack, and everyone who worked there treated him like family. He was like a beloved icon, the person who made life come alive when he entered a room.

And every time Jack visited, Mack had had a different girlfriend.

They all had one thing in common, though: They were fun.

Every girl Mack had ever introduced him to had been beautiful, funny, and down to have a good time. Jack had grown up watching the guy and wanted to be just like him. He'd wondered countless times over the years why anyone would rush to get married and settle down when you could live like that.

Mack wasn't the life of the party—Mack *was* the party, wherever he went.

"Here." The bartender set down Jack's food and said, "Need ketchup?"

Jack looked at the man and didn't recognize him. "No, thanks."

As he unrolled the utensils with the napkin wrapped around them and watched the TV behind the bar, he found it surreal that there wasn't some sort of accounting of the time his uncle had spent there, some kind of tribute to the man who'd been more mascot than customer.

A plaque, a picture, a retired barstool—there was nothing. No evidence Uncle Mack had ever been there.

It was like he'd never existed.

Taking a long pull from his pint, Jack thought back to the wake. The whole family had been at the mortuary, hanging out at the visitation and sharing stories, but no one else had shown up. He hadn't realized at first because the family was so big, but none of Mack's friends, no one from the bar, none of his girlfriends—not a single person from Mack's daily life had shown up to pay their respects.

It still pissed him off, and as he ate his dinner and the place thrummed with early-evening energy, he got more pissed for Mack. It was honestly depressing, that his uncle thought he'd been tight with his friends and this bar. Had he been wrong? Had they all humored him but didn't really give a shit? The women who had fawned over him—what were their stories? Where had they disappeared to?

As much as his mom liked to refer to her brother as a "hopeless bachelor," Mack had been more than that. He'd been the kindest, funniest, most generous person Jack had ever met, but since he'd chosen *not* to settle down, his life was just written off as less valuable.

Damn, Jack thought. He was getting far too introspective sitting here alone, and he needed more beer.

He finished his dinner, pounding a few beers while glaring at everyone who dared to hang out in that bar and watch football. All of a sudden, the place he'd considered to be one of his favorite restaurants in the world sucked. He didn't want to be at that asshole bar anymore, so as soon as the game ended, he paid his tab and went back to his hotel.

He was walking into his room when Hallie texted.

Hallie: Whatcha doin?

He dropped his key card, stepped out of his shoes, and fell back onto the bed.

Jack: Just got back.

Hallie: That was a long dinner. Did you meet someone?

Jack: The only person I met was the bartender who took my order.

Hallie: That sounds lonely.

Her text made him *feel* a little lonely. He texted: The whole night was weird. I don't really want to get into it, but let's just say I used to love this place because my uncle was here, and now he's not, so it feels like shit.

His phone started ringing, and it did something to his chest when he saw her name on the display. He answered with, "Piper. I said I don't want to talk about it."

"I know," she said, and he could hear the smile in her voice. "Which is why I'm calling. I thought I'd tell you about *my* night."

"Lay it on me." He got up and walked over to his suitcase. "Tell me everything."

"Okay. So." She cleared her throat, and he heard her cat meow in the background. "Alex picked me up and took me to the restaurant. It was nice, the wine was good, and then he ordered a vegan cheese ball as an appetizer and wanted me to try it."

"Is he vegan?"

"No, he's just had it before and it's really good."

"You didn't try it, did you?" There was no way that picky Hallie had tried a vegan cheese ball.

"He really wanted me to take a bite, so I did. I took the teeniest, tiniest little bite."

"And . . . ?" He pulled his shirt over his head and reached for the button on his jeans. "How was it?"

"I don't know, because about thirty seconds after I tried it, my throat got scratchy. Then my cheeks got red and my neck got blotchy."

"You're allergic?" Jack stopped undressing. "Are you okay?"

"I'm okay *now*." She sounded tired. "But I learned tonight that I'm violently allergic to cashews, which were apparently a core ingredient in the vegan cheese."

"Holy shit." He shucked off his jeans, dropped them into his suitcase, and went back over to the bed. "What happened? You sure you're okay?"

"Alex had to take me to the ER, and I'm pretty sure he heard me puking my guts out into a barf cone as I waited for the doctor."

"Holy shit," he said, wishing he'd been there to help her. "Also, what is a barf cone?"

"The nurse handed me this thing that was like a cardboard circle with a long, latex reservoir attached—barf cone. Vomit condom."

He started laughing, in spite of his foul mood and the fact that she'd had a health scare. "I'm so sorry you had to use the retch receptacle."

"It's okay . . . that I went HAM on the puke pocket."

"I would've held your hair," he said, still laughing. "If I'd been there."

"Well, I would've eaten with you so you weren't lonely, if I'd been *there*," Hallie said, and her words did something to him. For fuck's sake, *she* did something to him.

He cleared his throat and said, "So how's the cat?"

"Jack, he's amazing. How is it that I lived my entire life without him, but now, just like that, I can't even remember the before? Does that sound crazy, to be attached that fast?"

"No," he said, sitting down on the bed. "It doesn't sound crazy at all."

Chapter
FOURTEEN

Hallie

She watched through the window as Alex pulled up in front of Starbucks. They were grabbing a quick post-work coffee, and even though she was happy to see him, she'd kind of been in a fog of missing Jack all day.

She missed her best friend. He'd been gone for almost two weeks, and even though they talked and texted every day, it wasn't the same as him being there.

And things were going great with Alex—they were. He was attentive and funny and easy on the eyes, so she had no complaints. In fact, she'd decided while running that morning that she was going to do it.

She was going to ask him.

After he sat down and they talked about what'd happened at their respective jobs that day, she did it. She'd been dreading it for ages, but it wasn't going away and she really didn't want to go alone.

Hot mess shit show was still too fresh in her mind.

"I know we aren't really a 'thing' yet," Hallie said, awkwardly looking at her Frappuccino instead of Alex's face, "but would you want to go with me to my sister's wedding? It's a destination wedding at a resort in Vail—just family and a few close friends. You could be my plus-one, but there are no strings—"

"I would love that so much," Alex said, taking her hand. "I would really like for us to become a 'thing,' if that's okay with you."

"You would?" she asked, not sure if *she* was ready to be a thing. Even though—*shit*—she'd been the one to bring up whether or not they were.

"Absolutely," he said, smiling. He had a nice smile, complete with the crinkles at the corners of his eyes, and she knew he was a catch. Alex was a *great* guy. He leaned forward and pressed his mouth against hers. It was sweet, and she closed her eyes, trying to fall into it. His tongue touched hers briefly—they *were* in Starbucks, after all—before he pulled back and squeezed her hand. "I can't wait for us to go on a trip together."

She was thrilled that she wouldn't be dateless at her perfect sister's wedding, but after she got home, she couldn't shake the reality that she wasn't excited to go with Alex. Everything with him was great, but it was great in the way a Hallmark Christmas movie was great. Everything looked perfect—the clothing, the setting, the words—but none of it felt . . . real.

It felt forced, like they were each playing the part of two people falling in love.

She texted Jack, needing to shake off the unease and not think about it.

Hallie: Guess what? Alex said he'll go with me to Lillie's wedding.

Jack: You're taking him to Vail? You really want to do the family thing with him already?

Hallie shrugged in her empty apartment before texting: Maybe . . . ?

Jack: He's not the one, you know. You're not going to win the vacation with that guy.

Hallie: Have you ever thought that you might be wrong? What if he IS the one?

She waited for his response, feeling a little breathless with anticipation. Conversation bubbles started and stopped, started and stopped, and then, after an entire five minutes had passed, he texted: I guess time will tell.

She didn't know why, but she was disappointed with his response. She'd wanted him to care that she might be close to winning the bet. She'd wanted him to argue with her that the notion of Alex being the one was asinine.

But he hadn't.

And what was up with Kayla? He never really mentioned her, but she knew he was still talking to her. So what did that mean?

Was he falling in love with the beautiful grad student?

Hallie tossed and turned all night, kept awake by the uncomfortable realization that things with Jack could be changing. And as much as she wanted both of them to find their happy endings with their true loves, the thought of change, especially with Jack, made her stomach hurt.

Chapter
FIFTEEN

Jack

Jack pocketed his keys and headed for the door to Hal's building, a tiny little pouch of catnip in his jacket pocket. He'd landed a few hours before, and he'd had to force himself not to come running over to her place the instant he'd touched down.

Because he was dying to see her.

He didn't know exactly what he was going to do or say, but something had changed in Minneapolis. *He* had changed in Minneapolis. He'd realized that as scared as he was of screwing up what they already had, he wanted to move forward.

God, was he out of his mind?

He went into the lobby and pressed the up button on the elevator, wondering when the best time was to confess his terrifying feelings.

The elevator doors opened, and a blond guy stepped out. He took a step forward but paused when he saw Jack.

"Hey, you're Hal's friend. Jack, right?"

Jack looked at the man's face and realized who it was. Also, did he really have to call her "Hal," like it was that hard to say her full name?

"Hey, Alex. How's it going?"

"Good, good. Are you going up to see Hal right now?"

Jack gave him a nod and didn't think he could take it if the douchebag said *Hal* one more time. Also, where the hell else would he be going?

"Would you mind taking something up with you?" Alex put his hands in the pockets of his bomber jacket and said, "I bought a few toys for Tigger but left them in my car."

"Sure."

Jack followed the guy to his car, hating the fact that Alex was spending time with Hallie every day. Hating that he was buying toys for her damn cat, even as Jack's own pocket burned with the catnip he had taken care to bring. Alex popped open his trunk—a goddamn Camaro, of course—and Jack stood there, feeling lower than ever as Alex dug around, rambling about his life like they were buddies.

"Hal is such a sweetheart. I have no idea how I got lucky enough to land her as a girlfriend."

Jack squinted, forcing himself not to say that it was way too early for Alex to call Hallie his girlfriend, even though it absolutely was. "It's, uh, yeah—she's great."

The fact that she'd invited Alex to her sister's wedding was still mind-boggling to him, but he refused to think about it.

Alex kept digging—*how much shit could one person have in their trunk*—and said, "But I'm blown away that someone like her was even on the app, y'know?"

Jack felt like his jaw was going to break from clenching it so hard. "Yeah."

"I'm a huge believer in fate, in things happening because the cosmos wanted them to, so her reaching out to me feels epic, y'know?"

Alex stopped digging and said with a grin, "Listen to me—I sound like a fucking lovesick little girl."

"Now you sound like a fucking sexist."

"Right there I did, didn't I?" Alex laughed, which bugged the hell out of Jack. "Thank God there are no feminists loitering in the parking lot to overhear."

"That would be the worst, right?" Jack said, unsure if the guy was serious or not.

"The last thing I'd want to do is look bad in front of Hal, so for sure the worst. Although, honestly, she seems way too sweet to care about something like that."

"You'd be surprised," Jack said, remembering her at the speed dating event.

"No, I wouldn't." Alex looked one hundred percent confident in his opinion as he said, "Even though we haven't known each other very long, I feel like I already *know* know her."

Jack didn't even know what to say to that, so he just muttered, "Is that right."

"I think it's that fate thing."

Jack couldn't stop himself from saying, "I wouldn't really put much stock in fate on this one, by the way. Sometimes you get lucky, but this sure as hell wasn't because the stars aligned."

Alex said, "Says you."

"Says life."

"Nope." He shook his head and grinned like Jack was the

one saying ridiculous things. "It's fate, my guy, and you just don't get it."

"Listen, buddy," Jack said, really fucking irritated at this point. "Don't tell Hal I told you this, but we had a bet. We made a wager on who could find love first. So her feelings for you might be real and you might be the luckiest son of a bitch on the planet, but it wasn't the cosmos or your good karma that made her swipe right on you. It was the will to beat me and win a free vacation."

"Are you serious?" Alex's face fell, and Jack immediately regretted telling him. Regretted it, but still felt the tiniest twinge of satisfaction.

"Hundred percent."

Alex rubbed the back of his neck and muttered, "Huh."

Dammit. Jack sighed and said, "I mean, it sounds like she really likes you, so it still worked out, right?"

Alex looked distracted and upset. "I suppose so."

"If I were you," Jack said, backtracking because he wanted to respect Hal's relationship regardless of his feelings for her or his utter annoyance with Alex, "I'd forget you ever heard this and enjoy the ride."

"That's probably good advice." Alex smiled half-heartedly and handed Jack a grocery bag. "Here are Tigger's toys."

"Thanks." Jack took the bag, turned, and had only taken one step when Alex spoke up again.

"So . . . you and Hallie."

Jack stopped and turned back around. "What?"

Alex put his hands in his pockets and gave Jack a knowing look. "Is there something going on? Something more than friendship?"

Jack wanted to hit him again, which was weird because he rarely wanted to hit people. He gave his head a shake and said with total honesty, "No."

"Do you want there to be?"

"If I did," Jack said, exhaling, "I would talk to Hal about it. Not you."

Jack left Alex at his car and went back inside the building. He felt bad about getting in the guy's head and being a general asshole, but he'd apologize next time he saw him.

Right now, he just needed to see Hal.

Hallie

"You really need to buy a couch."

Hallie and Jack were sitting side by side on the floor with their backs resting against the wall, their legs stretched straight in front of them. They'd been watching another episode of *You* on Netflix, and it had just ended. She looked at him and said, "Is this hard on your old man back?"

"Funny girl." He put his hand on top of her head and tousled so hard she kind of tipped over, making her squeal and laugh. "It's hard on my one-year-older-than-you ass when your chunky boy won't get off of me."

Tigger had plopped his huge body on Jack's lap the minute he'd sat down and hadn't moved since.

"So I didn't even ask—did you have any fun at all in Minneapolis?" Hallie felt a little bad that she knew almost nothing about his job, but they had so much fun when they hung out that neither of their careers really ever entered the conversation.

"It sucked." He scratched behind Tigger's ear with one hand while grabbing the remote and flipping through Netflix with the other. "The work was fine, but usually when I go up there, I stay with my uncle and it's a whole big family thing. He passed away since my last trip, though, so it was just, I don't know, weird now."

His uncle Mack. She remembered his sister mentioning him. She didn't want to pry or make him sad, so she just said, "That really sucks."

He nodded and looked like he was casually watching the TV as he scrolled for something to put on, but his Adam's apple moved around a big swallow before he said, "I kind of wasn't prepared for what a gut-punch it would be, honestly."

She reached out a hand and squeezed his arm. "I'm so sorry."

He shook his head, like it was nothing. "It's no big deal, so quit looking at me like I'm a weepy little kid."

That made her pinch the arm she'd been softly squeezing. "I'm doing no such thing."

"Bullshit." He grinned at her and said, "By the way, Kayla dumped me over the phone yesterday."

"Oh, no." *Poor Jack.* "The PhD candidate?"

He nodded.

"Did she say why?" She couldn't imagine anyone not being into Jack. He was hilarious, charming, and damn pretty to look at; what the hell was wrong with Kayla? Even though he hadn't said a lot to Hallie about her, she suspected he'd kind of been hoping it would pan out into a real relationship.

"Ah, you know," he murmured, his eyes still on the TV.

"No, I don't know."

He shook his head and made a dismissive noise.

"Well, what did she say exactly?"

"Hal." He started laughing, and the sadness in his eyes went away when he looked at her, thank God. "Settle your ass down—she just wasn't feeling me. It happens."

She laughed with him, because regardlesss of everything else, she was so incredibly happy Jack was back that it was hard to stop smiling. She liked Alex as a romantic partner, but she realized she had the most fun hanging out with Jack. They'd gobbled down ice cream as they watched TV, and he hadn't even judged when she'd licked the bowl and then helped him finish his ice cream as well.

Her phone buzzed. It was a text from Alex, but she didn't feel like texting him until after Jack left. But when she looked at the text, it read: Can I call you? It's important.

Hallie swallowed and wondered what was up. Was he regretting saying yes to the weekend in Vail? She responded: Of course.

"I have to take a call—I'll be right back. Just sit and watch the movie," she said as she stood and went into the bedroom.

"Like this guy will let me do anything else," Jack muttered, scratching Tigger's big head.

She went into the bedroom, closed the door, and sat down on her bed. When the phone rang, she answered with, "Tigger loves his toys."

"Oh. Good." Hallie heard Alex clear his throat before he said, "Listen, I'm really bad at this stuff, so I'm just going to say it. You seem really great, but I don't think this is going to work."

Hallie's heart started beating in her neck as he continued

to speak uncomfortably. "Some guy is going to be really lucky, because you're an awesome girl, but I just don't think I'm that guy."

Hallie felt a little light-headed. "You're, um, you're breaking up with me?"

"I . . . I guess I am." Alex's voice sounded thick. "It's not you, it really is just a me thing."

"Okay. Uh, got it."

"Hallie, please don't—"

"Is this because I invited you to the wedding? Because if it's too soon, I'm fine—"

"No, the wedding sounded like a blast. I just . . . I just don't think we're meant to be together."

Hallie felt suffocated with the weight of rejection. She wasn't enough for him. He didn't want her. He didn't want to go to the wedding with her. He'd rather be single than be with her. She managed to croak, "Okay, um, I have to go. Take care, Alex."

"I'm sorry, Hal—"

She disconnected the call before she could embarrass herself further. Tears immediately filled her eyes, and she bit down on her lip to keep herself quiet. She felt like sobbing, like giving in to a big, sad cry, but Jack was on the other side of that door and she couldn't bear the thought of him seeing her like that.

Especially when he'd also gotten dumped and was handling it like a champ.

But every time she got close to having her emotions under control, she thought of her sister's wedding—where she and Ben would both be in the wedding party—and she lost it again.

The tears wouldn't stop, and after a while she forgot about Jack entirely.

Until she heard the knock on the door. "Hal? Are you okay? Did you fall asleep?"

She wondered if she were quiet he'd assume the latter and leave.

"If you don't make a noise in the next ten seconds, I'm coming in just in case you've fallen and can't get up."

"I'm fine," she said, but he must've heard the tone because he said, "I'm coming in."

The door opened a crack, and when he saw her, his face went from relaxed to dead serious. He swallowed and said, "Holy shit, what happened?"

He walked into the room, and in a second, his arms were wrapped tightly around her, which made her cry harder.

"It's no big deal," she said, kind of snuffling it out in a hiccupping sob, "but Alex broke up with me."

"Oh, God," he said, and she felt tension in his arms as he asked, "Did he say why?"

She shook her head and said, "Just the whole 'it's not you, it's me' bullshit."

She tried to sound unaffected as she said it, but she felt unlovable at that moment, which made her too sad to act cool.

"Well, it *is* bullshit. You know that, right?" He was talking into her hair, his voice low. "He's a moron, because you're incredible and any guy would be lucky to scoop your cat's fucking litter pan, do you hear me?"

That made her smile a little.

"Honestly, I didn't know you liked him enough for him to hurt you this way." He cleared his throat and sounded emotional when he said, "God, I'm so sorry that I didn't know how hard you'd fallen."

A tiny part of her was incredibly touched by that apology, by the fact that her friend felt bad for not reading her feelings better. But as Hallie lay there, staring into space, his first sentence gave her pause. *I didn't know you liked him enough for him to hurt you this way.* When she pictured Alex's face, she didn't feel *that* sad. When she thought about no more dinners with him, she didn't feel *that* disappointed.

"I didn't know, either," she whispered. "Hell, I don't even know now. Is it awful that I think I could be sadder about getting dumped than about actually losing Alex?"

"Not at all," he said into her hair, his arms staying tight around her. "I'm the same, Hal. Rejection feels like shit, even when it comes from someone who might not matter that much."

"Don't enable my bad behavior," Hallie said around a half laugh.

"It's true, though, horrible human."

She laughed again and started to face him, Jack's grip loosening so she could. She knew she looked hideous when he looked at her with a pitying smile. She said, "Shut up, I know I look good."

He gently swiped under her lower lashes with his thumbs. "No comment."

"The thing is," she said, blinking fast to stop more tears, "I just really hate starting back at square one; with Alex, at least I had hope that I was maybe on the way."

His eyes traveled over her face, and he said quietly, "I get that."

Of course he does.

"And now I have to go to my fucking perfect sister's wedding alone next week!" she cried, unable to stop herself from full-on bawling over that one. "I was so happy to call my mom the other day and casually drop that I had a boyfriend who would be coming with me, and now I have to roll into Vail with my tail between my legs."

"No, you don't."

"And I don't think I've ever told you about my ex, other than the fact that we broke up, but Ben is going to be IN the wedding. With me." She pictured his face and groaned. "I'm going to look so pathetic."

"You don't have to go alone," he repeated.

"Yes, I do. I don't have anyone." Her eyes filled with tears again.

"No. You don't. Listen," he said. "If you want, I'll go with you. You can pretend I'm your boyfriend, and we can be the greatest fucking couple they've ever seen until we return home from the trip and break up."

She sniffled and looked at his face. He looked serious. She asked, "You'd do that?"

He gave a little shrug and said, "Sure. I love Colorado."

"So," she said, unable to believe what he was offering to do, "you will let me tell them you're my boyfriend *and* you'll act like you love me?"

"Hallie Piper," he said, his voice low and husky as he looked at her, "from the second we enter the airport to depart until the moment we return home, I will be head-over-heels, worship-the-ground-you-walk-on, wildly obsessed and madly in love with you."

Hallie felt a little buzzed at the sound of those words. *God, he is good*, she thought as he looked at her like he meant every word. His jaw flexed as his eyes stayed focused on hers, and she sat up in the bed. "I can't believe you'd do that for me."

He shrugged again. "It's not a big deal. We're friends."

She could feel a smile coming as she said, "Thank you so much for being my friend, Jack."

"Right back atcha, TB."

Chapter
SIXTEEN

Hallie and Jack texted more than usual the following week as they finalized travel plans and lodging details. Her entire family was taking the same flight, so she was absolutely dreading *that*, but she made sure to request a room on a separate floor from everyone else.

She was a little nervous when she woke up at four a.m. on the day of the flight. Could they pull it off? Would Jack be able to pretend he was in love with her? Actually, as long as he managed to pull off a solid she's-kinda-cool disposition, Hallie would be thrilled.

She was zipping up her carry-on when Jack texted.

Jack: Good morning, my love. May I pick up a donut for you on the way to your place?

Hallie: Careful, I may ACTUALLY fall in love with you if you say things like that.

Jack: I will shower you in chocolate donuts for the rest of your life, my darling.

She laughed and texted: I think I just had a tiny orgasm.

Jack: On my way.

Just like that, her nervousness turned into excitement. She was going to Vail with Jack—how could it not be fun? She double-checked that she had absolutely everything she'd need and stacked her bags beside the front door.

She got a little choked up saying goodbye to Tigger, because she was afraid he'd feel abandoned. Ruthie was going to "take a crap-ton of Claritin" and come over every day to feed and play with him, so that made her feel a little better, but she still hated leaving him behind.

Jack, on the other hand, said he desperately needed a weekend away from Mr. Meowgi, who kept peeing on his bath mat.

Jack rang the buzzer when he got there, and she brought down her luggage. When she exited the building, he was waiting out front with his trunk open.

And he looked *hot* in his jeans and black hoodie. The man had the kind of chest you wanted to rest your palms on, if that made any sense at all.

"Good morning, boyfriend," she said, dragging her bags to where he stood. "Ready for a weekend away with the love of your life?"

His eyes narrowed as he looked down at her. Specifically, at the spot just above the V-neck of her black sweater. "Please tell me that I'm not inside that locket."

"Open it and see," she teased, the chilly wind blowing her hair in her face.

He rolled his eyes before reaching out and opening the silver locket that hung on a chain around her neck. She could tell he didn't think there would be anything in there, and his mouth dropped wide open in shock.

"You fucking weirdo—explain yourself," he said, laughing.

She grinned and moved around him to lift her bag into his trunk. "I took that selfie when you fell asleep on the floor watching *Pride & Prejudice*. I forgot to delete it, but then it was super easy to print and jam into my necklace. So yay for my horrible memory."

He just kept looking at her. "This is terrifying behavior."

"Says you."

"Says the laws of polite society."

"Whatever. My mother will lose her shit over this adorable pic of her daughter clowning with her boyfriend."

"Too bad I didn't think to snap a photo of you crawling out of my hotel room," he said, his eyes on hers as he grabbed the locket again. "Your mom would've loved that."

Hallie pictured him facedown and asleep in that bed as she looked at him and shook her head. "I still can't believe you saw that."

His eyes raised to hers, and his voice was quiet when he said, "Have I ever told you that I'm dying to know what you remember from that night?"

She stared into his blue eyes, and her voice came out a little breathy when she said, "What do *you* remember?"

"Every fucking thing." He said it fast and sure, and then his lips turned up. "But perhaps we should discuss this later. When we have time to compare notes."

"Yeah," she said quickly, pushing her hair back. *Compare notes.* "Later."

As they drove to the airport, they went over the details. Hallie thought she was going to have to coach him on stories, but everything about their actual relationship translated into their fake relationship.

They met at his sister's wedding, reconnected on a dating app, and had been texting and going on taco dates ever since.

It was too easy.

"So as soon as we hit the security line, we become boyfriend and girlfriend." Hallie wanted to make sure he realized that she needed him to be pretending the whole time. It wouldn't do for someone to see him chatting up some other girl outside the airport bookstore. "You know, just in case someone is watching and we don't see them."

"The minute we hit security, it is *on*."

"I just wish we didn't have to sit by all of them," Hallie said, picturing her aunt Diane's nosy stare. She loved her family, but they were always up in everyone else's business.

"We can upgrade to first class," he said, following the sign that directed him toward long-term parking.

"Shut up." Hallie had never been in first class. She turned toward him in her seat and asked, "Would that cost a lot?"

"As long as they have availability, it won't cost me anything."

"Because of all those miles you have?"

"Bingo."

"Oh, my God, Jack, you are making it so easy to fall in love with you."

He glanced over at her. "Glad to hear it."

By the time they headed for security, Hallie was cackling.

In the shuttle bus, the driver kept yelling at Jack to duck because he was just too tall and the guy couldn't see out the back. They hadn't been sure exactly what the driver had been looking for, but his inability to see through Jack and out the back window had really set him off.

The faces Jack made at her while getting screamed at left her crying with laughter.

Then, when they got inside the terminal, Jack realized he'd left his keys on the roof of his car, so he'd had to take a cab back to the long-term lot to retrieve his keys. When he walked back in, looking around for Hallie, his face was so full of irritation that it'd cracked her up again.

"You're a damn hero, Jack," she said as they approached the TSA line. "I appreciate you."

He looked offended when he said, "You shouldn't enjoy my suffering so much."

"I know. It's a character flaw."

"It really is."

When they joined the line, Hallie felt Jack's fingers slide in between hers. She looked up at his face, but he was looking straight ahead, as if holding her hand was something he was used to doing.

Ohhh. He's in character.

Hallie knew she should be good, but something inside her wanted to mess with him. Or play with this situation. Whatever the reason, she started moving her thumb, letting it stroke over the heat of his big hand.

"Hal," he murmured, still not looking at her.

"Hmmm?" she replied.

"I'm great with you doing that," he said, squeezing her hand a little tighter. "But just know that if you're still doing it when we get past the guy scanning boarding passes, I'm kissing you."

"What?" she squealed, a little too loudly.

He looked at her then, his lips sliding into a dangerous smile. "I like this game. I'm a big fan. What could make this day more fun than a one-up challenge?"

She grinned. "What's a one-up challenge?"

"A truth-or-dare of sorts. One-upping each other. I hold your hand, so you stroke that thumb of yours in a way that makes me fucking crazy. I kiss you, and you . . . one-up me, somehow."

"Somehow." Hallie couldn't look at him, turning her warm face so she was looking at the line in front of her. "Interesting."

"Isn't it, though."

They both stood in silence, her thumb still moving over his skin, as they got closer to the front of the line. She kept telling herself to stop, that it wasn't a good idea, but she was giddy with an electric anticipation as they stood in line to embark upon their vacation.

She swirled her thumb across his skin, making a figure eight, just as the man in front of them got his boarding pass scanned. Her heart was pounding as Jack let go of her hand so they could each hold out their passes to be scanned, and she realized he'd been kidding, because they'd reached the front and he hadn't kissed her yet.

"Thank you," she said to the TSA official, shoving her phone into her coat pocket.

"Thanks," Jack muttered.

Hallie had taken one step toward the area where they'd be removing their shoes when Jack grabbed her hand and turned her around. She looked up at his face, at those intense blue eyes, and before she could formulate a thought, his hands were on her face, his lips on hers.

She thought she heard him growl as he angled his head just a little and bit down on her bottom lip, and then she might've made a sound as he opened her mouth with his own and did something wicked with his tongue. Her hands came up to squeeze his upper arms—or grasp for leverage, she wasn't sure—as his tongue dipped into her mouth and he kissed her like he was sampling dessert, dessert he'd been denied his entire life and now he couldn't get enough of it.

Was starved for it.

He pulled back, looked down at her in a way that made her knees weak, and said, "We better move before we clog up the line."

She nodded. "Yeah. Um, yes."

Once they passed security, Jack grabbed her hand and pulled her off to the side of the foot traffic. He looked down at her with an unreadable expression, his eyes serious, and he said, "Are we okay?"

She nodded and said, "We're amazing."

His eyes softened then. "It was a fucking great kiss, wasn't it?"

"Holy shit, Jack," she said, shaking her head with a grin. "I almost passed out."

He threw his head back and laughed, a sound that made her want to curl up and take a nap in it, and he said, "I think I'm going to like being your fake boyfriend."

Chapter
SEVENTEEN

Jack

"So last I heard, you were messing with him on the app. Now you're actually dating?" Chuck, Hallie's best friend and also maybe her relative(?), whisper-shouted to her across the aisle.

As soon as Hallie and Jack got upgraded to first class, Chuck and his girlfriend, Jamie, had done the same. Which was good, because he wanted to get to know her friends, even if sitting with them made him a tiny bit nervous.

Feeling unsettled was quickly becoming his default state.

Because he had a lot—huge fucking heaps—of guilt about how things went down with Alex. He'd fully intended to mess with the guy, but he hadn't meant to get Hallie dumped, and he'd never imagined it would make her cry like that.

God, he hated himself for making her cry like that.

Every hour or so, he considered confessing, but selfishly, he didn't want to risk her rage when he was dying to tell her how he really felt about her.

"Yep." Jack listened as Hal told Chuck all about their bet and Taco Hut meetups, and he found himself riveted when she finished it with, "Then I realized that I was having a better time at our Taco Hut dates than I was having with any of the people I was seeing."

That was exactly how Jack felt.

"Wow," Chuck said. "And this is drunken hotel sex guy, right?"

"Oh, my God," Hallie whisper-shrieked. "Yes, but don't say it like I have more than one occasion of drunken hotel sex to my name."

Jack couldn't stop himself from laughing and adding, "Someday I'll tell you about her desperate search for her missing bra."

"Jack." Hallie rolled her eyes at him, and then shrugged. "Okay. Now I have to hear it. Tell me how ridiculous I looked from your point of view, because all I know is that I was trying to get the hell out of your room without waking you up."

"Holy shit, yes," Jamie said, tiny-clapping. "I need to hear this."

"You sure?" he asked Hallie.

"Go ahead," she said, laughing. "They already know my worst."

"Okay. Well." Jack looked at the freckles on the tip of Hallie's nose and wondered how he'd ever thought of her as just cute. "I don't know if she knew it or not, but our friend Hal here had, at some time during the night, fallen asleep on my feet. Like, my huge feet were her fucking pillow."

"No shit?" Chuck said.

"Oh, my God," Hallie groaned, already regretting that she'd asked to hear this.

"So I felt it the second she woke up, because blood flow returned to my extremities."

Jamie started cackling.

"I was about to lift my head and say something charming when she literally—*literally*—rolled off the end of the bed."

Hallie started laughing. "Oh, my God, you watched me roll?"

"I watched you roll."

"Was it hot or horrifying?" Chuck asked.

"Hilarious," Jack said, and Hallie gave him a look. Her eyes stayed on his face as she smiled, and he added, "In a hot way."

"Oh, bullshit," she said.

"So then . . . ?" Chuck prompted.

Jack was having a hard time not laughing. "So then she crawled over to her clothes and—"

"Wait." Hallie was grinning when she said, "I looked at you when I was putting on my pants, and you were sound asleep."

That made him laugh. "I closed my eyes pretty fast when your head swiveled in my direction."

She smacked him in the arm with a laugh, which made him grab her hand and sandwich it between his.

"She must've realized the bra was in the bed," he said, "because she tiptoed over and started moving her fingers on top of the sheets like she was trying to find it without jostling the bed."

They were all laughing. Hard.

"And then—my angel right here—she muttered 'fuck it' and ran out of the room."

Jamie and Chuck started applauding, and Hallie just

shook her head at him while wearing a grin. He felt her index finger slide over his palm—she was still playing—and he had no fucking clue how the weekend was going to shake out.

Because she really seemed to be enjoying the game, leaning into the fake dating thing, but he was already having a hard time remembering it was a game. Every time she leaned against his arm or held his hand, he was a little shook.

And the way she'd kissed him back at the airport—holy shit. He'd assumed it would be a flashback of their night in the hotel, but everything had changed since then, and it was totally different.

That night had been all about hot chemistry with a stranger.

Kissing Hallie in the security line—that was something else entirely.

That was like coming home.

Hallie

Jack is so good at this.

She put her head back on the seat and closed her eyes, relaxed by the sound of Chuck and Jack's conversation. There was something about hearing the deep voices of her two favorite people that made her feel all warm and fuzzy inside.

But as she listened to Chuck hit it off with Jack, she wondered if she should just tell him. He was *terrible* with secrets, but she hated lying to him.

Aside from Chuck, though, she would've thought she'd be

stressed or concerned about what they were up to, the whole fake dating bit, but she wasn't. At all.

It felt too good.

For once, when facing a family event, she wasn't even the tiniest bit stressed—and it was all because of Jack. It reminded her of when she was a kid and everything was somehow tolerable when her parents let her bring a friend along. He was her favorite friend, and his presence was making everything okay.

And that included the idea of seeing Ben.

She was very aware that once she was face-to-face with her ex everything might change, but at that moment, the thought of it didn't make her lose her neurotic mind.

And yes, Jack's PDA made her hot and bothered—she was only human, for God's sake. The man kissed like he was going to be murdered if he didn't pull off the world's hottest kiss, like a gun was pointed at his head and his only shot at life was to weaken her knees with his mouth.

Any human would need smelling salts after Jack Marshall's mouth touched their mouth.

But she was kind of attributing it to what Jack said before, about their bodies knowing each other. They *had* slept together, so it made sense that their sexual chemistry would skew less on the friends-faking-love side and more toward the raging-wildfire-scorching-thousands-of-acres end of the spectrum.

She wasn't even fazed.

In fact, she thought the one-up game sounded like the most fun she'd had in ages. She spent the rest of the short flight with her eyes closed, but she was far from sleeping. She was downright giddy as she thought about messing with him, of amping up the PDA in delicious ways.

And if she was giddy at the thought of her own actions, she was downright obsessed with the thought of his. What one-ups would Jack Marshall be capable of?

She heard him say to Chuck and Jamie at one point, "I think she's asleep."

Not asleep, Jack, she thought, forcing herself not to smile. *Just lying in wait.*

Chapter
EIGHTEEN

"Here's your room key, hon."

Hallie took the key from her mother as she climbed out of the van. The whole group had been met at the Denver airport by a fleet of passenger vans that drove them to their resort hotel in Vail. She'd planned on messing with Jack during the trek, but because of someone's kids' car seat needs, he'd gone in the van with Jamie and Chuck, and she'd been stuck in the one that was transporting her parents and grandparents.

Which, after twenty minutes of constant questions about Jack, required even more fake sleeping.

"Thanks," she said, smiling as she got out and stretched. The mountain air was amazing, and she felt surrounded by the yellow leaves of the aspen trees and the sense that autumn was arriving that very second.

She glanced toward the hotel entrance . . . and saw Ben.

God.

Her ex was maybe more handsome than he'd been be-fore, and her stomach filled with butterflies as she looked at that face, the face she used to know as well as her own. His brown hair was a little longer than he used to keep it, he had a short beard that looked really good on him, and it appeared that he was wearing the red plaid scarf she'd always loved.

Her heart started beating faster, but then she saw him laugh and noticed he was laughing with her sister. Her vision panned away from him and she saw that Ben, Lillie, and Chuck were all laughing at something Jack was saying.

She swallowed. *Might as well get this thing started.* She saw Jack notice her as she headed toward him, and *damn*, he was good at being a fake boyfriend.

Because even though he kept up with the conversation, his eyes landed on her with a focus so intense that even Lillie and Ben turned to see what he was looking at.

"Hey, you," she said, wrapping both of her arms around his right one and going up on her tiptoes for a quick kiss.

His eyes narrowed ever so slightly, like a question, before his lips kicked up into a smile and the question was replaced with his teasing, knowing glint. He kissed her back, a cute, normal-couple peck of hello, but instead of letting her go, he grinned at her and said, "Your glasses are smudged—here."

He gestured for her to hand them over, and she bit down on a giggle as he took the glasses from her fingers and did the whole hot-breath-smudge-wipe thing with the bottom of his shirt. *So chivalrous.* Instead of handing them back, though, he placed them on her nose and gave her an intimate grin that she felt in her toes.

"Better?" he said in a quiet voice.

"Much," she breathed, half hot and bothered, half trying not to laugh. All of a sudden, she was glad she'd decided to go with glasses for traveling instead of her contacts.

"Hey, Hal," Ben said. "Long time no see."

Hallie felt Ben's voice like a punch, and she shifted her gaze to his face. He looked beautiful and just like the boy she'd loved with her whole heart, and her throat was tight as she turned her lips up into what she hoped was a casual smile. "Right? How *are* you?"

"Fantastic," he said without a hint of awkwardness, like it was easy to face her.

"Great," she replied, suddenly unfamiliar with words. She didn't love him anymore, but his face was like a song: One look at it and she felt every single bit of sad emptiness from their breakup. "That's really great."

He nodded and smiled.

"Do you have our room key, babe?" Jack asked, knocking her back into the present.

"What?" Hallie tucked her hair behind her ears as Jack gave her a knowing look, like he was absolutely sure of where her head had just been. She nodded and said, "Yes. Key. I have it."

"Where are you guys?" Jamie asked. "We're in 326."

"Everyone's on three," Lillie said. "We blocked off the whole floor."

Chuck asked Hallie, "What's your room number?"

"Um." She bit down on her lip before muttering, "I'll text you."

"What?" Her sister put her hands on her hips. "Why are you acting all secretive? What room are you in?"

Hallie glanced at Jack, who was giving her that sexy smirk, before saying, "Can't a girl and her boyfriend move to a quieter floor without it being a criminal offense?"

"You've never been to this hotel. Why would you assume three is noisy?" Hallie could tell that for some reason, this pissed her sister off. Lillie asked her, "Did you change the reservation?"

"I did," Jack said, picking up his carry-on and putting it over his shoulder. "We, uh, just wanted a little privacy."

"Privacy?" Her sister looked confused. "You have your own room, for God's sake."

Jamie started laughing, and when Hal looked at her, it was obvious what she thought.

She glanced at the rest of the group and she could tell that they thought the same thing now, too.

They all thought that Jack had reserved a room on a different floor so he and Hallie could have a weekend of wild sex. She felt her cheeks get hot as they all stared at her, but she wouldn't have had it any other way.

Suck on that, Ben.

She picked up her own luggage, pulled out the room key, and said to Jack, "Shall we go get settled in, baby?"

He looked like he wanted to smile at the endearment they both knew she would *never* use for him, and he said, "It would be my absolute pleasure."

As they walked into the hotel, he quietly said, "Is Scarf the ex-douchebag?"

"Yes." She started laughing, so glad she'd brought him. "Scarf *is*."

Jack

"I'll just call the front desk." Hallie dropped her bags and walked to the phone on the nightstand. She pressed the zero key and said with a laugh, "But this is hilarious. I don't know that I've ever heard of this actually happening in real life."

Jack watched her kick back on the king-sized bed, twirling the phone cord like everything was fine. "You've never heard of a reservation getting screwed up?"

"I've never heard of an only-one-bed trope actually happening." She rolled her eyes at him and said, "It's a romance novel thing. You know, two people forced to sleep together in one bed because there's no other option . . . ?"

His collar felt tight. "That is ridiculous."

She rolled over onto her stomach and muttered, "You're ridiculous. Oh, hi. My name is Hallie Piper, and I'm up on . . ."

As she spoke to the front desk associate, Jack set down his suitcase and walked over to the window. The room was amazing—stone fireplace, overstuffed reading chairs, wood floor with a thick rug, king-sized bed—but the view from the balcony was even better.

He opened the door and stepped outside. The Rocky Mountains filled the horizon, a breathtaking panorama, and a wide, clear stream gurgled below with a thick border of yellow aspens on either side.

He braced his arms on the railing and took a deep breath of Colorado air.

"I have good news and bad news."

Jack heard her step out onto the balcony, but he didn't turn around. "Of course."

"The good news," she said, wrapping her arms around

him and leaning her cheek against his back, "is that we don't have to move to a room on the third floor."

Jack could feel every tiny movement of her fingers on his chest, could feel her voice rumble soothingly against his skin. He swallowed and managed, "Nice."

He looked down at the ten pink fingernails that were spread out on his chest. *Fuck.*

"But the bad news," she said, kind of giggling as she spoke, "is that we have to stay in this room."

"What?" He turned around and stared down at her face. She looked startled by his reaction, and her hands fell to her sides as he said, "You're telling me they can't find a single room?"

She blinked. "Well, they *do* have a couple of rooms, but they're on the third floor."

He said, "So let's move."

"By my family."

"So?" he asked.

"So we just made a whole big thing about wanting a private sex room."

She was seriously going to kill him with her Hallie-ness. He sighed and said, "We never said anything about a sex room, for the love of God."

"It was implied," she said, as if he were the ridiculous one. "So how do I explain the change of heart? We didn't want to have wild sex in the same bed, we like to use two? We prefer to sleep separately after we bang?"

"Will you stop saying 'bang'?"

"You don't like 'bang'?" She smirked and said, "You, Jack Marshall, don't like 'bang.' That's right; you prefer 'jostling' and 'railing.'"

He sighed. "No one will have to know we're down there."

"They'll know," she said.

He tilted his head and cracked his very-tight neck. "I'll make sure they don't."

"Can you just do this for me?"

"No," he barked.

"Why not?"

He knew he must sound totally unreasonable to her. He said, "I just think it's a bad idea."

"Why?"

"Why?" He very nearly yelled the word as he tried getting through to her. "Sharing a bed while pretending to be in a relationship? That doesn't seem like it's treading something that could fuck up a friendship?"

She shrugged, and something about the gesture made him want to pull her coat tighter around her body and make sure she was warm enough. She said, "I get what you're saying. I mean, even though we don't ever talk about it, this friendship means a lot to me and I'd hate if something got in the way of that. But . . . "

He clenched his jaw together as he waited for her to continue.

"We don't have a normal friendship. We became friends *after* we slept together. Sex and feelings can't get in the way, because we drove over them right at the beginning."

He swallowed. Why did it irritate him that she was so cool about it, so positive that more intimacy wouldn't add feelings?

Dammit, he knew he was all over the place and making zero sense.

But the reality was that he hadn't considered how much of a mindfuck the fake dating might be for *him*. He didn't like that it felt real when she wrapped her arms around him, and he didn't like the way he felt when he kissed her; it felt like everything he wanted. And since she was, in fact, faking it in accordance with their agreement, if he acted on his feelings under the guise of faking it, that felt like lying. Or fraud.

He wanted to tell her how he felt about her and then give her time to explore her own feelings and respond accordingly. But if he told her how he felt now, would she think it was part of the game? Or a result of the game?

Or, worse, would she confuse their pretend relationship with her true feelings for him?

The best thing to do, as much as he didn't want to, was wait until they got back to Omaha to discuss his feelings. They needed to fake date for her family like he had agreed to do, keep their hands off each other in private, and revisit what was really going on once they were wheels-down at home.

He said, "Hal, maybe—"

"You're overthinking this, Jack."

Something about the way she said it and the look on her face made him pause. "What do you mean?"

She looked a little bit shy but also entirely confident as she lifted her chin and said, "I *really* liked kissing you at the airport, and if it happens again under the guise of fake dating, I will enjoy every minute of it. But I also think sleeping in the same bed with you sounds like an absolute blast, like a grown-up platonic sleepover. We can handle it."

He had no idea how to respond to that tempting but terrible idea, and he could smell her perfume, which somehow made everything worse.

When they had made their travel plans, he'd imagined they would behave like roommates for the weekend. In that scenario, they would be watching TV from two separate beds on opposite sides of the room and telling jokes in the dark.

But talking in the dark in the same bed? Watching TV under the same blanket? His head felt like it was going to explode when he thought about it.

She said, "The minute we cross the security line back home, we can return to being friends who are each respectively searching for their soul mates."

He turned his head to the side and cracked his neck again, suddenly stiff as hell. "Well, I don't think—"

"Tell me one good reason why we can't make this work."

He had a very good reason, but not one he felt like sharing until they were home. He let out his breath and said, "Fine. We'll stay in this room, but if you touch me, I swear to God I'm screaming."

Hallie

Was it weird that she found this side of him adorable? Teasing, hilarious Jack was being uncharacteristically uptight and genuinely worried about jeopardizing their friendship.

He was sweet under all that Jack.

She really didn't want him to be uncomfortable, though, so she asked him, "Are we good?"

He rolled his eyes and tousled her hair. "Fuck right off with the coddling, Hal. I'm fine; I'm just trying to protect this."

"Great." Hallie smacked his hand, stepped away from him, and straightened her hair while feeling punched in the gut by the emotions behind his words. *Protect this.* Something in the way he said it made her feel . . . unsettled, but it was probably the fact that she didn't like admitting how important his friendship had become to her.

"So do you want to go do Vail or what?" he asked, sounding like a total grump.

"Let's do it," she said. "Care if I change first?"

"Yeah, I will, too."

She went into the bathroom and changed into a black turtleneck sweater, jeans, and hiking boots. She rolled her clothes up into a ball to hide her underwear, the same way she did when she had to visit the gynecologist.

God forbid people knew she wore underwear.

"Listen, Jack," she started, pulling open the bathroom door, "maybe we . . ."

The words died on her lips when she saw him standing in front of his suitcase in just his jeans—jeans that were hanging low enough that the waistband of what appeared to be boxer briefs was visible.

Dear God.

He had that jutting-hip-bone thing that she had thought only existed on the covers of cowboy romance novels.

"Yes?" he asked.

She looked up from his stomach. "What?"

He smiled a little. "You said *maybe we* . . . and then you trailed off."

"Oh. Yeah." She gave a breathy laugh and said, "God, you caught me off guard. I forgot how, um, how *that* you are."

And she gestured with her free hand toward his naked torso.

"'That'?" he repeated, with one eyebrow raised.

"Yes, *that*." She rolled her eyes and said, "You know exactly what I mean, Jack Marshall."

He repeated, grinning, "*That*."

As she opened her suitcase beside his and dropped her clothes inside, she said in an octave lower than her usual voice, "My name is Jack. I'm so hot. I'm so *that*."

He started laughing.

"Please put on a shirt before I kill you," she said, grabbing her jacket from a hanger and sliding into it.

"Because my . . . *that* is bothering you?"

She shook her head and narrowed her eyes into her meanest squint. "Y'know what? Don't wear a shirt. See if I care. Go hike naked. I'll laugh my ass off when the bears eat your *that*."

"I'm pretty sure I can outrun you," he said, still laughing as he pulled his gray Henley over his head and threaded his arms through the sleeves. "So I'm confident my *that* will remain intact."

"But," she said, "as soon as you attempt to *outrun* me—"

"Piper." He reached out a big hand and fisted the front of her jacket, his eyes still smiling as he playfully yanked her a little closer. "I don't believe for a second that you'd let a bear eat me."

"No?" she asked, her heart doing a little stutter in her chest as she was instantly aware of the distance between his mouth and hers.

"No." His eyes dropped down to her lips, like he was thinking the same thing. For a beat they were both frozen in possibilities, neither moving nor speaking, but then Jack cleared his throat and said, "Because I'm the only one who gets your taco order right."

"True." Hallie nodded, and her lips slid into a smile of their own accord as she felt all warm inside. "No one else understands that it's ridiculous to put the cheese on top."

"I mean," he said, his grin matching hers, "what is the point of cold, hard cheese?"

Chapter
NINETEEN

They spent the afternoon, just the two of them, walking all over Vail. She forced him to go down the hill with her to the nearest Starbucks before they visited the charming shops, and after that they snagged beer and slices outside an adorable pizzeria.

They'd intended to hike up into the mountains, but the village of Vail had been so picturesque, the afternoon so autumnally gorgeous, that they'd just strolled instead.

Hallie felt happy because, in spite of his concerns, fake dating Jack was her new favorite pastime. Alone in the mountains, they wouldn't have to pretend. But in the picturesque little town, anyone attending the wedding could see them.

Which was why she held his hand while they walked around, hopped on his back when her legs got tired and he offered a piggyback, and why she kissed him.

It was absolutely necessary.

When they stopped in front of a store that looked like a

tiny chalet and Hallie attempted a French accent, Jack gave her the mockery she deserved.

"That is atrocious, Piper," he said, laughing at her, and she realized that his smiling face was only about an inch or two above hers. Just . . . *right* there.

So close.

He swallowed as their eyes held, as if noticing the same thing, and she said, "I think I see my uncle Bob coming."

"You're looking at me. How would you see that?" he asked, his eyes dipping down to her lips.

"It's like an intuition thing," she said in a near-whisper. "Just in case, we should probably kiss."

He said in a deep, quiet voice, "Hallie Piper, do you even have an uncle Bob?"

"I just want to so badly," she breathed, unsure if she was talking about kissing or having an uncle Bob.

"Well, if you want to," he said, reaching out with a finger to trace the arch of her eyebrow, his eyes all over her face, "maybe you should."

The words were nothing, but his tone was challenging. Daring.

So she tugged on the collar of his coat, pulling him down a little closer as she went up on her tiptoes. Instead of going for his mouth, though, she kissed the side of his neck, breathing in his scent while scraping his throat with her teeth. She could feel his intake of breath, and she reveled in the tiny groan as her lips and tongue tasted his warm skin.

Images shot through her head as she imagined what it would be like to do that when they *weren't* on a public street in a charming mountain vill—

"Hal. You need to stop. That. *Shit*." Jack grabbed her upper arms and set her a step away from him, his voice a little gravelly. He ran a hand down his face, breathed in through his nose, and said, while not looking at her, "Come on. I need to walk."

She felt like a sex goddess as they started walking, like she'd rendered him weak with her seductive necking skills. She hadn't realized she'd been smiling, though, until he nudged her arm and said, "Quit that."

It was barely an hour later when they kissed again, but this time it was all Jack. They were in the outerwear store, and Jack went back to the men's section while Hallie shopped in the women's.

The store employee was totally a ski bro: young, adorable, athletic, and into skiing. He chatted her up about the slopes, and then he put a cute hat on her head.

"You need to get the pink Patagonia. Totally makes your gorgeous greens pop."

She rolled her eyes and shook her head at the dude. "Stupid sentences like that aren't going to get you the Patagonia commission. Not from me, at least."

He smiled and adjusted the hat, pulling it down onto her forehead. "It's not nice to call my heartfelt compliment stupid."

She laughed and said, "I'm not buying the hat."

Suddenly, Jack was right beside her. She felt his presence before she saw him, and she smiled up at him as he reached out a hand and tugged on one of the hat's dangling strings.

"I like it," he said, looking at her in a way that seemed obscene in public. His eyes didn't waver from hers, and the heat in them nearly scorched her irises. She didn't even know how to respond. He turned his attention to the sales guy and said, "We'll take it."

They moved to the cash register, and as soon as Jack paid for the hat, he maneuvered her through the small store and into a changing room. "I think I see a relative."

"You need a number for the changing room," the sales guy shouted.

Before she could say a word, the door closed and Jack's mouth was on hers, feeding her wild kisses that made her pulse beat hard as his hands rested on the wall on either side of her face. The mirror was at her back as he pressed against her—every hard bit of him—and she kissed back with as much hunger as she felt from him.

He cursed against her lips and raised his head. He gave her a dirty grin and said, "I think they're gone."

"You sure?" She raised her thumb and dragged it over his lower lip. *Had it always been this full?* "I mean, they could still be lurking."

His eyes were heavy-lidded as he lightly bit down on her finger—wow, how did *that* feel hot—and then took a step back from her. He dragged his hands through his hair. "I'm afraid your boyfriend out there's gonna call the cops on us, and your sister will kill us if we get arrested."

"Oh, yeah." She kept forgetting about the wedding. "What time is it?"

He glanced at his watch. "5:05."

"We should probably head back so we can shower and get ready for the rehearsal."

"After one more coffee stout at the brewery . . . ?"

"Fine." She rolled her eyes and said, "You better chug, though, because it takes a long time to make this girl look presentable."

"Just wear the hat and call it good. The guy is right—makes your gorgeous greens pop."

"On that note," she said as they left the fitting room and walked toward the exit, "can you please not interrupt next time I'm being complimented by a bro? I might've gotten lucky if you hadn't stepped in."

He messed up her hair and put his arm around her neck. "Sorry, my bad."

After they got back, Jack decided to go work out. That way, he said, she could have the room to herself for an hour to get ready before he needed to shower.

"You sure?" She crossed her arms and watched as he grabbed running shoes, shorts, and a T-shirt. "I was kidding—I can get ready pretty fast."

"I'm dying to get in a quick mountain run," he said, walking toward the bathroom. "And I need to lift. I can get ready for dinner in fifteen minutes, so the timing will be perfect."

After he left, Hallie took a long, luxurious shower. She was having the time of her life playing boyfriend/girlfriend with Jack, and she wished the weekend would never end.

Part of her felt like she should slow down and examine the "why" of her enjoyment, but she quickly pushed that thought out of her mind.

Hallie did her hair and then applied some eye shadow for a smoky eye look while half watching a *Top Chef* marathon. When she was finished, she steamed a few wrinkles out of her dress and put it on.

Her sister, the attention whore, was having all the bridesmaids wear white to the rehearsal, while she wore a scarlet gown, and then the colors would be flipped for the wedding.

She'd been obsessed with the idea since Taylor's version of *Red* came out, and she'd found a man who was all-in on her theatrical side. It *would* be amazing for the photos, but since it was her sister, Hallie just considered it annoying and melo-dramatic.

She did love her dress, though.

It was long and white, a flowy fabric that hugged her body but wasn't stuck to it. One shoulder had a white ruffle that cut diagonally to her waist, while the other shoulder was bare. Hallie thought it looked like something she'd wear to one of Diddy's white parties if she were famous enough to be invited, if he still did those . . . and, now that she was think-ing about it, if he was even still called that.

She was putting on her pearl earrings when she heard Jack at the door. She was ready for him to make fun of her for looking positively bridal, but when she opened the door and said "Marry me" in her best Maeby Fünke voice, he didn't crack a smile.

His eyes moved all over her, from her hair to her face and down the length of her dress, before he just said, "Wow."

"I know," she said, rolling her eyes. "She's making all the bridesmaids wear white tonight. It's so over-the-top, but she's the bride."

She turned away from him and went to grab her beaded handbag from the nightstand. "I'm going to go down to Chuck's so you can have some privacy—"

"No."

"Huh?" She looked at him over her shoulder, and as he cleared his throat, her eyes dropped down to his neck, his sweat-dampened shirt, and then his legs.

Oh, God, those legs. He had thick, chiseled calves.

She was such a sucker for a good calf.

He had very bitable calves, if that was a thing.

He said, "Just stay. I need ten minutes tops in the bathroom and I'm ready."

"You sure?" She straightened and turned around, but she was having trouble with words. Out of nowhere, she was zapped with the awareness that he was going to be showering, naked, just through that door in mere minutes, getting all wet and soapy and—oh, my.

"Yep."

"Okay. Cool." She walked over to the mirror that hung between the hotel fridge and the desk and leaned a little closer to check her lipstick.

"Don't move." Jack walked over and stepped behind her, and they looked at each other in the mirror. "You're only halfway zipped."

"Oh." Hallie sucked in a breath when she felt his fingers on her zipper, his other hand on her lower back, and the heat of his body behind her. Through the mirror, she watched his eyes on her back as he slowly slid up the zipper. She saw the clench of his jaw and the flare of his nostrils, and how his left hand lingered after the zipper reached the top, resting on her lower back. After a moment, he stepped back, cleared his throat, and said, "Okay—how long do I have?"

She blinked, confused for a second, before looking around him in the mirror at the clock. "Uh, fifteen minutes," she said.

He nodded and walked toward the garment bag that was hanging next to the bathroom. "Easy peasy," he said, before going in the bathroom and shutting the door behind him.

Jack

He was pretty sure the weekend was going to kill him.

He turned on the shower, but no matter what he did, he couldn't get the image of Hallie in that white dress out of his head. Her wavy hair, red lipstick, pearl earrings—she looked like a fucking bride.

What was that expression—a man plans and God laughs?

Yeah, someone was cackling at that moment at his idiotic fake relationship plan.

He toed off his running shoes and pulled his shirt over his head before he grabbed his phone and texted Hallie.

Jack: I should've said this before, but you look incredible.

He knew she was wrinkling her brow as she read the message.

Hallie: Why are you texting me from the bathroom?

Jack: Because I don't want this sentiment to get caught up in our games. Your buddy Jack—not fake boyfriend—is telling you in a purely subjective statement that you look absolutely stunning.

Hallie: Well if I'm being honest with my real-life bestie, not my fake bf, I'm having the best time vacationing with you and I don't want it to end.

Jack: Same.

He put down the phone, shed his remaining clothes, and got in the shower.

He wished he had any fucking clue what Hallie was thinking. What she was feeling.

Because it appeared to him that she was enjoying their little game just as much as he was. But she seemed casual as hell about it—blasé, even, which made him think she was still his wingwoman and just "leaning in" to the weekend of pretend, whatever she even meant by that.

And if that was the case, he couldn't bare his soul to her and risk losing her as a friend.

He quickly shaved, brushed his teeth, and combed his hair before getting dressed, and when he walked out of the bathroom and looked at her in that dress again, leaning back on the bed and looking at her phone, his necktie felt like it was strangling him.

His phone buzzed as he slid his feet into his dress shoes, and he pulled it out of his pocket.

Hallie: Don't let this go to your head, but you look handsome AF. Like, I want to call you beautiful, but I feel like you'll be insulted.

Jack tried to swallow, but his throat was fucked up all of a sudden.

He texted back: Are you ready to go, TB?

He kept his eyes on his phone but heard her giggle as she texted: I am. But I feel like I should warn you—your girlfriend gets a little handsy when she drinks wine.

He couldn't *not* grin, and he responded with: Then I feel like I should warn YOU—when my girlfriend gets handsy, I usually find the nearest broom closet or elevator and make her scream.

He did look at her then, half smiling because he knew he'd shut her up, and he instantly regretted it. Because first, her mouth dropped open and her cheeks got red; the response he'd been shooting for. But then—holy balls—she puckered her crimson lips, tilted her head, looked him straight in the face, and raised an interested eyebrow.

Fuck my life, he thought, as he pulled open the door and held it for her.

Chapter
TWENTY

Hallie

"So we want the bridal party out in the hallway," Hallie's mother shouted, "and everyone else in the ballroom."

Hallie rolled her eyes and said to Jack, who was holding her hand and patiently waiting for the rehearsal to get under way, "I'll be back."

"I'll be in the ballroom, apparently."

She started pulling away, but he jerked her back and kissed the tip of her nose. His eyes were warm as he smiled down at her, and her stomach did the tiniest little flip as she had no choice but to smile back.

She was grinning as she walked out into the hallway, lost in her own thoughts. So much so that she didn't even see Ben until he said, "Hey, Hal."

She stopped walking and looked at him, irrationally irritated by his use of her shortened name. "Ben. Hi."

He smiled and said, "You look great."

"Thanks." She rubbed her lips together and looked at a spot

just past his shoulders, because she didn't want to see his warm brown eyes. She said, "Yeah, you, too."

Of course Ben was the kind of perfect guy who couldn't abide the elephant in the room, so he said, "Listen, I don't want this wedding to be awkward—"

She held up a hand. "It won't."

"—so I hope you'll accept my apology."

She dropped her hand and did look at his eyes then, shocked by his words. Apologizing had never really been his thing, even when he'd ripped her heart out. Hallie crossed her arms, suddenly cold, and said, "For . . . ?"

"For everything." He squeezed the Fiji water bottle he was holding, like he was nervous, and said, "I'm so sorry."

She looked at him and was seriously conflicted. Part of her wanted him to suffer forever, because she could still feel the pain of his rejection. She might not want him anymore, but she'd be lying if she said that certain songs didn't take her right back to that September and still fill her with an aching melancholy.

But a larger part of her also didn't care. She looked at him, at his beautiful face, and all she felt was nostalgia.

She swallowed and said, "It's history, Ben—all is forgotten."

His eyebrows went up and he turned his head a little, like he wasn't sure he'd heard her correctly. "What?"

"I'm over it, so we're cool."

"Wow." He smiled, looking totally surprised, and she wondered if she'd ever be able to look at him and not feel a tiny bit sad. She'd never want to get back together with him, but she'd probably also never feel *nothing* for him, either. "I can't believe you're being this nice about it all."

"Why?" she asked, and they both shared a smile. Because the last time they'd spoken, she might've called him Satan (amongst other choice words) and taken his beloved World Series baseball.

She shrugged and said, "You weren't that hard to get over, Scarf."

Jack

Jack: Are you cold or just really happy to be at this rehearsal?

Hallie: First of all, you will not make me look down at my own breasts with your childish behavior.

Jack laughed quietly and looked up from his phone long enough to see her stick out her tongue at him. She looked down at her device and started typing again.

Hallie: Second of all, I got sent to the principal in junior high because when Jon Carson said that exact same thing to me, I went on a rant in the lunchroom about how he obviously knew nothing about nipples. I got in trouble for saying NIPPLES and he got off.

Jack: I bet he did.

Hallie: You're an idiot.

"Hallie, for God's sake," her mother said, putting her hands on her hips and yelling, "can you put down your phone for five minutes so we can have a damn rehearsal here?"

Hallie rolled her eyes and set her phone on the empty seat beside her.

Jack laughed again from his spot in the gallery. The wedding was going to be outside the following day, but they were rehearsing inside because another wedding was going on today.

Everyone else in the room had a role in the wedding, but Jack's only job was to sit and watch the train wreck. Hal's mom and sister both seemed to be intense about every single detail, and Hal's ex wouldn't stop staring at Hal, but she had spent the entire time looking bored because she was on her phone.

Texting him.

Busted, he texted.

He watched her absolutely ignore her mother's warning as she glanced at her phone and quickly sent: Quit getting me in trouble.

Hallie

"That is disgusting."

Hallie looked up from her phone and at Carolyn, her sister's maid of honor, who happened to be standing next to her and grinning with her nose wrinkled. "What?" she asked.

"The way your boyfriend watches you. I want to vomit with jealousy."

Hallie followed Carolyn's gaze to Jack, who was giving her that sarcastic little smirk she loved. "He's actually being a brat—that's what that look is."

"I don't mean this minute," she said, glancing toward Hallie's mom, who was having a shitfit about the violinist. "I mean that since we got here, your boyfriend has been sitting there staring at you as if you're the most amazing thing he's ever seen."

Hallie needed to remember to tell him to tone it down a little so he didn't come off as a clingy creep. He *was* good at looking at her like she was amazing, though; the look he was giving her at that moment did wild things to her stomach.

She opened her mouth to downplay it, but remembered that she did actually want everyone to think Jack was the perfect boyfriend who worshiped the ground she walked on.

"He's just, um," she said, trying to think of the right words. "Jack is just very focused."

"Well, bravo, Hallie," Carolyn said, looking downright wicked as she gazed at Jack. "A focused man is hard to find."

"Okay, so I bribed the server to put us at Chuck and Jamie's table."

"What?" Hallie asked as they walked into the lodge's great room. Jack had immediately reached for her hand when the rehearsal ended, and she'd yet to find a way to one-up him in their current situation.

"The server told me that there isn't a head table, so you and I were already seated together." His thumb stroked over her palm and she felt it everywhere. "I just had her flip it so we get to sit by your friends instead of your uncle Marco and aunt Tam."

Hallie looked up at his mischievous face and wondered how he could be so perfect. Marco and Tam were loud, obnoxious people, and that would've been the worst. She said, "My sister's going to kill you."

He said, "Are *you*, though?"

"You are the greatest boyfriend in the world. I could never."

He pulled out his phone and sent a text, and her phone buzzed.

She pulled it out of her pocket and read the message.

Jack: But you could kill ME, yes?

She smiled, pulled her hand free, and replied: I've spent hours daydreaming about that very thing.

Jack: Freak.

Hallie: I'm not, but your girlfriend told me you like teeth on your neck.

Jack: Don't tell her what I'm about to tell you—this is just between Hal 'n' Jack

Hallie: Yay! The country 'n' is back!

Jack: Told you we'd revive it.

Hallie: You're nothing if not dependable. Anyway, what don't you want me to tell your beautiful, charming girlfriend?

Jack: When she kissed my neck today, I was *this* close to begging her to go back to the room with me.

At the thought, Hallie's stomach dipped and she felt a little light-headed. So . . . you wanted her to go back for more biting?

Jack: Biting 'n' more. 'N' much more.

"Would you two put your phones away?" Chuck yelled from his seat. "Come on, it looks like you're at our table."

Hallie and Jack walked over to the table, and Hallie was glad the moment had been broken, because she'd been about to beg her best friend for "'n' more" all night long. She took the seat between Chuck and Jack and immediately reached for the glass of wine beside her plate and drained it.

"You drank that very fast, young lady," Jack said in a low voice next to her ear.

She glanced at him and rolled her eyes when he gave her

that funny little squint that called her out on her flustered state.

The room was set up to put Hallie's sister in the spotlight. There was a table in the center of the room covered in white linens to accentuate her and her husband-to-be's bloodred formal wear (yes, Riley had opted for a red suit to match his bride). A huge, glowing chandelier hung over their table, literally putting them in the spotlight.

Everyone else was seated at white tables dispersed around the room in near-darkness, aside from the candelabra centerpieces.

Hallie had to hand it to her sister; the girl knew how to create a mood.

"So what'd you two do all day?" Chuck had already loosened his tie, and it was *very* crooked. "I figured we'd run into you somewhere."

"We just walked around the town," Hallie said, thinking about the way Jack had been nervous about their facade and their sleeping situation. The way he'd referred to their friendship as something to protect. "What about you guys?"

Chuck and Jamie launched into a story about getting stuck hiking with family, but Hallie couldn't focus. Her skin was prickly with awareness of Jack's proximity, of zippers and calves and soapy showers.

What was wrong with her?

The minute they finished their story, Hallie stood and said, "I'm getting a drink."

She walked over to the bar, regretting that decision instantly because she'd been able to avoid relatives all day by sneaking away with Jack, but now she had no escape. By the time she finally had a vodka cranberry in her hand, she'd spoken to a handful of cousins and three uncles.

And none of that had cleared Jack out of her head.

The meal was finally served, but she wasn't even hungry. She was too . . . antsy to eat. She mindlessly participated in dinner conversation, and she was beyond grateful that Jack had swapped their seats, because Chuck and Jamie were keeping him entertained, so Hallie was able to silently spiral in peace.

I was *this* close to begging her to go back to the room with me.

"Hal."

"Huh?"

Jack was looking at her questioningly. His blue eyes searched her face for something and apparently didn't find it, because he said, "Come outside with me for a sec?"

Her heart started pounding in her chest and she just nodded.

"We'll be right back," he said to the table as he linked his fingers tightly between hers and led her out of the room and into the hallway. Her mind was spinning, but she couldn't think of anything specific, which was bizarre. She just felt . . . nervous . . . ?

He didn't take her outside, didn't stop until he reached an unlabeled closet. He pulled open the door, led her inside, then closed the door behind them. The closet smelled like a mix of bleach and clean laundry, and it was dark except for the tiny bit of light coming through the door vents.

She could barely see his face.

"What are you doing?" she said as he turned so her back was against the door.

"Why are you freaking out, Hal?" he said, his voice deep and a little husky in her ear.

She wanted to deny it, but this was Jack. He knew her too well. Her breathing felt shallow as she said, "I don't actually know."

She could smell whiskey when he spoke. "Does it have to do with what I said about begging you to go back to the hotel room?"

She swallowed. "I mean—"

"I knew our games were a bad idea." She could feel the closeness of his body, even though they weren't touching, and he said, "I'm not losing you over sex. For the rest of the weekend, I think we should fake date without any of the PDA bullshit."

Disappointment surged through her; his suggestion was kind of the opposite of what she'd been thinking. She said, "Well, wait a minute—that's a little rash, don't you think?"

He chuckled darkly in her ear. "Then what do *you* suggest?"

"Um," she said, not wanting to give up the intimacy they'd shared since arriving in Colorado, "maybe we just set a hard and fast rule about sex."

"That it has to be hard and fast?" he growled, and she felt his teeth on her earlobe.

"You know what I mean, perv," she said in a near-whisper.

"I do." He nuzzled his nose against her neck, his breath streaking over her skin. "We solemnly swear not to have sex this weekend, no matter how many times you bite me."

"Exactly." She laughed. "And no matter how nice your calves are."

He lifted his head. "My calves?"

"I'm so distracted by them, you don't even know," she confessed.

He started laughing, and the sound filled the darkness.

"We should probably go back now," Hallie said, not wanting to but knowing her mother and sister wouldn't put up with her absence for long. "I'm sure someone will be giving a toast soon."

"Wait." His phone lit up the darkness, and she heard his message send before her phone buzzed.

She pulled it out of her pocket.

Jack: Since we've doubled down on this weekend being a one-off, can I kiss you?

She stared at the text for a long moment, wondering how to respond, and then she turned off her phone and slid it back into her pocket. She said, "We've kissed multiple times since you picked me up this morning. You're asking permission *now*?"

The hard line of his jaw was caught in the light of his phone. "I'm not asking as your fake boyfriend."

Hallie's heartbeat picked up again. She felt a chill on the skin of her neck as she said, "So . . . *you* want to kiss me?"

His phone's display timed out and turned off, and she heard a roaring in her ears as she waited for his answer.

"Just once," he said, his voice gravelly. "Jack and Hallie for real, before things go back to normal."

She seriously thought she might faint. She struggled for words and all she came up with was, "My hands are shaking."

She felt his hands on the sides of her face, and she could hear her own trembly breathing. His mouth came down on hers, but instead of the hot, arrogant kisses she'd become accustomed to since the airport, this was . . . different.

It was an intimate, sexual kiss, the kind of kiss that was usually shared in a darkened bedroom, with one body stretched out on top of the other. Wide-open mouths, slanting for the perfect connection, the warmth of his breath on her lips, the feel of his fingertips on her skin.

His tongue tangled with hers and teased, his teeth nipping at her lower lip, and she felt herself rearing up, desperate to meet him kiss for kiss, and to do whatever it took to keep him from ever stopping.

She reached out and grabbed the lapels of his suit jacket, pulling herself closer to him, pressing her body against his. He grunted, and she felt his hands squeeze her waist, slide down to her ass, and it was her turn to let out a noise when she felt his hardness grind against her.

"Don't you dare stop," she breathed into his mouth, and she let her head fall back as his lips moved down to her throat.

"I have to, Hal," he panted into her neck, sucking her skin as he pressed his body into hers. "Before we mess up everything."

"Yeah," she said, agreeing while also moving her hands so she could feel his thick hair between her fingers. "Good idea."

"So . . . are we stopping?" He lifted his mouth, but she could still feel his breath on her throat when he spoke, and he sounded like he'd do whatever she said.

"Yes," she said, letting go of his hair and saying on an exhale, "I guess so."

"Thank God," he replied, his voice a sleepy drawl. "Because I have a roll on my plate that I haven't gotten to yet."

"The rolls are trash," she said, her hands still shaking as she fumbled to get herself together in the dark.

"Why do you have to ruin everything for me?" he asked, his voice teasing in the quiet darkness.

She touched her hair and said, "How are we going to exit the closet without looking like a couple of horndogs?"

"That's easy. Just step out with authority, like we had every legitimate reason to be in here."

Hallie touched her lips and then remembered she'd been wearing red lipstick. "Crap, can you see my face?"

Jack's face moved closer. "A little . . . ?"

"I might have makeup smeared all over my face. Shit."

"Here." Before she could stop him, he raised his phone and took a picture from point-blank range, and the flash was blinding in the tiny closet.

"Gah, what are you doing?!"

"Trying to help—"

He didn't finish the sentence, because he looked at his phone and started laughing. The display illuminated his face, and when he couldn't stop laughing long enough to explain, he turned it around and showed her.

The picture of her was positively garish.

Her eyes were half-open, her lipstick was smudged, her nostrils were flared, and the photo was so up close that you couldn't see more than her eyes, nose, and upper lip. She looked like the ghost of a drunk clown.

"I'm not laughing at you—" he tried, but couldn't finish.

"I know," she said, looking at the picture and losing it. She started belly laughing with him, and neither one of them could stop. He rested his forehead on the door above her while he tried to calm down, and she could feel tears ruining what was left of her smoky eye as she cackled.

She almost couldn't breathe.

Every time she tried to stop laughing, she pictured it again.

She screamed when the door flew open behind them, dropping them both out of the closet and onto the lobby floor.

A housekeeper stood there, blinking at them with her hand on the doorknob.

Hallie quickly scrambled out from under Jack and into a sitting position as the bright lights assaulted her eyes. She looked at him, lying on the hotel floor with red lipstick smudged all over the bottom of his face and hair sticking up everywhere. He looked as shell-shocked as she felt.

He sat up, and then he looked at her.

That grin crawled all the way up his face before he threw his head back and started laughing all over again, even as the hotel employee stared blankly at them.

That was the moment she knew.

Chapter
TWENTY-ONE

Jack

"So it's cigars and scotch on the east patio for the gents and cosmos on the west patio for the ladies."

Jack watched Hallie's sister put the microphone back on the stand, and he thought it was interesting how different they were. Lillie seemed great, but Hallie was just so . . . *Hal*.

"Are you freaking kidding me?"

Speak of the devil.

He turned around as Hallie approached, looking put together again. No more eye makeup smears, no more red lipstick all over. He missed the mess. He played innocent on her remark and said, "Pardon?"

"Where are we—Victorian England? *The gentlemen will retire for scotch and cigars while the ladies rest their delicate constitutions?*" She watched as the rehearsal guests started heading for their respective patios. "What if *I* want a cigar?"

He looked at her lips. Couldn't keep his eyes off them, all of a sudden. He asked, "What exactly *is* a constitution?"

Hallie shrugged. "I don't know, but I'm positive mine is just as strong as yours."

"You wish." He patted down a piece of her hair that was sticking up. "Do you even want a cigar?"

"Not really," she said, smoothing down the same piece of hair while finally meeting his eyes. "But I don't want a damn cosmo, either."

"C'mon, Jack," Chuck said, walking over and giving a chin nod toward the east exit. "Time for us gents to get our stogies on."

"I want to go with you guys—"

"Get over here, Hal," Hallie's mother half shouted from the west exit. "Please?"

"Git," Chuck said, giving Hallie a tiny push. "Go be a good little female."

"Screw you," she said to Chuck, and then she pointed at Jack and said, "Be ready to hold my hair tonight, because if I have to drink cosmos with *my mother* and talk about what happens on the wedding night, swear to God I'm getting hammered."

He and Chuck were still laughing when she turned and marched away, and there was nothing he could do but watch her go.

What a fucking force.

"So, can I ask you a question about Hal?"

Jack slowly shook his head and exhaled a puff of cigar smoke, watching it rise in the night sky. "If you must, Chuck."

Chuck cleared his throat and said, "So, things are good with her?"

Jack tilted his head and looked at the guy. He really, really liked Chuck. Chuck was nerdy and nice and funny as hell. Jack said, "Yeah."

"So you like her a lot?"

"Yeah." Jack looked at the other side of the patio, where the groomsmen were playing some stupid drinking game, and said, "I do."

"Here's the thing." Chuck frowned and said, "Did she tell you anything about Ben?"

"Who's Ben?" he asked, fully knowing it was Hallie's ex.

"*Who's Ben?*" Chuck lowered his eyebrows and said, "Ben Marks, her ex . . . ?"

"Oh, that guy." Jack raised the cigar to his mouth and looked over at the man in question, who was talking to Hallie's dad. He looked like the kind of guy who enjoyed talking about what he smelled in his wine. "I don't know much about him."

"I'll give you the dirt, but you never heard this from me, okay?"

Jack gave a nod.

"Hallie and Ben dated for a few years and were living together."

Holy shit. "Years?"

Chuck nodded. "He's this wannabe sophisticate, passive-aggressive asshole who made her feel like shit about herself. Convinced her to do things like play tennis and buy a Volvo."

"A fucking Volvo?"

"Yes. *Shit.* I hate that guy and also Volvos." Chuck leaned back in his patio chair and looked up at the dark sky. "It seemed like he made her feel like her Hallie-ness was embarrassing or something—I'm paraphrasing, by the way. This is my analysis after seeing them together for years."

Jack fucking hated that guy.

Didn't really mind Volvos, though, he thought as he took a long drink of whiskey.

"One day, out of the blue, Ben came home and told Hallie that he'd had an epiphany. He realized that he was in love with the idea of her—what he thought she could be—but not actually her."

Jack lowered his glass. "What the fuck does that even mean?"

"That he didn't love her. That he loved what he wanted her to be but she never, like, got there for him."

"Shit." Jack pictured Hallie crying after Alex broke things off and felt like an even bigger asshole for causing that. She might not have had deep romantic feelings for him, but she didn't need another guy to make her feel like she was less than.

Because she was fucking everything.

"Between you and me," Chuck said, leaning a little closer and lowering his voice, "I disconnected Ben's car battery like three times after that, just to fuck with him and make him late for work."

"That is awesomely psychotic," Jack said with a laugh, puffing on his cigar and looking at the asshole Hallie used to love. "I think I really like you, Chuck."

"You know that fucker had no idea what was wrong when it wouldn't even turn over," Chuck said, chuckling.

The conversation soon turned to Volvos. Chuck was clearly a car guy—and a Volvo hater—and saw something in

Jack that made him think they were of a like mind. Jack just listened, enjoying the cigar and trying to imagine not finding Hallie to be enough. He couldn't.

"Hey, jackasses." She came out of nowhere in the darkness, just walking across the grass, and Jack found it a little hard to breathe. Hallie was still wearing the white dress, but her curls had come undone, leaving her hair a little wild and wavy, and she was no longer wearing any jewelry. Her smile was big and her eyes were twinkling and her high heels were dangling from her fingers.

"I'm telling, you scandalous piece of shit," Chuck teased.

"Shhhh," she said, glancing toward the rest of the groomsmen, who had now switched to playing cards. "I ran all the way around the building and had to climb that fence."

Jack was looking at the fence she'd pointed to when she snatched the cigar from between his fingers and sat down on the ground between his and Chuck's chairs. She looked up at him, her head leaning back in a way that exposed the entirety of her graceful throat, and she said, "You don't mind, do you?"

He watched her take a puff and thought it was on-brand for Hal that she looked completely natural smoking a cigar.

"You know, you're going to ruin the back of your dress, sitting on the cement like that," Jack said.

"I already got chocolate all over the ruffle—see?" She moved the ruffle, which appeared to be affixed in place with silver duct tape, and he saw that its underside was splattered with a big, brown stain.

"Please explain the duct tape."

"The bartender helped me. Bartenders always have a handy tool kit," she said.

"And the chocolate?"

"I had DoorDash bring me a Frappuccino and then I dropped it on the patio."

Chuck snorted. "You've been fucking busy since we saw you an hour ago."

"Yeah, I have," she said. "Also, Jamie told me that if I ever made it to the other side, I was supposed to tell you that her phone is dead, she faked sick, and now she's up in the room."

"Sweet." Chuck stood and, without another word, just left.

"Listen, Jack," Hallie said, looking at his collar instead of his face. She seemed casual, but something weird was going on with her. "My mother is going to be looking for me very soon, and I'm not going back—they can't make me. I think I'm going to just call it a night and go up to the room."

"Hal."

"Yeah?"

"Look at me."

Her green eyes looked bright as she looked at him and said, "What?"

"Are we cool? You okay after the whole . . . closet thing?" He noticed the goose bumps on her arms and instinctively began taking off his jacket.

She rolled her eyes and gave him a grin as he draped it over her shoulders. She stood and pulled it tighter against her, looking even tinier as she burrowed into the jacket. "I'm fine, and thank you for the jacket, you chivalrous delight."

He set down his glass and stood. "Let's go."

Her eyebrows dipped down. "You don't have to leave the party just because I am."

He shrugged, wanting nothing more than to be alone with her in their only-one-bed room, even if sex was off the table. "I want to."

Thankfully, no one noticed as they left the patio and went back into the hotel. He wanted Hallie all to himself.

Chapter
TWENTY-TWO

Hallie

Hallie rambled about the patio party as they walked to the room, her heart pounding in her chest as she thought through her plan. She was scared to say anything for fear of messing up their friendship, but she was equally scared of letting the perfect weekend end without ever daring to make something happen.

Without possibly taking a step forward.

"And they actually took the microphone away from you?" Jack laughed as they stepped into the elevator. "What a bunch of buzzkills."

"Okay, well, I was actually being really obnoxious."

"You? Impossible."

She loved the way his eyes got crinkly around the edges when he was teasing her. She hit the button for their floor and said, "I discovered that falsetto made the mic squeal, so I might've selected a Bee Gees song and hit it *hard*."

He rolled his eyes and said, "Why would they ever let *you* sing karaoke?"

"Why wouldn't they? I have the voice of an angel."

They got off on their floor and walked down the hallway. Hallie kept trying to get herself to just say it, to calmly tell him how she felt and what she wanted, but she couldn't bring herself to utter the words.

They were stuck in her throat, so she rambled incessantly about nothing.

Jack opened the door and they went into the room, and as Hallie looked at that one very big bed, the words wouldn't come out.

Say it, Hal.

Say it, you pussy.

Sayyyyy. Itttttt.

She spun around and looked up at his handsome face. "Um, Jack?"

He started loosening his tie, and she felt light-headed. "Yeah?"

"I think, um, well, I was thinking. That."

He raised one eyebrow. "That . . . ?"

"That since we're both staying in this room, uh, together, maybe we should, um. Maybe we should . . ."

He whipped off the tie and dropped it by his suitcase, his gaze intense. "Should what?"

She swallowed. "We should, um, take turns using the bathroom."

His eyes narrowed as he unbuttoned his top button. "As opposed to . . . using it at the same time . . . ?"

"No." She rolled her eyes. "I just have to wash my face. Can I have the bathroom first?" she asked.

He gave her a weird look. "Of course."

"Awesome." Hallie went over to her suitcase and pulled out

the super-safe, not-sexy pajamas she'd decided to bring on the trip: her oversized, knee-length flannel nightshirt and a pair of tall, fuzzy socks. She walked past him and went into the bathroom, and it wasn't until the door was closed and locked that she silent-screamed and wanted to smack herself in the face.

We're adults, Jack, and we've slept together before. Since we don't have emotional baggage, why not sleep together again? We obviously have sexual chemistry, so I say we do whatever feels right this weekend and then leave it all in Vail. As long as we don't feel anything other than sexual attraction, it won't be a problem, right?

She felt a hell of a lot more than that, but no way was she going to put it out there. No, her plan was to throw every single thing into the fake relationship this weekend, and maybe by the time they returned home, they would share their mutual feelings for each other.

Crazier things had happened, right?

But she had to say it casually enough so he wouldn't get freaked again. Obviously he was worried she'd get emotionally attached—hence the closet conversation—so she needed him to believe that she wouldn't.

She took off the white dress and changed into—ugh—the world's least sexy pajamas. She fluffed up her hair, put on vanilla lotion, spritzed her belly button with Chanel No. 5, and pulled on her tall tube socks.

Wow, not even an inch of exposed skin.

When she came out of the bathroom, she was surprised to see Jack standing out on the balcony, in the dark. The lights from their room illuminated his tall form, and she could see he'd stripped down to his white undershirt, dress pants, and bare feet. "Which side of the bed do you want?" she asked.

He turned around, looked at her, and scowled. "*That* is

what you're sleeping in?" He stepped back inside, sliding the door closed.

"Shut up," she said, rolling her eyes. "I know it's—"

"You don't have any pants you can wear?"

She paused. "What?"

"Pants." He pointed to her legs, his eyebrows all bunched together, and repeated, "Pants. You don't have any you can sleep in?"

She narrowed her eyes. "No . . . ?"

He sighed. "We can't sleep in the same bed if you're not wearing pants. Come on, Hal."

"Are you kidding me right now?" She heard her voice rise to an irritating pitch. "You think my pajamas are, what—inappropriate?"

He said, "They're not inappropriate unless we're sharing a bed."

"*Then* they're inappropriate?" she asked, wondering if he was losing it.

"Yes."

"*Yes?*"

"Yes."

She put her hands on her hips. "What is wrong with you?"

"Hal, I didn't bring any pajama pants," he said, as if that totally explained his reaction to her pajamas. "I sleep in my boxers."

"So?"

"So . . . ?" He gestured wildly with his right arm, like a point had just been made.

"So, I've seen boxers before, Jack."

He made a noise that was a cross between a groan and a growl. "You're being obtuse on purpose."

"I'm not." So much for gathering the courage to beg him to sleep with her. She sighed and said, "I'm going to get in bed while you go wash up. I will be buried under covers when you come out, my inappropriate flannels hidden from the world, and you can just squeeze your eyes shut and duck under the covers on your side. We will be fine."

He dragged a hand through his hair and said, "I just think we need to proceed with caution."

"Go change." Hallie walked away from him, going to her suitcase to find the book she'd brought for the trip. He didn't say anything as he brushed past her and went into the bathroom, and after the door closed, she rolled her eyes at him so hard they probably *would* get stuck, just like her mother had always warned.

She was lying on her side reading when the mattress dipped and Jack got under the covers. He smelled like Irish Spring soap, and her entire body tingled at his closeness. She thought he was going to just sleep, but he quietly said, "Hal?"

"Yeah?" Her voice was almost a whisper, stuck inside of her tight throat.

"I didn't mean to overreact." His voice was low and gravelly, and it did things to her when he said, "I'm sorry."

She turned over, and just like that, his gaze was focused on her as they lay side by side, face-to-face in bed. As if that weren't enough to make her spontaneously combust, his naked chest was just *right* there. She said, "You're looking out for us—I get it. We're cool."

One side of his mouth kicked up a little. "Oh, well, thank God we're cool."

They shared a smile, more intimate than any they'd ever shared as their heads rested on matching pillows, and she reached out her index finger and traced the center line of his strong nose. "If I say something, do you promise to forget it if you disagree?"

A crinkle appeared between his eyebrows. "Okay . . . ?"

"Okay." Hallie lifted her head and moved her pillow closer to his so their pillows were touching, and she laid her head back down. She looked down at his chest, because she couldn't dare look at his face. "I know what we said in the closet, but I think we can have sex and it will totally be fine."

Chapter
TWENTY-THREE

Jack

He felt like he'd just been jolted with a cattle prod. "What?"

What in the actual fuck?

The smell of her swirled around his head as she leaned on her elbow and said, "Hear me out. I think we can absolutely have a weekend full of amazing sex, and nothing has to change."

He lay there, frozen in place, as she started rambling.

"We're adults, Jack, and we've slept together before. Since we don't have emotional baggage, why not sleep together? We obviously have sexual chemistry, so I say we do whatever feels right this weekend and then leave it all in Vail. As long as we don't feel anything other than sexual attraction, it won't be a problem, right?"

He was pissed and turned on and disappointed, all at the same time. Because every molecule of his being wanted Hallie Piper. She was all he ever thought about anymore. And when he'd turned around and saw her in that stupid flannel nightgown and hot-as-hell knee-high socks, he'd wanted to drop to his knees and beg her to love him forever.

So yeah . . . it was a sweeping understatement to say he wanted to have a weekend full of sex with her. Especially now that she was lying inches away from him under the same heavy blanket. He wanted to get rid of that nightgown, leave the socks, and explore every inch of his tiny bartender.

But he couldn't enjoy the thought, because she kept saying shit like *we have no emotional attachment* and *it's purely physical*. She smiled that funny grin—his favorite one—and said, "So why not spend the rest of the weekend doing *everything* a couple does, Jack? We can promise to tell each other if we start to feel something. Then, if that happens, we'll stop and go back to how it was before."

He sighed.

"Think about it. If you start wondering if you have feelings for me, you can just say 'I might feel something' and we'll flip it right back before it becomes a thing. It'll be like tapping out."

Too late to fucking tap out, he thought, so he said, "It's a terrible idea, Hal."

A flicker of something crossed over her face—hurt?—but just like that, her smile was back in place. "Can I ask you a serious question, then?"

God, he wanted to kiss her so badly. He looked at her mouth and said, "Sure."

"Are you worried about me, or you? Because I am absolutely positive I will not catch feelings for you. A thousand percent. So . . . are you afraid of falling for me?"

He ground his teeth together so hard that his jaw felt like it might break, but he managed to give her a smile. "Fuck, no."

Her chin raised. "So why not, then?"

Jack's chest burned as he looked at her fierce, ornery face as she promised to never fall in love with him. He shrugged and said the truth.

"Because it's too good with us for it not to become a habit."

She wrinkled her forehead. "I don't—"

"How much do you remember about that night, Hal? For real."

Hallie

Shit.

She'd been casual about the hotel night since it'd happened because she'd been mortified by her poor decisions. She'd teasingly acted like she only had fleeting memories because it was easier to blow the whole thing off, but the truth was that she remembered all of it.

Every. Single. Hot. Minute.

She cleared her throat and said, "Um . . . all of it?"

"Wait." His eyebrows went straight up. "What?"

She bit down on her lip and nodded.

"You lying little shit," he said, laughing, tugging on a strand of her hair. "Well, then you have to know what I mean."

She did. She knew exactly what he meant. But she wanted him so badly that she said, "I don't, actually."

His eyes narrowed, calling her bluff without saying a word.

"What?" she said.

"Okay. Y'know what we're going to do instead of having sex tonight?"

She rolled her eyes. "Sleep, like sex-hating losers?"

He moved his face a little closer and nipped at her chin, then pulled back. "We're going to talk about that night. In great detail."

"Why would we do that?" She watched her hand as it reached out, seemingly of its own accord, and wove its way into his hair.

"Because when we're done, you'll concede my point that if we sleep together again, we'll start sleeping together all the time until we die."

"Cocky much?"

He put a finger over her lips and said, "It all started in the kitchen. You remember? You were sitting on the counter and you said 'My lips are cold from the Rumple Minze,' and I said—"

"'Let me warm them up.'" She remembered his charming grin. "And then you said, 'God, please.'"

His lips slid into a flirty half smile. "Instead of answering, you climbed onto my lap."

Hallie's cheeks warmed as she thought about that moment, about how charmed she'd been by Jack. "I did."

"Swear to God, I nearly lost it right there," he said, looking sexy and sweet all at the same time with his head on the fluffy pillow. "You were so fucking hilarious, but then you pulled some wizard shit and turned into a damned seductress."

"Shut up," she said, rolling her eyes.

"Seriously." He looked up at the ceiling, like the scene was being replayed for him. "Just like that you were on my lap, in my hands, and my tongue was on your minty lips."

She felt like closing her eyes and just listening to the sexy bedtime story, but instead she added, "Which was great until you tripped over the box of bananas."

They'd started kissing and he stood, holding her while she wrapped her legs around his waist. He'd started walking, intending on taking them somewhere, but then he tripped.

"I could've crushed you," he said around a quiet laugh.

"But instead you recovered and stumbled your way to the service elevator." Hallie closed her mouth, positive she couldn't talk about the elevator without spontaneously combusting.

"Finally. The *service* elevator." Jack gave her a wolfish grin before scooching just a little closer to her on the bed. "I would really like to hear it from your point of view, Tiny Bartender. Tell me about the elevator."

Jack

Jack would never forget what'd happened.

Between kisses, they'd joked that they should just stop the elevator and go at it. He'd had her pinned against the wall, kissing the hell out of her, and then she'd done it.

She'd hit the button and stopped the elevator.

"We were grinding like teenagers," Hallie said, grinning, bringing him out of his flashback. "And I stopped the elevator. That's it. We kissed in that elevator for a very long time."

"Really."

"Yes," she said, nodding.

"That's your recollection," he said.

"*Yes,*" she said, laughing.

"I think it's more of a matter of *what* we kissed, don't you?"

"Oh, my God, Jack!"

"That's what you said in the elevator," he said, laughing, "when I was kissing your—"

"No." She put her hand over his mouth, her cheeks red as her eyes danced. "That's enough."

He moved his face from behind her hand. "Are you ready to admit that we would become friends-with-benefits addicts if we slept together?"

She rubbed her lips together. "I will concede that you might have a tiny point."

God, why was he suddenly obsessed with her mouth? All of a sudden, he was like a predator and her lips were his prey.

He prompted, "And . . . ?"

"And fine. No sex."

"Are you sure?"

"Am I sure?" She looked at him like he was crazy. "What are you doing here?"

"I just mean if you want to discuss this further, I'd be more than happy to talk about sex against hotel room walls, and sex on hotel room desks—which, if I recall, was your absolute favorite—"

"Why can't you shut up?" Hallie moaned, shoving her hands over his mouth. "I said you were right, so stop talking!"

He tickled under her arm to get her to let go, and then he rolled on top of her. *Instant mistake.* He'd done it to remind her he was the winner, to lord his victory over her and pin her down, but the feel of her body underneath his was too much.

She blinked up at him, looking like she felt exactly what

he was feeling, and whispered, "It was really, really good, wasn't it, Jack?"

He looked down at her face, her funny, stubborn, beautiful face, and he couldn't find his voice.

So he just nodded.

Chapter
TWENTY-FOUR

Hallie

Hallie leaned over the bed and whispered, "Jack."

He opened his sleepy blue eyes, and she wanted to rub her hand over the morning scruff on his jaw. The blanket had ridden down to his waist, and she was having trouble focusing with his half-naked torso laid out before her.

"Quit dripping on me," he said, rubbing his eyes and sitting up.

"Sorry." She moved her head, but that just dripped more water on him. "Just got out of the shower."

"Did you? I couldn't tell."

"Are you always grumpy in the morning?" She sat down on the edge of the bed and thought he looked like an adorable little brat as he was waking up. "This is fascinating."

"I'm only grumpy when I find myself in a real-life only-one-bed trope."

She laughed at that. "Don't blame me. If we'd railed last night, you probably would've slept like a baby."

"I don't think 'railed' is the proper derivative of getting railed," he growled, and she thought it was funny how much deeper his voice was in the morning.

"If you'd railed me—is that better? If we'd railed the hell out of each other?" She snorted at that and said, "Ooh, that's a good one."

"Why are you so perky this morning?"

"Well," Hallie said, and paused. She was ridiculously peppy because she'd had a blast spending the night with Jack. Had they shared a night of passion? Nope, not even close, really. But sleeping in the same bed as him, hearing the snuffly sleeping noises he made, waking up to his arm resting over her in his sleep—she'd loved every bit of it. "There are donuts in the lobby."

He shot her a look. "This elfin mood is donut-inspired?"

"Absolutely." *Lies.* She was also in a good mood because she'd decided that since Jack was the AntiSex, she was going to play the one-up game big-time for the entire day. After all, it was the last day of the trip. They were going home tomorrow. She stood and said, "That's why I woke you up. Want me to snag one for you?"

"No, thanks." He pushed back the covers and got out of bed, and Hallie's eyes went straight to his calves. Okay, not straight to them. They may have made a pit stop at his boxer briefs, but as she watched his legs flex with every step he took toward his suitcase, she decided she was grateful he liked running. "I don't usually eat until after my run."

Hallie tilted her head. "Are you sure you should be running around the mountains by yourself this early in the morning?"

He unzipped his bag. "Why would that be an issue?"

"Bears. I don't want you to get your face eaten off."

"Awww. So sweet." He reached for a pair of basketball shorts. "I'll be fine, Hal."

"I'm going for donuts, then."

"Enjoy." He looked at her then, like he was finally awake enough to see her, and when he gave her a slow smile, she felt it in her fingertips.

That was really the last time they were together that day. While Jack was running, Hallie was summoned to her mother's room to help tie ribbons on tiny bottles of bubbles. After she finished, she was informed she only had an hour before she had to head to the salon with the rest of the bridesmaids.

When she got to her hotel room, Jack wasn't there.

She texted: Where are you? Please tell me a bear didn't eat you.

Jack: You'd miss me, wouldn't you?

Hallie: I was really looking forward to embarrassing you with my offensive PDA today.

Jack: I ran into Chuck, who wanted me to go with him to get edibles since they're legal here.

Hallie: That reminds me, I need to text Ruthie and check on Tig.

Jack: Do you want any edibles?

Hallie: Baby, I'm a shit show on my own. I don't need help.

Jack: Baby?

Hallie: Weird, sorry, that came out naturally and I'm not being sarcastic.

Jack: Does that mean I can use a pet name for you?

Hallie: Like what?

Jack: Umm . . . sunshine?

Hallie: No

Jack: Punkin?

Hallie: That's offensive to redheads.

Jack: My apologies. Um . . . how about Shortcakes?

Hallie: That's so Fonzie.

Hallie: OKAY. The reason I was texting was to let you know that I'm heading to the salon, and then we're getting our nails done and having a special bridal party luncheon.

Jack: When will you be back, Pudding Pop?

Hallie: Probably won't be, Numb Nuts. Are you okay meeting me at the wedding?

Jack: Of course.

Hallie threw herself into bridal party mania, opting to be the excitedly enthusiastic sister as opposed to the cynical dick she'd been about the wedding thus far. She got her nails done, got a blowout, and pretended a chicken salad was the most delicious meal she'd ever had.

At lunch, her mother waved her over to where she was animatedly chatting with two of Hallie's aunts.

"Hey," she said, feeling a little nervous as the trio smiled at her in a weird way.

"Alma has a question about your boyfriend," her mother said, gesturing toward Hallie's tiny aunt with flame-red hair.

Uh-oh. Hallie gave a polite smile and said, "Yes?"

"Did he really design the Larsson Center in Zurich?"

"What?" She looked at her senior aunt and had no idea what the woman was talking about. "Zurich, as in Switzerland?"

"Well, of course, Hal," Hallie's mother said, looking irritated. "What other Zurich is there?"

"Well, I'm sure there's probably a Zurich, Indiana, or Zurich, South Dakota, somewhere," she said, trying to figure out where this Jack information was coming from.

"Uncle Bob was talking to Jack about his job, and after he said he works for Sullivan Design, well, your uncle googled him."

"He googles everyone," Hallie's mom said, and her two aunts nodded in agreement.

"He really does."

"It's a problem."

Hallie said, "Okay . . . so . . . ?"

"According to the website, he's designed parks and urban areas all over the world. We wanted to ask you, though, because your mom thought he was a landscaper."

Hallie stood there, stupefied, as she mulled it over. She'd *assumed* he did landscaping when she saw he was a landscape architect, but was that not accurate? He *did* dress nicely and put in a lot of hours, and he *had* said he had a ton of frequent flyer miles because of business travel.

She lied and pretended to know what they were talking about, but as she walked away from them, she googled him as well. And holy shit, he was a senior associate who had indeed designed urban areas all over the world.

He had a master's degree in landscape architecture, for God's sake.

What in the actual?

She didn't have time to give it more thought, though, as the wedding day started cranking up to full throttle. Hallie did everything her sister asked of her, and by the time she zipped herself into her crimson-red bridesmaid dress in the huge white prep tent on the mountaintop, she was ready for a drink.

Just before the wedding planner lined everyone up, Hallie hugged Lillie, and for the first time since the engagement, she felt nothing but happiness for her sister.

Ben caught her eye right after the hug and gave her a fatherly *aww-that's-so-sweet* smile, and she accidentally flipped him off.

Old habits and all that.

She got in line beside Chuck and actually felt a little nervous as the music started. Her detail-oriented sister had selected one of those amazing Ed Sheeran songs that has the power to make anyone cry, but she wasn't lame enough to just play it on a Bluetooth speaker—oh, no. She had a string quartet playing the music along with the recording, so it genuinely sounded like ol' Eddie was hiding in the bushes somewhere, crooning his little English head off.

As they stepped out of the tent to make their way down the aisle, Hallie's breath caught in her throat as she linked arms with Chuck. The air smelled like autumn leaves, and the white flower petal path stretched out in front of them, leading to an arch that was set in the middle of a stunning copse of aspen trees. To their left was a clear, flowing creek, and to their right, beyond the rows of white chairs and guests, was a tall mountain, towering over them with its stretching pines.

It was breathtaking.

"Damn," Chuck muttered.

"Damn, indeed," Hallie said, giggling, but then her giggles died when her eyes landed on Jack's face.

Jack

The quartet started playing and he stood, along with the other guests, turning to see the bridal party's procession. He was impatient, though; he hadn't seen Hal all day, and he wanted to get the ceremony over with so he could spend more time with her at the reception.

He was distracted by his thoughts of her as his gaze turned to the creek, memories of the night before playing back in his mind, when he felt her presence.

The strings were climbing to higher pitches, and the singer was crooning about telling someone he loved them.

And just as Jack felt the words in the middle of his chest, there she was.

Hallie was walking down the aisle, dressed in red and carrying a bouquet of white roses, and she was smiling at him. *At him.*

Shit.

He felt like he couldn't breathe as he looked at her, which wasn't that different from how he'd felt the night before as they'd shared a bed. As they'd gradually moved closer to each other over the course of the night, under the warmth of the heavy down comforter.

When he'd woken up at three a.m. and her backside had been snuggled against him, her breathing soft and sweet, he hadn't moved. He was pretty sure his job, as the man in an only-one-bed trope, was to suffer.

Well, suffer he had.

He'd lain there like a chump, wide awake for what felt like hours. The weirdest part was that her body's closeness had tormented him *less* than the overall closeness of her, the feeling of Hallie sleeping beside him. Eventually he'd just thrown his arm over her and held her there, like it was normal for them to be sharing a bed.

Which, coincidentally, was when he'd finally fallen back to sleep.

"They're so beautiful," Jamie said, crying beside him as she smiled at Chuck. Something about the way those two oddballs loved each other made him feel . . . fuck, something he didn't like. Pathetically envious.

Because as great as it was to play the game of pretend with Hallie, kissing her and holding her hand like she was his, he couldn't forget her words, words she'd said with total certainty.

I am absolutely positive I will never catch feels for you.

The ceremony was sweet and made him a little softer than weddings usually did, if he was being honest. Hallie got the hiccups during her sister's vows, and between her tiny squeaks, her whispered sorries, and the resultant laughter from both Hal and the wedding guests, he was pretty sure everyone in attendance fell for her just as hard as he had.

Chapter
TWENTY-FIVE

Hallie

"My mind is blown," Chuck said, tossing back one of the shots Hallie had poured for the two of them and set on the table in front of them. "You guys are incredibly convincing."

Hallie took her shot, feeling the whiskey burn down her throat. "It's easy, because we're best friends and we have sexual chemistry."

"So. Um." Chuck grabbed his water bottle and took a long drink before wiping his mouth and saying, "Tell me again—why aren't you *really* dating if you have chemistry and you're best friends . . . ?"

Hallie tilted her head. "It sounds simple, doesn't it?"

"Incredibly." Chuck looked toward the door of the multi-purpose changing/gathering room, through which most of the bridal party had just exited. Pictures were over, and they were ready to party.

"It's complicated. Jack thinks we have too much chemistry and we won't stop bonking if we start being friends with benefits." Hallie slid her feet back into the red pumps and pulled her compact out of her bag. "He thinks that we would have sex until we were dead and ruin our friendship. I, on the other hand, think he's one of those guys who *needs* to be in a relationship, so I don't want to be his low-hanging fruit, the person he gets into a relationship with because it's easy and we had a good bonk."

"He's not your douchey ex." Chuck leaned over and checked his hair in the compact she was looking into. "And I feel like he actually does like you."

She opened her lipstick and raised it to her mouth. "I think we both like each other, but not enough or in the right way to risk the friendship."

"Listen to me right now." Chuck stood as she finished applying her lipstick. "Risk the fucking friendship."

She stood as well and showed him her teeth. "Lipstick-free?"

"You're good," he said, then bared his teeth, to which she responded, "You are, too."

"Seriously, though, if you two are perfect for each other, fuck everything else."

Hallie picked up her bag and said the words that hurt her soul. "I can't bear the thought of losing him, though, Chuck. I can't."

The breakup with Ben had been awful. Out of nowhere. She'd assumed they were close to getting engaged, and she'd been absolutely in love with him, and then he'd told her that he didn't love her and she wasn't enough.

She'd been devastated and destroyed, but she felt like losing Jack as a friend would be a thousand times worse.

"Hal." Chuck grabbed her bag from her fingers and tucked it under his arm; he knew she hated clutches, which was what made him an above-and-beyond friend. "You won't lose him. You won't. And don't you think the possibilities of love are worth the risk?"

"Shit. Yes." She took a deep breath and nodded. "I need another shot if I'm going to make him fall in love with me tonight. Care to join me?"

"I'd be delighted."

Because of bridal party obligations, it took forever before Hallie was finally able to meet up with Jack. After the pictures, she and Chuck had to sit at the head table while everyone made toasts, and then she had to sit there while everyone else got their food first.

Thank God for phones.

Jack: You look bored.

Hallie: That's because I am bored.

Jack: Wanna play a game?

Hallie: Absolutely I do.

She glanced in the direction of his table, but it was hard to see him because people were milling about the ballroom.

Jack: Let's call it yell, beat, or kill.

Hallie: wtf you animal.

Jack: Choose one person here to publicly yell at, one whose ass you'd like to kick, and one you'd like to murder.

Hallie: Wow.

Jack: I'll start. I would like to publicly yell at your cousin Emily, who is seated beside me and will not stop telling me about her food allergies.

That made Hallie grin; Emily was a *lot*. She texted: I get that. So what about the ass-kicking?

Jack: That's easy. I would like to kick your new brother-in-law's ass, because his fraternity friends are a bunch of blowhards who've wasted far too much of our time with their stupid toasts. He should have better friends.

Hallie: I back you on this. May I assist?

Jack: Of course. Choose your weapon.

Hallie: Cake knife.

Jack: Excellent choice.

Hallie: And now, for the murder . . .

Jack: This obviously has nothing to do with you, but I would really love to wring the neck of Ben Marks.

Hallie looked up from her phone and craned her neck to find Jack. She couldn't, but she was a little taken aback that he even knew Ben's last name.

Hallie: It was the scarf, wasn't it?

Jack: Certainly didn't help. But every time I look at him, I want to hurt him for making you feel like you weren't enough.

Hallie wasn't laughing anymore. She texted: Did I tell you that?

Jack: Chuck did, but he was drunk and it was a slip. Please don't get mad at him. But here's the thing, Hal. It's fine if it wasn't meant to be for you and Ben, but you have to know that you are more than enough. You're perfect, and if he was too fucking stupid to see that, it's on him.

Hallie could no longer read the text in front of her as tears blurred her eyes. She blinked fast to clear her vision before texting: You're not allowed to be this nice. You're screwing up my makeup.

Jack: So how should we kill him?

Hallie shook her head, and at that moment the crowds

cleared just enough for her to see Jack's face as he smiled at her. She texted: I think death by poison is a very humane way to put Scarf out of his misery.

The toasts finally ended, and Hallie and Chuck bailed on the wedding party and went to sit by Jamie and Jack. As they approached the table, Hallie took a minute to admire Jack while he wasn't looking.

His suit and tie were black, and something about the whole look was ridiculously sexy. He looked like a cologne ad. He looked like the guy who'd be on the cover of a romance novel about billionaires. He was dashing and gorgeous, and her heart stuttered a little when he looked up at her from his chair.

"So," he said, his eyes crinkling around the corners. "Those hiccups."

"Why didn't you scare me or something?" She grabbed the chair next to him and scooted it closer, pushing back the warmth she felt for him over what he'd said about Ben. "I thought you were my friend."

"What exactly should I have done—shouted?"

"Sure." She grabbed his hand in both of hers and started playing with his fingers while she leaned in close. "Anything would've helped."

A tiny wrinkle formed in between his eyebrows as he looked down at their hands.

She said, "I don't want to sound like a creep, but you look incredibly hot."

He looked at her and raised an eyebrow. "Are you hitting on me, TB?"

"Little bit. By the way, Chuck and I decided that we're not going to dance together for the bridal party dance—he's going to dance with Jamie and I'm dancing with you."

He raised an eyebrow. "Do I have to?"

"Oh, my God, you don't know how to dance, do you?"

He smirked and said, "Actually, my nana made me take ballroom dancing."

"Shut up."

"Seriously." He picked up his glass and said, "For three years."

"So you can, like, waltz?"

He raised his drink to his mouth. "So hard."

"You can waltz the crap out of me?" she asked, laughing.

"And then you'll beg me for more, honey."

As it turned out, he wasn't lying.

When the DJ finally called for the wedding party to hit the dance floor, Jack led her around like he was Fitzwilliam Darcy at a Netherfield soiree.

"Dear God, are you literally Prince Charming?" Hallie said.

Jack put his mouth to her ear and said, "Yes, but don't tell anyone. People lose their shit over royals."

"My lips are sealed." She laughed, squeezing the warm hand that held hers. "By the way, I love the feel of your mouth on my ear, in case you're wondering."

"Is that right?" he asked, his lips moving over the shell of her ear, clearly on purpose.

She shivered as he took his time to pull back his mouth from her skin. "Maybe I'm just sensitive, though. Tell me, does it do anything for you?"

She raised her head and brushed her lips against his earlobe, then nuzzled his neck with her nose, wanting to bury her whole self in him.

"Quit it." He looked at her hotly, his eyes intense. "You know it does."

"I can't help myself." She laughed again, thinking the couples of yesteryear might've been onto something with this whole dancing thing. "Making you look at me like *that* is downright intoxicating."

"You enjoy making me weak?" he asked as he guided her around the dance floor.

"I enjoy making you feel."

"Sadist."

The shots were kicking in. She didn't feel fuzzy, or anywhere close to drunk. Just relaxed enough to say, "If I tell you something about feels on our last night of fake dating, do you promise to forget it later?"

He didn't answer but just looked at her, and the heat of his hand on her lower back teased her skin through the dress.

She said, "It's not going to change anything, and it's not like I'm falling for you so don't get all weirded out. But I'm pretty sure I feel something."

"What?"

"It won't affect our friendship, and I don't want—"

"Say it again."

"Jack—"

"All of it, Hal." He pulled up and stopped so they were just standing on the dance floor. His eyes were unreadable. "Tell me."

She regretted opening her big, fat mouth, because she had a feeling he was freaking out. Still, she said, "It's not a big thing. I just think I might have some feelings for you that I can easily forget tomor—"

He kissed her.

Right there on the dance floor, as the wedding party moved to a sweet song about forever, Jack wrapped his arms around her waist and kissed the hell out of her. Her arms slid around his neck and she angled her head just a little, absolutely fine with letting him devour her mouth in the middle of her sister's wedding reception.

She didn't want him to ever stop.

"Hal," he said against her lips, not even attempting to stop kissing her to speak.

"Hmmmm," she sighed.

"You are *so* getting railed tonight," he growled.

That made her start laughing, and when she opened her eyes, he was squinting down at her in that way she adored.

The rest of the reception went by in a blur because she couldn't focus on anything but Jack. She suddenly had this greater awareness of him, this buzzing electrical connection, and she had no interest in anything but him.

Cake cutting, "Electric Slide," chocolate fountain—they were all just white noise in the background as Jack grinned at her in a way she felt down to her toes.

Jack

"Hey, Jack, can you do me a favor?"

Jack, who'd been standing next to the bar, watching Hallie do a stupid line dance with Chuck and her sister, looked at Hallie's mom and said, "Of course."

"Since food service is done, the caterers left, but I want to make sure this cake topper gets put in the freezer so Riley and Lillie can have it for their anniversary. Here's the kitchen key—can you put it in the freezer for me?"

"No problem." Jack set down his glass, took the key, grabbed the section of the cake she wanted to save, and took it into the kitchen. He found a shelf for it in the back of the freezer and was closing the cooler door behind him when Hal walked in.

"Hey." She grinned at him like he was exactly what she'd been looking for. "You."

She pushed his chest, giving him a little shove so his back was pressed against the freezer door.

Goddamn. He liked her so much it was stupid.

"There's a lot of booze in that smile," he said, looking down at her hand. The sight of her short red fingernails on his chest did something to him. Ever since she'd said she had feelings for him, he felt like a wild animal on a leash, straining to get at her.

"It's only ten percent wine," she corrected in that breathy voice he'd only ever heard when he was kissing her. "Ninety percent happiness."

And then, because of her high heels, she easily reached up and pressed her lips to his. He instantly fell into her, tangling his fingers in her hair and losing his damn mind. Her mouth was soft and tasted sweet, like champagne, and he wanted to sip at it until he fucking drowned.

God help him.

Her hands flexed on his chest, grasping, and it was like an electric shock that he felt everywhere. He trailed his mouth down to her throat, where her skin smelled like the Chanel No. 5 she'd left on the vanity in their room, and he wanted to consume her.

The skin on her throat, just under her ear, underneath the curtain of hair on the back of her neck—he wanted to taste every inch of it. She made a noise in the back of her throat, a demand, and he moved behind her, lifting her hair in his fist so he could drag his teeth over her nape.

"Jack," she said around a sigh, slapping her palms against the freezer door, "that is . . ."

She trailed off, and he said against her skin, "Hot?"

"Mmmm," she breathed, pressing her backside against his front. "I was going to say 'wicked.'"

He wrapped a hand around her waist and pulled her back, closer, so she was flush against his body. "You make me that way."

"What time is it?" she asked, making a little noise as he nibbled at the skin between her shoulder blades. The red bridesmaid dress exposed half of her back, and he would be eternally grateful to Lillie for selecting the style.

"Almost ten," he said, unwilling to leave her body to verify.

"Dammit, we only have a few minutes before the bouquet toss," she said, her voice almost a whisper. "Please hurry, Jack."

Her words almost made him dizzy with lust, and he clenched his teeth as he said, "By 'hurry,' you mean . . ."

She answered him with her hands on his belt.

Hallie

Apparently that was all it took.

Jack muttered a string of obscenities as he hurried to multitask things like belts and zippers. She felt she was going to die waiting as he slid his hands up her dress, his fingers drawing a line up the sides of her thighs as he raised the skirt and bunched it in his hands.

And then he was *there*—oh, God.

They groaned in unison, and after that his hands were on her hips and she might've lost consciousness as he drove her absolutely wild.

"This doesn't count," he said, his voice thick and hot, "as our first time post-hotel."

"Don't," she replied, bending a little lower and arching her back, making him growl, "be bossy."

"Honey," he rasped, and then her knees nearly gave out as he touched her with a talented hand. "At this moment, I will be whatever you want me to be."

"Jack?"

They both froze at the sound of Hallie's mother's voice. She started knocking on the kitchen door, pounding, and Jack said, "Shit."

"Don't you dare stop," Hallie said.

"Your mother—"

"Is locked out."

He groaned into her neck and said, "I didn't lock the door."

"I did." She looked at him over her shoulder.

He lifted his head and his eyes were hot blue on hers. "You did?"

She nodded.

"You fucking hero," he said, making her gasp as he started moving again.

She laughed and moaned at the same time.

He muttered into her hair, "I want to see your face."

"What?"

"Your face." He turned her, breaking contact for only a split second before sliding right back inside her.

"Well, hello," she breathed, her eyes heavy as he smirked down at her.

"Better," he said, his face going all intense as his hands found her ass and he lifted her, pinning her against the freezer door with his big body.

"So much better," she whispered, letting her head fall back against the door as she grasped at his back and he continued moving in a way that made her want to scream.

"Like the hotel," he panted, at the exact second she whispered, "This is just like the hotel."

She opened her eyes and smiled at him, but it quickly fell away as his body pushed her harder, drove her deeper, as his blue eyes penetrated hers in the hottest way.

"Hal," he bit out, his nostrils flared, the muscles in his neck straining above his shirt, "God, I—"

She raised her mouth and swallowed whatever he was going to say in a desperate, wild, hungry kiss.

"Your mom thinks I'm evil," Jack said, looking over Hallie's head toward where her mother was seated.

They were standing beside the gift table, where Hallie had been instructed to count how many packages would need to be carried up to her sister's room.

"She just didn't understand why the door was locked," Hallie said, grinning. She was having trouble *not* grinning as she talked to Jack like they hadn't just had screamingly hot sex in the banquet kitchen. "And why it took so long for us to open it."

"You're enjoying this," he said, managing to look disgusted and amused all at the same time.

"Am not." She looked at his handsome face, heard the notes of "A Groovy Kind of Love" coming out of the DJ's speakers, and was a little nervous about how happy she felt at that moment.

"Then why are you smiling?"

She rolled her eyes. "Because I'm happy."

He tilted his head and narrowed his eyes. "I don't know if I trust happy Hallie."

"You should." She grabbed his tie and pulled him a little closer. "Because she's obsessed with the way you move around a kitchen and is desperately thinking of a way to lure you back in for round two."

"If you're there," he said, sweetly brushing a tendril of hair behind her ear, "I'm there."

At midnight, the reception was still raging. Hallie had planned on helping with cleanup, but every time Jack looked at her, she toyed with the idea of being the worst sister in the world. She was seriously contemplating just sneaking away with him when her father appeared with Ben at his side.

"Hal, your mom sent me to get you. She's in the prep room, trying to figure out whose stuff is whose. Can you help?" her dad asked.

"Um." She glanced at Ben, simultaneously irritated by his presence and absolutely neutral, emotionally speaking.

Her dad gave her a knowing look and said, "Ben volunteered to help. Isn't that nice?"

"*So* nice," Jack muttered, and it definitely didn't sound like a compliment.

"Yeah." Hallie didn't care about Ben and just wanted to

know how quickly she could be up in the hotel room with Jack. She asked her dad, "How long do you think it'll take?"

He sighed. "You know your mother."

"Ugh." Hallie turned back to Jack and said, "Just head up to bed. God only knows when I'll be done."

"Can I help?" he asked, and as their eyes met, she realized it was their last night there. Their last night fake dating. Their last night sharing a room.

The look he gave her said he was thinking the exact same thing.

They were down to mere hours.

"It's not your problem, man," Ben said, giving him a charming smile. "You're just a wedding guest. If I were you, I'd take that excuse and run. Make the wedding party do their jobs."

Jack looked at Ben like he wanted to hit him.

Then he looked at Hallie—really looked—almost as if he was searching for her decision.

She had no idea what to say. She wanted Jack by her side no matter what she was doing, but she didn't want him to feel forced to help, either.

"Do you have your room key?" Jack asked, his eyes unreadable.

"Oh." She narrowed her eyes and tried to remember if she'd grabbed it while also trying to analyze the nuances of their situation. "I don't know."

"No worries. I'm a light sleeper." He cleared his throat and said, "I'll hear when you knock."

They exchanged another look—lust and longing and something else she couldn't put her finger on—before he said good night to her dad and then left the ballroom.

Hallie hadn't even made it to the prep room when her phone buzzed.

Jack: I miss your mouth already.

She smiled and typed: My words of wisdom?

Jack: No, your gorgeous lips and the way they feel when you suck my tongue into your mouth.

Hallie: Damn, Marshall—this is a PG-13 show.

Jack: Then someone's going to be pissed when I tell you that I can't stop thinking about the way your ass looked when your hands were on that cooler door.

Hallie felt that in her stomach.

She texted: Confession: that might be the hottest I've ever had.

Jack: MIGHT? Hal.

Hallie: I just mean I can't decide between up-against-the-freezer-door and on-top-of-the-hotel-room-desk.

Jack: Confession: My favorite part of hotel night was actually your Rumple Minze lips.

Hallie: Mere kissing??

Jack: That falling-off-a-building feeling the first time you kiss someone is just perfection.

Hallie set her hand on her stomach when she read that. God, Jack was a heady drug. He would be a lot to recover from, and it was terrifying. She texted: So you're saying it could've been anyone.

Jack: Anyone who knew how to make a perfect Manhattan, tell a ridiculous joke about the Kansas City Chiefs, climb on my lap to get my attention, and have the name Hallie Piper.

Hallie: Nice save.

Jack: Thank you very much, TB.

She was about to drop her phone into her pocket when

she saw texting bubbles. She stared at the screen as she walked, and when the text finally came through, she felt breathless as she read his message.

Jack: It couldn't have been anyone but you.

As she followed Ben and her dad, Jack's words kept playing through her head, over and over on a loop.

I miss your mouth already.

My favorite part of hotel night was actually your Rumple Minze lips.

It couldn't have been anyone but you.

Chapter
TWENTY-SIX

Jack

Jack took off his jacket and dropped it on the bed, tired and frustrated at the situation.

Hallie was here for her sister's wedding, so that was the priority, he reasoned as he undid his tie and yanked it off. Of course she would stay and help out, he mused, untucking his shirt with a jerk and undoing his buttons. What kind of a sister would she be if she didn't?

And the fact that her douchey ex-boyfriend was helping, too, had nothing to do with his sudden foul mood.

He knew it was all part of being a bridesmaid, but as he continued to undress, he had to admit to being selfishly disappointed. The entire weekend had led up to that night, for them, and after hearing her say that she had feelings for him, he'd been champing at the bit to spend the entire night worshiping her in their king-sized bed.

He wanted a whole night before the weekend came to an end.

Jack slid off his belt and was unbuttoning his pants when he heard the knock at the door.

It couldn't be her. He wanted it to be, but there was no way she was finished with her post-reception tasks. If it was her, it just meant she needed something from the room.

He dropped the belt on the pile of his clothing and walked over to the door.

When he pulled it open, Hallie was standing there. She looked focused. And . . . nervous? He raised an eyebrow. "What'd you forget?"

"That we only have a few hours left." Her eyes went down to his chest, then his stomach, and he felt her gaze like a touch as she looked at his unbuttoned pants. She took a deep breath, raised her eyes to his face, and said, "I want to feel everything before we go back to normal, Jack."

He wanted to say they didn't have to go back to normal. He needed her to know that what he wanted from her was a hell of a lot more than texting and being each other's wingmen. Instead, he heard himself say, "Don't you have to help your mom?"

She shrugged and said, "I told them I had to go do something important."

"Such a little liar," he said.

"I wasn't lying." She raised her chin, and that tiny defiant motion made him feel some kind of way. "And my favorite part of hotel night was when you offered to let me use your toothbrush, by the way."

"What?"

"We were, um, finished," she said, stepping into the room as he moved back and held the door, "and instead of passing out or doing whatever a buzzed person might do during a one-night stand, you asked me if I was okay. You looked into my eyes and waited for my answer, and after I said I was fine, you offered to let me use your toothbrush."

The door slammed shut behind her, and he said, "I still can't believe you remember that night."

She said in a breathy voice, "I think about it all the time."

He felt warm, like he was burning up, and all he could see was her. Hallie Piper was surrounding him, filling him, and he could feel her in his every molecule. His arms went around her, to her zipper, as his mouth came down on hers.

"Jack," she whispered, and the sound of his name on her lips made him fucking insane. He opened his mouth over hers, needing to taste her, and as always, kissing Hallie felt like some kind of reward.

Hot, wet, and like a gateway drug, her kisses sucked him in with the promises of things he'd yet to feel. Her teeth and tongue responded to him like they'd been jolted awake, and he groaned into her mouth as she made him burn.

He started lowering the zipper on the back of her dress, his fingertips grazing her soft skin, but then he froze when he felt her fingers on the button of his pants.

Hallie

One twist, and the luxurious suit pants fell to the floor.

Her heart was in her throat, not because she was some nervous teenager but because it had never felt this . . . *intimate* between them before. No tipsiness, no jokes, no rush to the finish; it was just Jack and Hallie, alone in the dark hotel room with their true feelings.

"God. Hal," he bit out, his voice tight and teeth clenched as she touched him.

As Hallie ran her hands over Jack's body and his mouth came down over hers, her dress slid to the floor. He wrapped his hands around her waist and led her to the bed, where he was lightning-fast at getting her stretched out on the big mattress, naked.

It was every bit the wild storm of the kitchen and the infamous hotel night, but more intense because of the absolute thoroughness. Jack wasn't just touching her, he was reaching every single nerve ending in her body with his hands and fingers and mouth. She writhed and arched and sighed and moaned as Jack explored every inch of her.

"Jack," she said, exhaling his name as his mouth traveled back up her body and hovered above her lips. His eyes were heavy-lidded and sensual, and he looked downright wicked as he traced her lower lip with his tongue and replied with a low growl.

She didn't want to beg, but she needed him inside her. She scratched her nails over his back and arched up, trying to get closer.

"Hal. *Shit.*" His eyes closed for a split second and he looked pained, but when they opened, he gave her a dirty smile and then he was there, hot and hard, exactly where she wanted him.

"Yes-yes-yes-yes," she chanted in a whisper, losing herself in the sinful feel of Jack sliding deep into her body. She moved with him, digging her fingernails into his back as she attempted to hold him against her own body as tightly as she could.

She felt like she was going to go into cardiac arrest from the heat. Not only was it impossibly good with them, physically—*so good, holy shit*—as he moved inside her, but every movement was enhanced by this overwhelming new emotion she felt for him.

She didn't know exactly what it was, but suddenly, he felt like *more*.

His face was dark and full of intensity as he looked into her eyes and moved faster, deeper, and she was having a difficult time reconciling the fact that this fantasy lover was her one-night-stand-turned-best-friend.

"Nothing has ever felt as good as you," he said, his voice thick and low against her skin as he kissed her neck and his big hands gripped her hips. "As this."

Nothing in the world *had* ever felt that good, but she only managed to moan Jack's name and bite his shoulder in response. She was too lost in him and what he was doing to her body to form actual words and coherent sentences.

He groaned and gritted his teeth, looking slightly animalistic as he slid his hands underneath her, changing the angle and bringing her even closer. She wondered if it were possible to black out from pleasure too intense as he drove her toward that delicious edge between ecstasy and pain.

She might've said his name, or screamed it, but the flash of the white-hot ending was blinding in a whirl that removed her from the room altogether.

Jack

"This is the most ridiculous thing I've ever done in bed," he said, watching Hallie cross the room in his dress shirt and her knee-high socks (as per his request).

She grinned at him and brought the tray over, the combined light of the muted TV and the roaring fire in the fireplace illuminating her approach. "Somehow I doubt that, but I'm honored to introduce you to one of my bedding specialties."

He shook his head slowly. "This is just a terrible idea, TB."

"No, it's not." She laughed, setting down the room service tray on their bed. "As long as you pull the comforter tight, no crumbs get in the bed. You shake out the top layer when you're done and you're good to go."

He watched her sit down criss-cross-applesauce in front of the tray, and he realized that that was one of the things that made her so . . . whatever the fuck she was that he was obsessed with. Hallie never tried to be cool or anything other than what she was, which, at the moment, was a hungry sex goddess who'd ordered french fries from room service at three in the morning.

"You have to be hungry, too," she said, taking the heavy lid off the plate. "You've been working very hard for hours."

"As have you," he said, and she gave him a stupidly huge smile.

He messed up her hair and stole a fry, to which she responded by delivering a stinging hand slap.

They turned up the volume on the TV and watched a rerun of *New Girl* while they consumed their french fries, arguing about who was the best character. He thought it was Winston, while she thought Nick, but they both teetered on the edge of making Schmidt their number one.

After they killed the food and started getting tired, she led him to the bathroom, where they brushed their teeth side by side because Hallie was convinced the vinegar and sugar in ketchup would rot their teeth while they slept.

Every time she tried gargling, she got the giggles because Jack was watching her and then she choked on the mouthwash. They were both laughing their asses off by the time he threw her over his shoulder and hauled her over to the bed, and when they finally lay down and shut their eyes, he couldn't remember a time he'd been that fucking happy.

Chapter
TWENTY-SEVEN

Hallie

"Hal."

She opened her eyes, and there was Jack, smiling down at her. Sunlight was coming through the window, but he was still buried underneath the covers beside her, like he had been all night. His hair was a mess, his eyes were tired, and he was so gorgeous it was almost hard to look at him.

"Good morning," she said, reaching up a hand to touch his jaw.

"Good morning to you," he said, and the way he looked at her made her feel adored. "You told me to wake you up at seven, and it's seven. But I'm about to hop in the shower, so if you want to snooze, I'll wake you up when I'm done."

"No run today?" she asked.

"I'm too pathetically into my fake girlfriend to leave for an hour," he said, kissing her forehead before getting out of bed. "Go back to sleep, and I'll wake you when I get out."

She watched him walk across the room and she thought

you could probably bounce a quarter off that tight, muscular ass of his. She'd probably test that later, just to make him laugh and get naked again.

God, how was she having those thoughts? How was she suddenly thinking that she and Jack would move forward as more than friends? She could still hear his sexy growl when they'd been going wild in the bed—*nothing has ever felt as good as you*—and she almost had to pinch herself to believe it was real.

She was in love with Jack, and things were looking incredibly promising.

She giggled, the noise echoing off the wood beams of their room, and she felt like singing.

Jack

He stuck his head directly under the spray, letting hot water slide down his face and neck.

Jack was exhausted in the best possible way.

He pushed his hair back and squirted body wash into his hands, rubbing them together before lathering his hair.

"I can't believe you use body wash as shampoo," Hallie said, and Jack felt a pinch in the center of his chest as he turned around in time to see her stepping into the shower. She was so fucking hot, his naked dream girl with the wild red hair, but it was the smile on her lips that made him melt for her.

She grinned at him like she knew him better than anyone else in the world, like they shared a massive secret, and there was something about the look that almost dropped him. It was everything, and he wanted to keep her with him in that hotel room forever so only *he* could enjoy it.

"It's all the same," he said, but his throat was dry and scratchy. "Soap is soap."

Her hands reached for his, her fingers sliding through his to steal the lather he'd built. She tilted her head up, waiting for him to kiss her, as she set her slick hands on him. His breath whooshed out of his body—*shit shit shit shit*—and he covered her mouth with his, voraciously devouring her as she moved bubbly fingertips everywhere he'd ever dreamed about her touching.

His fingers speared through her hair as her mouth became his feast, became the centralized spot for him to unleash his passionate response to her wicked hands. He scraped his teeth along those sexy lips, desperate to consume every single bit of her.

His legs were shaking as she kept sliding those slippery fingertips over him, and when it was too much, *too close*, he wrapped his arms around her waist and lifted her. Startled, she stilled her hands as he hauled her out of the shower.

Steam filled the bathroom as hot water continued falling from the rain forest showerhead, and Jack set a towel on the vanity with one hand before lifting her on top of it. Her eyes were heavy-lidded, like she was struggling to keep them open, and they fluttered closed when he stepped between her legs and slid inside her.

They moaned at the same time, hers a needy request while his was deep and guttural.

He fucking loved that sound, loved that *he* was the one drawing that reaction from her.

She leaned back on her arms, letting her head fall back

as he drove her to madness with his strong body. His mouth took advantage of her position, lifting water droplets off her wet skin while he explored her with his tongue, and he knew he'd never forget the hot look in her eyes as she watched him lick all over her.

He felt her heels dig into his lower back, and she wrapped her arms around his shoulders while her body tightened and flexed around him. Every movement they shared was fucking sexual perfection—scorching intoxication that he was totally under the influence of—and he had the fleeting realization that he'd never had sex like that before.

In his entire life.

It was great sex, the kind of sex you couldn't quit even if the world was ending around you, but it was laced with a disconcerting sentimentality that made him want to pull Hallie closer and kiss her on the forehead.

Which ignited something inside him that made his already sweaty body feel hot all over.

Jack tightened his grip on her hips and gave himself up to all of it, going wild with Hallie as she panted like a sprinter and clutched at his shoulders. He buried his face in her neck as the finish rushed through him, and he'd barely refocused on his surroundings when he heard Hallie say, "Now that was a brilliant start to the morning, Marshall."

Hallie

"I can't believe how pissed your mom looked," Jack said as they boarded their flight.

"Yeah, she unloaded on me in the bathroom, and I'm

fairly certain she thinks you're my bad influence." Hallie giggled, and couldn't believe that her mother's rage wasn't stressing her out at all. "Before you I was an angel."

"Wonderful," he said.

"It'll be fine. Next time we talk I'll tell her you saved me from drowning or something, and it'll be cool."

"This sounds absolutely like something that won't work," he teased, squeezing her fingers.

She loved that he'd immediately grabbed her hand at the airport, even without relatives in sight. Their fake dating was officially over—everyone else was leaving the following day—but he was still treating her the same.

And after the night and morning they'd just shared, she wasn't surprised; it had been intimate and perfect, way more than just a roll in the only-one-bed hotel room.

But a tiny part of her was concerned because they hadn't had time that morning to really talk about what their relationship would be upon returning home. Neither of them had said exactly what they wanted, but she was too afraid to bring it up.

Once they were in the air, she leaned her head on his shoulder and fell sound asleep. She slept through the entire flight, and when her eyelids fluttered open as the flight attendant announced their descent, Jack smiled at her in a way that made her remember every hot detail from the night before.

"Why are you so tired, Tiny Bartender?" he asked, his voice deep and gravelly as he ran his hand up and down her spine. "Long night?"

"I don't want to overshare," she whispered, raising her mouth to his ear, "but I met a guy at a wedding and he railed me all night long."

"He sounds fit," Jack said.

"You have no idea," she said. "It was like a sexual boot camp, but with french fries and TV."

That made him throw his head back and laugh, the same way he had when they'd fallen out of the closet during the rehearsal dinner, and she knew it was over.

She was head over heels in love with Jack Marshall.

Chapter
TWENTY-EIGHT

"I'm going to the restroom, and I'll meet you at baggage claim."

"Deal," Jack said, grabbing her carry-on from her shoulder and putting it over his.

"Don't ditch me," she said, laughing, and then he stepped onto the escalator and headed downstairs. She walked toward the closest bank of public restrooms, but she felt more like skipping, she was so happy.

"Hallie?"

Hallie stopped and turned. It was Alex.

"Oh. Hey. What are you doing here?" She stood there as he ran to catch up with her, but she was surprised at how unaffected she felt. Not even her bruised ego cared anymore about this blond man, smiling and approaching cautiously like he was afraid she'd slug him.

"Last-minute work trip—talk about a small world. Do you have a quick second, since we both ended up in the same place?"

She looked behind him, then back at his face. "Well, I mean, I kind of have to go—"

"Just one second. Please? Obviously the universe wanted us to meet up."

She shrugged and stepped out of the foot traffic, settling beside the airport bookstore. She knew she looked rough with no makeup and a messy bun, but she really didn't care.

"I just want to apologize," he said, looking incredibly serious. "I am so sorry, Hallie."

What was with all the men from her past apologizing to her all of a sudden?

She waved a hand and said, "It's okay."

"I regret it so much, and I don't know if you'd ever consider it, but I'd love to take you out to dinner."

She gave a tiny shake of her head. "That's very nice, but I don't think so." She paused, and because she was genuinely curious, she said, "Can I ask, though, what's changed since you thought we weren't meant to be together last week?"

He swallowed and said, "I was an idiot. Remember how we talked about dating apps and organic chemistry, and how—"

"How you thought fate was more important than anything else? Yeah." Hallie was starting to get impatient because she knew Jack was waiting for her. Also, she still needed to use the restroom. "I remember."

"Well, when your friend told me about the bet, I got mad, to be honest, because things were going so well that I wanted to believe it was fate. When I found out it wasn't—"

"What?" Alarm bells started ringing in her head at his mention of the bet. "What are you talking about?"

"Jack. I ran into him when I was leaving your place, the day he brought you the cat toys I had in my car . . . ?"

"Oh, yeah." Hallie felt a little confused by what he was talking about, but she remembered Jack bringing up the toys Alex had gotten for Tigger. "Um—"

"We were shooting the shit in the parking lot, and when I gushed about you and it being fate, he told me about the bet."

"What, um—"

"Your bet on who'd find someone first."

"Oh." Hallie felt like she was missing something, but she wasn't sure what it was. "He mentioned that to you?"

"I think he just wanted to set the record straight that you and I were definitely not fated."

Hallie narrowed her eyes and looked at Alex. Why would Jack tell him about their bet? Jack had known how much she had liked Alex. Why would he interject that into a conversation with a guy he barely knew?

And why hadn't he mentioned it to her when Alex had dumped her?

"Listen, Alex, the bet was just our way of motivating each other to keep trying to find someone. There was nothing—"

"Oh, I know—that's what he said, too," Alex said. "Honestly, I got the impression he was trying to make something happen with you, and I was in the way. But that doesn't matter."

She smiled even though she felt unsettled by their entire conversation. "It doesn't?"

"No, the screwup was all mine. Listen, can I text you later?" He leaned in a little closer and said, "This is a weird place to chat, and I would really like to finish this conversation."

She nodded and said, "Sure."

After she walked away from him, Hallie started filtering through everything in her head. She was on autopilot as she went to the restroom, washed her hands, and stepped onto the escalator. Jack's words, Alex's words, Olivia's words—they all looped through her mind, and by the time she approached the baggage claim area, she had it figured out.

And it fucking sucked.

She'd been Jack's low-hanging fruit, just like Olivia had predicted, and when he'd seen her connecting with someone else after he'd gotten dumped, after he'd spent two weeks in Minneapolis being sad and lonely about his uncle Mack, he'd ruined it for her.

Why else would he have kept his conversation with Alex a secret?

When he'd been holding her in her bedroom, making her feel better about her breakup while she bawled, the right thing to do would've been to say, *I told him about the bet—that's probably why.*

But he hadn't said a word.

He'd let her cry her eyes out without even mentioning it.

And then he'd offered to swoop in and be her Prince Charming.

She had no idea what to make of this information after everything that had happened between them last night. It had been an amazing, perfect night for *her*, but what exactly had it meant to him?

God, was she just overthinking everything?

She knew she was, but on the other hand, she'd thought Ben was about to propose when he actually had realized that she wasn't someone he could love, as hard as he tried. So what if Jack was happy right now with his easily picked, low-hanging fruit? Would it last? Or would he ultimately realize that as hard as he'd tried to make her the solution to his loneliness, she wasn't the one?

"I thought you got lost."

Hallie turned around, and there was Jack, grinning down at her with their luggage piled in front of him. His smile made her stomach drop, and as she turned her lips up into a smile, she kind of wanted to cry.

She said, "I just saw Alex."

His smile disappeared. "The blond clown?"

She nodded. "He wants to call me later. He said he regrets breaking things off."

His Adam's apple moved when he swallowed, but that was the only change to his countenance. He didn't look like he had anything at all to confess. "You gonna wait by the phone, TB?"

She shrugged and tried to sound teasing when she said, "I guess time will tell."

He slid his fingers between hers. "I'll just have to keep you too busy to hear the phone, then."

They took the shuttle to his car, and Hallie thought it felt like it'd been years since they'd left town. Jack kept hold of her hand, but they were both quiet, and it felt like there was a huge, unspoken issue hovering over them.

When they got to his car, she called Ruthie to check on Tigger and tell her they were on the way. Ruthie said she couldn't bear to part with her cat baby and might have to borrow him the next day.

"So he finally stopped hitting her?" Jack asked.

"Apparently so."

They settled into silence as he pulled away from the parking lot, and Hallie was relieved when he took a work call. She was able to get in her own head and think while he discussed the concrete finish that was going to be used in an upcoming project.

The one lesson she'd learned from the Ben breakup—*thank you, Dr. McBride*—was that the most important thing was for her to be honest with herself about how she felt about every little thing, good or bad.

So her first honest admission: She loved Jack. She wanted Jack. What she wanted, more than anything in the world, was to pretend she'd never talked to Alex at the airport. She wanted to throw herself into being with Jack, living like they had over the weekend.

But her second honest admission: She would rather lose any romantic possibilities with him now than go through what she'd gone through with Ben later. That had been hell, and she was positive it would be ten times worse with Jack.

Her third honest admission: She wasn't mad he'd told Alex about the bet—it wasn't a super-sworn secret or anything—but she was livid that he hadn't mentioned it sometime between Alex dumping her and now.

"You okay?"

Hallie glanced over at Jack as he drove along the freeway—she hadn't even realized he'd disconnected the call.

"Oh. Yeah." She smiled and her throat was tight. "I'm just so tired."

"Same."

She laid her head back on the seat and closed her eyes, preferring to feign exhaustion over making conversation.

Because her fourth honest admission was that she knew exactly what she had to do.

And it made her want to weep.

Jack

Fuuuuuck.

He wasn't usually insecure, but Hallie had been quiet and distant since running into Alex. She seemed weird about him calling her later, almost as if she was open to it, which made Jack want to toss her phone out the damn window.

He couldn't stop his brain from thinking, over and over again like a fucking demonic chant, *She still wants Alex.*

Jack pulled into the parking lot of her building and grabbed her luggage from the trunk, and they went up to her apartment. Ruthie spent twenty minutes telling Hallie everything Tigger had done in her absence while Hal snuggled the huge tabby, so he had a few minutes to get his shit together.

When Ruthie finally left and Hallie closed the door behind her, he pulled Hal into his arms. They were great together, and Alex showing up at the airport was just a blip they'd both forget after five seconds together in her apartment.

But instead of being her playful self, Hallie looked dead serious as her wary eyes stared into his. So serious, in fact, that he actually felt a pang of nervousness slice through his belly.

"What's up, Tiny Bartender?" He kissed the tip of her nose, the center of the constellation of mini-freckles. "You look troubled."

She swallowed and said, "Nah, I'm just a little . . . introspective as we leave the fake dating behind."

"Introspective, huh?" His heart started pounding—stupid, that—as he got ready to tell her exactly how he felt. If she was ready to talk about their relationship, God help him, he was ready to put himself out there and confess to every overpowering feeling he had for her.

She nodded and set her hands on his chest. "This is our last night of pretend, and part of me is going to miss it."

"It *has* been fun," he said, a little confused by her referring to that night, that moment, as pretend when it was only the two of them in her apartment.

Also—*what the fuck*—the night before definitely hadn't been pretend for either one of them.

"Agreed." She looked sad as she said, "The lines got a little blurry over the weekend, but you were the perfect fake boyfriend, and I'm so grateful."

He didn't say anything, because his throat was too tight to speak. It was all there on her face, in the fatalistic way she looked up at him.

Holy shit.

She was ending things.

It was over before it'd ever started.

Hallie

She was dying inside and wanted so badly to crawl into her bed and cry her eyes out. But not before having one last night with him as more than friends.

"I totally get it if you want to go home and get back to

normal. There are probably girls in the dating queue right now, waiting for your response." She tried to surround it in a sarcastic laugh, but none came out. "I personally will not be getting back on the app until tomorrow, because I'm far too tired."

"Hal." His blue eyes were stormy. "What the hell are—"

"But if you're interested, I'm game for one last night of pretend. One last night of Hallie and Jack, the couple at the wedding, having mind-blowing sex."

It sounded desperate to her ears, but she was when it came to Jack. She was desperate for one final night.

His jaw flexed, and he looked pissed as his eyes traveled all over her face. It took a long moment before he said, "Let me get this straight. That whole fake dating game is over and we're back to being friends, but you want to *fuck* one last time?"

"Forget it," she said, mortified by the insulting way he'd said it. "I didn't—"

"I'm in," he growled, and then his lips were on hers.

It was angry and hot, his mouth opening hers and kissing her with a wild aggression. His hands came up to hold her face so he could absolutely go feral with his teeth and tongue, and she grabbed his biceps because she felt like she needed something to hold on to.

He made a sound in the back of his throat before sucking her tongue, before treating her mouth like it was a juicy, ripe peach that he wanted to eat whole.

Just like that, she was in his arms and he was carrying her into the bedroom as she wrapped her legs around his waist. His eyes were dark as he dropped her onto the bed and crawled up her body, his mouth only leaving hers long enough to remove clothing.

Her hands were shaking as she fumbled with the zipper of his jeans, and then everything changed.

His expression stayed just as serious, just as hyper-focused and intense, but his body gentled. His touches softened. His mouth grew worshipful instead of ravenous.

It broke her heart, because it was too much.

And when he finally slid deep inside her, she had to close her eyes to hold back the tears. It was so good, like it always was with Jack, and she tried to just lose herself in the physicality of it all.

Don't think, don't think, don't think.

"Open your eyes," he said, his voice gruff. "Please?"

She did, and his throat moved as he swallowed and looked down at her. She saw the flare of his nostrils, the flex of his jaw, and as their eyes locked, they exchanged powerful unspoken words. *Goodbye. One last time.* She reared up to kiss him, needing his mouth on hers. She locked her hands around his neck and sealed her mouth on his as he made her dizzy with the way he moved in her body.

Then they reached the point of no return, where emotions ceased to matter as raw lust took over, and when she shifted her weight to flip them, so she was on top, he cursed like a sailor.

His fingers held her hips, digging into her skin as he watched her move, but when he sat straight up and kissed her, taking her face in his hands, she was done.

She moaned into his mouth as every muscle in her body clenched and flexed, and a second later he was biting her lower lip and groaning into hers.

Jack

He turned and moved, sliding them on the sheets so they were lying side by side. Hallie's eyes were closed, her breathing labored as they both came back to themselves. He felt emotional as he looked at the freckles on her nose, the bow of her lip, and like a pathetic fool, he touched the curve of her cheek and said, "Are you sure you want to be done with this, Hal?"

Her eyes opened, and he hated the way they looked. Hurt, distant—he couldn't put his finger on what he saw, but it wasn't good. She blinked fast before she said in a pinched voice, "Absolutely."

He gave a nod and sat up, getting out of bed and grabbing his pants from the floor. There was a roaring in his ears, and even though he knew he didn't want to know, he heard himself ask, "Is this because of Alex?"

He shoved a foot into one of the pant legs, unable to say the guy's name without gritting his teeth. Because honestly, he was so fucking jealous it was almost painful.

"Um, I guess you could say that," she said, her tone flat, and her response ripped his heart out of his chest.

He turned back to the bed and she was standing now, the sheet wrapped around her body, her arms crossed over her chest. He swallowed and muttered, "Awesome."

She squinted at him and said, "Why didn't you tell me that you told him about the bet?"

His hands stilled on his button. "What?"

"Before the wedding." She glared at him and said, "It sounds to me like you got dumped by Kayla, so you decided to tell Alex about the bet to get *me* dumped."

He felt everything rush to a halt as he realized how it looked. What she thought. How it seemed. He shook his head and said, "No, it wasn't like that at all. I just told him about the bet because that jackass thought fate brought you two together. That you were meant to be."

"Why did you care?" She inhaled through her nose, her eyes flashing, and she said, "And it *was* like that, Jack, because you're wholly responsible for him breaking up with me."

He ground his teeth together so hard it felt like they might shatter. Why did he care? *Because I have huge fucking feelings for you, Hallie Piper.*

Not that he could tell her that *now*.

She said, "I can't believe you let me cry over him without telling me the truth."

He wanted to apologize, because he *did* feel like trash about that, but his mouth couldn't form the words when she was looking at him like that.

Like she was livid because he'd ruined her relationship with that guy.

Because she wanted Alex, not him.

"My apologies, Hal," he said as he finished putting on his pants, feeling like a chump for grabbing at the chance to sleep with her one last time. He hadn't been able to resist being close to her again, even knowing he'd regret it afterward.

Hell, if he were being honest, he'd been half hoping it would change things.

"Sure," she said, biting down on her lower lip and yanking up the sheet a little higher.

Looking at her suddenly felt physically painful, and he had to get the hell out of there before he made a fool of himself. "I've got to go move my car before it gets towed."

He pulled on the rest of his clothes, and as he grabbed his keys from the kitchen counter, she said, "Bye, Jack."

And then she went back into the bedroom and closed the door.

Well, fuck.

Chapter
TWENTY-NINE

Hallie

Jack: Can I call you?

Hallie dropped her phone on her desk, sighed, and hated the way her heart was racing at the sight of his name on her phone.

Because it had been two weeks.

Two weeks of radio silence.

At first, she'd been glad he hadn't texted—she needed a clean break, emotionally speaking, from their games. She'd cried through her shower and halfway to work the morning after their last time, whereupon she decided to nut up and knock it off.

Jack was her very best friend, and that was all that mattered.

But then . . . he never came back. He didn't call her and he didn't send a single text.

In her wildest dreams, she wouldn't have imagined he would just disappear from her life.

She missed him so much it was almost unbearable. She closed out of her spreadsheet and texted: It's 6pm and I'm swamped and trying to finish so I can leave.

Before she could add to that, her phone started ringing.

"Son of a bitch," she whispered, just before she answered with a terse, "Hello?"

"Hey. How's work?"

How could the sound of his voice be so overwhelming? She looked at the wall clock and said, "Great. What's up?"

"Do you maybe want to get some food tonight?" He sounded serious, and she hated that that was what they'd become: serious people who didn't talk anymore. "I was hoping maybe we could eat and kind of figure out what's going on with us."

Her brain screamed, *Where the hell have you been for two weeks?!*

She sighed. "I'm behind and have to play catch-up. Sorry."

"What about tomorrow night?" Jack asked.

She wasn't sure why she said it, but she said in her breeziest voice, "I actually have a date."

"Oh." She heard him clear his throat before he said, "Through the app?"

"Yeah."

"Still trying to win the bet, then?"

As if. As if she even felt like dating again. And how dare he tease her, like they were friends or something. She tried sounding lighter still when she said, "Of course I am. I need a vacation, Jack."

"Not as much as I need that World Series ball. Want to get Taco Hut afterward?"

Are you freaking kidding me? She powered down her computer and said, "Sounds good, but I think this date might be a good one, where tacos won't be necessary."

"Is that right?" His voice was deep.

She swallowed. "Yes."

The silence felt loud and slow-moving, and she opened her mouth to say something, anything, when he said, "I guess we'll play it by ear, then."

"I guess so."

"Where's the date? Charlie's?"

"Yes, but—"

"See you tomorrow, Hal," he interrupted, and then he was gone.

She hung up the phone and cursed loudly since her office door was closed. *Dammit dammit dammit!* Had she lost her mind? She'd agreed to meet Alex to talk, but it wasn't a date, and she definitely didn't want to see Jack.

Shit.

She should've just told him no, but her brain had shorted out the minute she'd heard his voice.

Jack

"Oh, my God," Olivia screamed, staring at him like he'd sprouted a second head. "So you haven't talked to her since that night?"

"Shut the fuck up, Liv," he muttered, flipping off his sister as she freaked the hell out over his ridiculous situation. He looked at Colin and said, "How do you not bang your head on the wall every damn day for having to deal with her?"

Colin grinned and looked at Olivia. "I find better ways to channel my aggression."

"I am going to puke." Jack picked up the bottle of Dos Equis and said, "For real. That's disgusting."

Colin and Olivia laughed, and as much as it pained him to admit it, they really were a great couple. Somehow their differences made them perfect for each other.

Fuckers.

"So you're in love with Hallie."

"*No.*" He groaned and said, "I mean, kind of. Yes. Yes, I am."

Livvie said, "But she only wants to be friends."

"Maybe not even that."

"Even though you slept together while pretending to be a couple."

"I'm sorry—are you going to continue synopsizing my situation? Because it's really fucking annoying."

"Sorry," she said, laughing. "I'm just trying to figure it all out."

"If you ask me," Colin said, "this is all about the blond clown."

"What?" Olivia asked.

"What?" Jack repeated, shocked because he hadn't even told them about the post-sex conversation. He'd casually mentioned they'd seen him at the airport—that was all.

"Everything was great until she saw the other dude at the airport." Colin raised his whiskey to his mouth and said, "She obviously either has feelings for him or is trying to figure out if she does."

That made Jack want to punch something. He'd started to text Hallie about a hundred times since they'd last been together, but every single time he stopped himself, because shit, what if she was already official with Alex?

He didn't know if she wanted him at all, but something inside him needed to give it one last shot.

Olivia said, "No, don't listen to him, Jack. I think she doesn't know what to do with her feelings for you."

"You guys are no help whatsoever." He'd stopped by their place solely because he didn't want to go home and be alone, but he realized as he sat there that he didn't feel any better when he was with people, either. "I'm going home."

"You need to tell her how you feel," Olivia said.

"I think she's right, God help me," Colin said. "Just tell her how you feel, because your friendship is already fucked. You will never have it back the way it was before, so you've got nothing to lose."

"Wow, you're really shitty at this," Jack said, terrified Colin was right about his and Hallie's friendship. Ironically, it was what he'd been afraid of from the beginning. "Now I just want to go sob into my pillow."

"You'll be fine," Olivia said, walking to the freezer and opening the bottom drawer. "I just made ice cream cake."

He set down his beer. Everything sucked, but maybe ice cream cake would make him feel better, right?

Wrong.

Because the minute he looked down at the bowl Olivia set in front of him, he remembered eating ice cream with Hallie on the floor of her living room and the way she'd licked her bowl like a damn cat.

There was no one quite like her, and he was terrified he'd lost her forever.

Chapter
THIRTY

Hallie

"You get it, though, right?"

Hallie nodded and smiled a little too brightly at Alex, forcing her eyes not to roam the establishment in search of Jack. "I do. It makes perfect sense."

She could hear the rain pouring on the roof. It'd been one of those chilly autumn days where the rain fell in sheets and didn't stop. Since the second she'd opened her eyes that morning, it'd seemed like the perfect weather for her stupid non-date date night.

Alex picked up his water and took a drink before saying, "It was dumb, honestly."

"We all have our expectations that we," she said, her heart pounding in her chest as she saw Jack walk in, "um, expect."

Alex nodded. "Right? It was a dumb thing to get hung up on."

"It is what it is," she said, watching as Jack bellied up to the side of the bar. He was wearing jeans and a thick fisherman sweater, and he sat down on a stool that put him directly in her line of sight, which was a blessing and a curse. He was so attractive, and her lovesick eyes were dying to drink him in, but he was also the world's biggest distraction.

Especially when he looked over at her and gave her a chin nod.

She looked back at Alex.

"Listen, I've got to be honest with you," she said, not wanting to lead him on. "I really like you. You seem like a great guy. This has nothing to do with you, but I'm really not looking to date anyone right now."

His eyes narrowed, like he was trying to figure her out, but he didn't look mad. "Okay, so I'm going to ask you what you asked me at the airport. What's changed since before?"

"Well," she said, not sure how to explain it, "let's just say I kind of fell for someone else. It didn't work out, but it left me with very strong anti-dating feelings."

"Got it." He reached out a hand and set it on top of hers. "Is it your bestie at the bar?"

Her eyes shot up to his. "What?"

He shrugged. "I saw him come in. Actually, I saw *you* see him come in."

"Alex, I am so sorry—"

"Nope." He smiled and said, "I got a vibe from him both times we met, so I can't say I'm surprised."

She swallowed. "There's nothing going on with us, I promise. And there wasn't when you and I were dating, either."

"I know." He swirled the liquid in his glass and said, "Are you okay, by the way?"

She smiled. He really *was* a nice guy. "I will be. You know how it is—love just sucks."

"Truer words have never been spoken," he said, smiling back at her. "We can still have dinner as friends, though, right? I feel like we've earned it."

She lifted her glass of wine and nodded. "We *have* earned it."

Jack

"Can I get another water, please?"

Jack slid his empty glass toward the bartender as he tried getting his shit together. After downing a whiskey while watching Hallie smile at Alex, he decided he'd better switch to water before he ended up dying of alcohol poisoning.

But what in the actual fuck?

First of all, how the hell did she look so beautiful and so fucking happy? He'd imagined, like him, she was struggling to move on without their friendship. He'd imagined that she missed him at least a fraction of the amount he was missing her.

But she looked like everything was perfect.

He hadn't planned a date for that night, because what was the point of dragging some nice person along when all he was interested in was Hallie? But he'd expected her to be with some rando, not Alex.

And he definitely hadn't expected them to be fawning all over each other like they were having the best time. He kept sitting there, pounding water and waiting for her to look like she might want to bail, but the sound of her laughter kept slicing through him like a fucking machete.

He pulled out his phone and was about to text her when she lost it. She started cracking up at something the guy said, with that same contagious belly laugh that she'd laughed in their hotel room bathroom when she tried to gargle, and Jack was done.

He was out.

He laid a couple of bills on the bar, stood, and left.

Hallie

He's leaving?

Hallie jumped up, her chair squeaking on the floor as she stood. Her eyes landed on Alex, and he gestured for her to go. She started toward the door, having no idea what she was going to say, but how could he just bail on her?

She pushed the door and went outside, the rain immediately pouring down on her. She looked to her left and saw the back of his sweater as he walked away.

"Wait!" Hallie started running as she yelled, "Jack!"

He stopped and turned, his hair already soaked.

"Where do you think you're going?" she yelled, finally stopping when she was a foot away from him. "You're just bailing?"

His eyebrows went down as the heavy rain drenched the two of them. "You didn't look like you needed my help."

"You were the one who said you wanted to do this—*you* called *me*—yet you're ditching me. Again. What is wrong with you?"

"What's wrong with *me*?" He squinted at her like she was out of her mind and said, "You failed to mention that your date tonight was with Alex. Why would you let me meet you at the bar just to watch you have a fucking love connection?"

"Are you *mad*?" He was the one who was out of his mind, she thought. "At me?"

"Yes, I'm mad!" he yelled. "I thought we were going to talk about us, but instead you're canoodling with that guy right in front of me!"

"What 'us'?" She poked a finger into his chest and said, "What *us* is there? I haven't heard from you in *weeks*, and now you think you have a right to say the word 'us'?"

"Hallie—"

"Why didn't you at least text me?" She hated the tears in her eyes. "After that night, why wouldn't you at least send me a text to say 'Hey' or 'I hate you' or 'Ramen is on sale at the fucking supermarket'? Anything would've felt at least like something between us. How could you just leave me all alone?"

"I was trying to figure out my feelings, Hal." He pushed back his wet hair before adding, "I wanted to be sure of what I felt before talking to you about how *you* felt."

"What does that even mean?"

"Do you want Alex?" he yelled down at her through the rain.

"Jack—"

"Do you?"

"No." She shook her head, her soaked hair slapping more water in her face. "I never did."

He grabbed her arm and pulled her closer to the building they'd stopped in front of, so they were under an awning. He looked down at her and said, "Christ, Hal, this isn't how I wanted to tell you. But the thing is—I think I'm in love with you."

Jack

He watched as her mouth dropped open in shock, and then it snapped shut. She looked up at him with those big green eyes, but no words came out.

She just stared at him.

"Maybe say something, Hal," he said.

"Okay, I'll say something." She was shivering a little, but her face was full of hot anger. "That is a terrible thing to say, you dick."

Her words hit him like a punch in the stomach, and he tried reading her expression as he said, "I tell you I love you and you call me a dick?"

"You didn't tell me you love me, you said you 'think' you're in love with me." She was gritting her teeth, looking mad as hell as she shivered in the damp night air. "Who do you think you are—Darcy in the rain, telling Elizabeth that he loves her in spite of her inferior birth?"

He had no clue what to say to that.

"It took you two weeks of radio silence to come up with the genius epiphany that you may possibly be in love with me but you really aren't a hundred percent sure?"

Fuck. Wrong word choice.

She said, "I knew I was in love with you the minute you fell out of the stupid closet at the rehearsal dinner. It didn't take me a fucking fortnight to get to 'possibly.'"

Hope shot through him, even as he opened his mouth to defend himself. If she'd been in love with him at the rehearsal dinner, she had to still have feelings for him, right? And why the hell hadn't she said anything that night? He said, "If I'm Darcy in the rain, then you're Mr. Smith, too stubborn to hear what I'm trying to tell you as you ramble on about the way I worded my feelings."

She squinted at him. "Who in the hell is Mr. Smith?"

"Boiled fucking potatoes are an exemplary vegetable—*that* is Mr. Smith!"

"Wait." Her mouth formed a big, gaping O. "Are you calling me Mr. *Collins*?"

He nodded and said, "I'm trying to tell you something, but you're too caught up in your own thoughts and opinions about everything to hear my words, *Mr. Collins.*"

Jack couldn't believe he was communicating in Hallie's bizarro language, but they were talking, and she was finally listening, so he was going to roll with it.

Hallie

Hallie's mind raced as she listened to him insult her in the most wonderful way. She still felt hot and angry, but she also felt like something was happening.

He said, "Forgive me for not wanting to put a label on my feelings, but I don't know shit about love, okay? All I know is that you've ruined every single thing about my life."

She scoffed. "*I* have?"

"*Yes.*" He swallowed and said, "I can't drive by a Burger King without thinking of french fries in bed; I can't hear a British person speak without remembering your fucking awful accent; I can't see a diamond ad without picturing your stupid grinning face at the Borsheim's counter; and I can't hear my phone buzz without wishing it would be some asinine text from you."

"Jack." She felt a little light-headed. It wasn't a romantic confession of undying love, but it was everything she'd ever wanted.

He said, "Everything in my life was fine before, but now it's so different and I hate it."

"I hate it, too," she said, stepping just a tiny bit closer.

He ran his thumb over her wet cheek. "I'm so sorry I haven't called you."

She shivered. "Me, too."

"I know I've screwed everything up, Hal," he said as he pushed her wet hair off her forehead. "But I miss you so much I can hardly breathe."

"Me, too," she repeated.

"And I know I didn't say it the right way, but I am *so* in love with you. And not just *in* love with you, by the way. I also like you more than anyone else in the world. You're funny and smart and beautiful, and whenever anything happens to me, funny, awful, or wonderful, you're the first person I want to tell."

She laughed as her eyes filled with tears again. "Oh, my God, did our 'its' get switched?"

His face came closer, his eyes seeming to get brighter as he, too, remembered their conversation about what they'd been looking for in a partner. He said, "Well, that would mean that you feel like I complete you."

She wasn't going to say it, but she raised her chin. She looked into his dark blue eyes and said, "Yeah, it would."

He made a noise that was somewhere between an exhale, a laugh, and a groan before he softly placed his fingers under her chin, raising her head as he lowered his. It felt like coming home when his lips were on hers and she was breathing his breath.

It turned hot fast—teeth, tongues, and wild, seeking mouths—and Hallie was down for all of it as the rain continued to pour around them. She raised her arms to his shoulders and she pressed her rain-soaked self against him, needing to be closer. She was lost in every little bit of Jack Marshall. He pulled back slightly, looked down at her, and said, "There's a great little taco place down the street. Do you want to grab a bite and talk?"

She nodded. "I'd like that."

He pointed to the Urban Outfitters across the street. "Can I buy you a dry outfit first?"

"That would be lovely." Hallie grinned as he grabbed her hand, and they stepped back out into the rain and started walking in that direction. She yelled over the rain, "Thank you."

"Anytime," he replied, also yelling over the downpour.

"I'm buying a dry outfit for you, too," Hallie said, "and you have to wear whatever I choose, okay?"

He didn't answer as they sprinted across the street, and she assumed he hadn't heard her over the deluge. But as soon as he threw open the door to Urban Outfitters and they both got inside, he pulled her to a stop. His mouth slid into his wide, full-throttle smile as they both pushed back their hair and wiped their dripping faces, and Hallie felt herself warming from the inside out when he said, "Hallie Piper, I am yours. Dress me however you see fit."

Jack

"I don't think you can be mad at me ever again." Jack took a sip of his beer and gave the Taco Hut waitress a polite smile.

She was looking at him and openly laughing as she set down their food. "I think I've earned your eternal forgiveness."

Hallie shook her head seriously, but her eyes were dancing when she said, "You think just because you're wearing that, we're square?"

He stood, just so she could look again at what she'd done. Animal-print workout pants, crop top, fuchsia pashmina, yellow Chuck Taylors, and a red fedora with a patch that said *EAT ME*. He did a spin and held up his hands, waiting for an answer, and Hallie started laughing again.

"I can't believe you wore it."

"Of course I wore it," he said, sitting back down and giving her a look. He seriously would dress like that every day if it meant he could have her. "I love you."

She rolled her eyes and teased, "Are you sure, though? Maybe you just *think* you love me."

As hard as it had been for him to get his head around his feelings, everything—just like that—had become crystal clear. Maybe it was her absence in his life for the past couple of weeks, but he suspected it was common sense kicking in after being late as fuck to the party.

"Listen, Tiny Bartender." He grabbed the plate of nachos and slid it in front of her, because they both knew she loved selecting the first chip. "You have bewitched me body and soul, and I love you three times. Please tell me my hands are cold so we can get on with our lives already."

She picked a chip that was dead center, covered in beef and cheese. As she carefully lifted it, trying not to lose any of the red onions (but she always did), she said, "But what if I only *think* your hands are cold, Jack? I mean, how can I be sure?"

"You're never going to let this go, are you?" he asked, loving her stupid grin as she lorded his screwup over him.

She shook her head, and her grin turned softer. Less teasing, more sweet. "I'm going to be bringing this up for a long, long time."

There was a promise in her words, and Jack felt like the luckiest guy in the world.

So he pulled out his phone.

Jack: I'm on a date, and I think she's The One. Is it bad form to rush her through dinner because I'm dying to get her in the sack?

He watched her pull her phone out of her pocket, read the message, and smile.

She texted quickly.

Hallie: Seriously, dipshit, "in the sack" is awful.

Was it weird that he kind of wanted to cry with happiness?

He responded with: How about "I'm dying to do the deed with her"?

Hallie: I feel like that implies you want her to help you murder someone.

Jack: I've got it. I'm dying to engage with her in the physical act of love.

"Put the phone down before I puke," Hallie said, setting her phone on the table and laughing as she took a bite of her chip. "I know your date, and she's all-in for getting railed after dinner. So hurry up and eat."

He set down the phone, grabbed his fork, and scooped half of the entire nacho platter onto his plate. "From your lips to Ditka's ears."

EPILOGUE

Christmas Eve

"This is amazing!" Jack's dad kept staring at the baseball, turning it around in his hand so he could see all the signatures. "I can't believe you got me this, Jackie boy! Did you see it, Will?"

Hallie and Jack shared a grin from where they were sitting on the floor by the Christmas tree. Since they'd both found each other on the app at the same time, he won the ball and she won his airline miles.

"Yeah, Dad, I saw it," Jack's brother said, muttering *Jackie boy* under his breath like it was an obscenity.

"I knitted you a scarf with my own hands," Olivia said, glaring at her dad from her spot on the couch beside Colin. "But sure, a stupid baseball is amazing."

"You don't get it," Jack said, shaking his head. "You weren't there."

"Because you didn't invite me," Olivia said.

"You hate baseball."

"Doesn't mean I wouldn't like to be invited," she said, rolling her eyes. "Assbags."

"Language, Olivia," Jack's mom said, looking at Hallie with wide eyes like she was shocked by what Olivia had said. "I apologize for her."

"It's okay," Hallie said.

"Yeah, Hal curses like a damn sailor," Jack teased.

"I do not!"

"Jackson Alan," his mother warned, "knock it off."

Hallie's mouth dropped open before she whispered, "Your name is Jackson Alan? Like the country singer, only flipped?"

"My mother loves country music," he said, sounding embarrassed.

They had Christmas Eve dinner with his family, and when they were finally finished and on the way home, Jack said, "Your present is in the glove box if you want it."

"Classy," she said, yanking open the glove box as fast as she could.

She didn't see anything wrapped in holiday paper, but there was a manila envelope with her name on it. She glanced over at him and said, "If you're suing me for something, Marshall, I swear to God I will cut you."

"Open it," he said.

She ran a finger under the seal, then reached in a hand and pulled out the papers. She started flipping through them, one by one, and she was blinking back tears by the time she figured it out.

"You're taking me back to Vail?" It looked like he'd made reservations for the same room they'd been in the first time, only this time they were getting there by train. "For *seven nights*?"

"Ten-day trip total." He glanced over, put his hand on her knee, and said, "It was the best vacation I've ever been on, except for the whole terrified-of-blowing-my-cover-and-losing-my-best-friend stress. So how about we go back without all the worry and family and ex-boyfriend?"

"This is the very best present ever!" she squealed, clasping all the paperwork to her chest with one hand and putting her other hand over his. "Thank you, Jack."

That's only part of the present, he thought, picturing the ring box in his closet as she teasingly rained kisses over his face while he drove. He knew it was probably too soon, but he also couldn't stop himself. Hallie was everything he'd never known he wanted, and it seemed unwise for him to drag his feet when his forever girl was right there in front of him.

"You're welcome," he said, watching the neighborhood Christmas lights rush by as he drove.

"You have to wait until Christmas morning," Hallie said, turning up the Michael Bublé song playing on the radio, "for your best present ever."

And it occurred to him, when he woke up under the Christmas tree the next morning with Hallie's cat sitting on his neck and her knee in his back, that he already had it.

ACKNOWLEDGMENTS

Thank YOU, reader of this book, for reading this book! You are a part of my dream come true and I'm forever grateful. Seriously. I don't want to sound like a creep, but I love you, man.

Thank you to Kim Lionetti, for putting up with my exclamation point–laden emails and for being a genuinely great human whom I adore. You are more than I knew I needed in an agent and I'm so lucky to have you.

Angela Kim—your title should be Super Editor, or perhaps something like Vice President of Awesome Editing. (You're good enough to be president, but who wants that job, right?) I love working with you and am thrilled that the party isn't over.

The whole Berkley team, honestly, but especially Bridget O'Toole, Chelsea Pascoe, and Hannah Engler; thank you so much for working so damn hard. And Nathan Burton—I love your covers so much. Please never say no to us because I will cry big, fat tears of sadness (and I'm an ugly crier).

Thank you so much to Bookstagram and BookTok. You are incredible creators, doing amazing work in the name of books, and we don't deserve you. Special thanks to Hailie

Barber, Haley Pham, and Larissa Cambusano for being especially kind to my little babies.

And THE BERKLETES. I adore you all so much, and I can't quite believe I get to call you my friends. Please don't ever kick me out of your club.

Random human beings who make me happy: Lori Anderjaska, Anderson Raccoon Jones, Cleo, @lizwesnation, Caryn, Carla, Aliza, Chaitanya; messages from you make my days brighter. Thank you for being you.

Also—my favorite Minnesota relatives, the Kirchners: I just felt like I should mention you here because we had a blast visiting you, we love you, and I swear we didn't mean to bring you COVID.

And the family [Alexa, play "We Are Family" by Sister Sledge]:

Thank you, Mom, for everything. Without you, none of this would've happened for me. I love you more than you'll ever know.

Dad—I miss you every day.

MaryLee—you truly are the NICEST person in the world, the Good Sister, and I can't wait for our next road trip.

Cass, Ty, Matt, Joey, and Kate—remember that time I half-listened to you while working on my laptop? Yeah, I'm sorry. For all those times. But I'm sure you got away with a lot when I was handing out "uh-huhs" willy-nilly, so we're good, right? You are my favorite people and I tell everyone we're best friends.

And lastly, Kevin. I dedicated this book to you, so I feel like I don't really have to add anything more, do I? I mean, I like the way you're happiest when you're reading books outside. I like the way you tell me to drive defensively and watch out for inattentive drivers EVERY TIME I leave the house. I like the way you don't seem to mind that I suck at homemaker-ing. I think I like every little thing about you. Thanks for being cool.

Keep reading for an excerpt from

HAPPILY NEVER AFTER

from Berkley!

Sophie

The moment my dad raised my veil, kissed my cheek, and handed me off to Stuart, I wanted to throw up.

No—first, I wanted to punch my groom right in his besotted smile.

Then I wanted to vomit.

Instead, I took his arm and grinned back at him like a good bride.

The pastor started speaking, launching into his cookie-cutter TED Talk about true love, and my heart was racing as I waited. I swear I could feel four hundred sets of eyes burning into the back of my Jacqueline Firkins wedding gown as I heard nothing but the sound of my panicked pulse, pounding through my veins and reverberating in my eardrums.

Was he already there, seated among the guests? Was he going to burst through the doors, yelling?

And—God—what if he was a no-show?

The photographer, kneeling just to my right, took a photo

of my face as I listened to Pastor Pete's love lies, so I turned up my lips and attempted to project bridal joy.

"You look so nervous," Stuart whispered, giving me a small smile.

I honestly don't know how I didn't throat-punch him at that moment.

"Welcome, loved ones," the pastor said, beaming at the congregation as he spoke. "We are gathered here today to join together Sophie and Stuart in holy matrimony."

I felt my breath hitch, unsteady, as he kept yammering, leading us closer to the moment. *Oh, please, oh, please, oh, please*, I thought, panic tightening my chest. With every word he spoke, my anxiety grew.

Stuart squeezed my trembling hand, the ever-supportive fiancé, and I squeezed back hard enough to make him look at me.

"Should anyone present know of any reason that this couple should not be joined in holy matrimony, speak now or forever hold your—"

"I do."

A collective gasp shot through the large chapel, and when I turned around, the man standing up was not at all what I expected. He was big and tall and impeccably dressed: charcoal suit, white shirt, gray tie, and matching pocket square. He looked like Henry Cavill's stunt double or something, but with darker hair and more intense eyes.

Honestly, I'd imagined he would be a party bro, like Vince Vaughn in *Wedding Crashers*, but this man looked more like he belonged in a boardroom.

"So sorry to interrupt," he said in a smooth, deep voice, "but these two should absolutely *not* be married."

"Who is that?" Stuart hissed, daring to give *me* an accusing stare as a low rumble of whispers emanated from the pews.

"Oh, she doesn't know me, Stuart," the man said, looking one hundred percent comfortable in his uncomfortable role. He raised one dark eyebrow and added, "But my friend Becca knows *you*."

I gasped, my response entirely authentic even though I'd actually practiced it beforehand. I'd known this man was coming, but I hadn't expected him to be so . . .

Good.

The man was *good*. The way he spoke made me feel just as shocked as I'd been two nights ago, when I'd discovered Stuart's *Becca* on his phone.

"Listen, pal, I don't know—"

"Stuart. Shut up." The man looked down at his wrist and straightened his cuff, as if the mere sight of Stuart bored him. "The lovely Sophie deserves so much more than a cheater for a husband. I would imagine most of us here know it isn't the first time; wasn't there a Chloe last year?"

"I don't know who you are, but this is *bullshit*." Stuart's face was red as he glared at the man, and then his darting eyes came back to me. I looked at his face, remembering how it'd looked when he'd sobbingly begged my forgiveness over his Chloe transgression, and he actually had the gall to say to me, "You know it's not true, right?"

My gut burned as he feigned innocence and I said, "How would I know that? Isn't Becca the name of the girl who texted you in the middle of the night, and you said it was a wrong number?"

"It *was* a wrong number," he said with wild eyes. "This guy is obviously trying to ruin our day, and you're letting him, Soph."

"Then give me your phone," I said calmly, and Pastor Pete pulled at his collar.

"What?" Stuart's flushed face twisted and he glanced at the congregation as though looking for backup.

"If you have nothing to hide," The Objector said, still standing and talking in that deep, steady voice like this whole scenario was completely normal, "just give her the phone, Stuart."

"That's it, fucker!" Stuart yelled, rushing toward the guy. All hell broke loose as his groomsmen followed, though it was unclear if they were trying to hold him back or incite the forthcoming brawl.

It was a cacophony of male yelling and gray tuxedos in motion.

His mother yelled, "Stuart, no!"

Just as Stuart punched The Objector square in the face.

"Oh, my God," I said to no one in particular, watching in disbelief as The Objector took the punch without his body moving, as if he hadn't even felt it.

Stuart's father looked right at me as he loudly muttered, "Jesus Christ."

And Pastor Pete apparently forgot that his lapel mike was on because he sighed and said, "Are you fucking kidding me?"

"To dodging the Stuart bullet," Emma said, holding up her shot glass.

"To dodging Stuart," I repeated, tossing back the Cuervo.

It burned going down—*man, I hate tequila*—but I welcomed its effects. My head was spinning from the wedding collapse, and I desperately wished for impairment of any sort. It'd been four hours since the ceremony brawl and an hour since Stuart had removed his things from the honeymoon suite, yet I still felt like everything had just happened.

"Whoo!" Emma shouted, slamming her glass down on the bar.

Yes, she is one shot ahead of me and way more relaxed.

The honeymoon suite had a fully stocked bar between the two balcony doors, and we'd been bellied up to it since the moment Stuart had left.

"I still cannot believe how perfectly it went down," she said, giving her head a shake. "I mean, technically it's exactly what we paid for, but the dude made everyone at the ceremony *haaaate* Cheating Stuart and totally sympathize with you."

Cheating Stuart. I appreciated her villainizing him—that's what friends did, after all—but I was still devastated by Stu's infidelity. Yes, he'd cheated in the past, so I hadn't been completely blindsided, but I'd wholeheartedly believed that it was a one-time mistake and I'd chugged the Kool-Aid of happily-ever-after like a damn fool.

Until I saw his phone two nights ago.

"I'm just *so* relieved the canceled-wedding blame falls solely on Stuart instead of me and my parents," I said, leaning forward on my stool to grab a Twinkie off the bar.

Until Emma found her unorthodox solution, I'd been resigned to marrying Stuart and seeking an annulment after the fact. I knew it was totally bonkers to go through with the wedding, but it was the only way to ensure my father didn't pay the price for my failed relationship.

I unwrapped the snack and shook my head, still in awe. "I can't believe the plan actually worked."

"I know," Emma agreed, reaching around the box of Twinkies to grab more tequila. "Thank God for The Objector."

Max

I knocked on the hotel room door and waited.

This was my least favorite part.

More often than not, the bride who desperately wanted out of her own wedding was an emotional mess afterward, shocked by the end of what she thought would be the beginning of the rest of their lives together.

And I was not the reassuring kind. Back pats and handkerchiefs were not my thing.

I just needed my money and to get the hell out of there.

On a side note, who the hell doesn't have Venmo or PayPal?

I heard a noise just before the door flew open.

"The Objector!" A blonde in a Red Hot Chili Peppers T-shirt that went down to her knees grinned at me. "I'm Emma. We talked on the phone . . . ?"

Ah, yes. The bride's best friend. "So you're Tom's sister."

"Yes!" She grinned again, and I realized she was totally buzzed. "Come in!"

She held open the door and I followed her inside what was obviously the bridal suite. Huge living room, bedroom to the left that appeared to have rose petals everywhere, and a silver bucket on the coffee table with a bottle of champagne inside.

Typical.

I shifted my gaze to the right and saw the bar, with an

open bottle of tequila in the center and two shot glasses on the surface.

Less typical.

"You were *amazing*," she squealed, shaking her head like she couldn't believe it as she went right over to the bar and grabbed that bottle. "Tommy told me to trust him, but I had no idea that you'd be such a professional."

I smiled and muttered a thanks, but I was never sure how to respond to that. It wasn't like I was proud of my performance. I wasn't an actor looking for good reviews, for fuck's sake.

It was just something I occasionally did for money.

At that moment the balcony door flew open and the bride—Sophie—ran in, saying to Emma, "I need one more."

At least it *looked* like the bride.

Walking down the aisle, she'd been stunning. Her dark hair had been tidily piled on top of her head, accentuating her bright green eyes and long, graceful neck. She'd looked like everything I imagined a bride would want to look like on her wedding day.

Her hair now, though, was *everywhere*. Technically a lot of it was in a messy bun on top of her head, but long strands of curly hair hung all around her face like she'd just wrestled a bear. She was no longer wearing any makeup, which made her look like a teenager, and she'd switched out the wedding gown for a Celtics jersey and leggings.

She stopped in her tracks when she saw me, and then a big smile slid across her face. "You. Are. My. Hero."

I opened my mouth to speak, but she cut me off with an index finger. "Gimme one sec. I have to finish a project."

I watched in disbelief as Emma tossed her a Hostess Twinkie, and then she disappeared back out onto the balcony.

"Do I want to know?" I asked, my eyes still on the sliding door.

"Twinkies won't hurt the Volvo's paint, so it's a harmless crime," she said, turning to look at the bottles of liquor on the shelf behind the bar. "That's all you need to know."

I contemplated just exiting the hotel room at that moment, because I didn't need the hassle of whatever this was, especially when it was just past seven and I was starving.

But when I saw the bride pull her arm back and launch that snack cake off the balcony like a professional quarterback, I decided to stick around for another minute.

"Want a drink?" Emma asked, looking ready to pour herself a tequila shooter.

Before I could answer, the bride came back inside, saying as she closed the sliding door behind her, "We need to switch to something else."

"What? Why?" Emma asked, pouting. She held up the bottle of tequila and said, "Jose is our friend."

"Nope." The bride shook her head and said, "As much as I want to get ripped, I don't want to end up with my head in a hotel toilet. Pretty sure that's how you get dysentery."

Pretty sure that isn't right, I said under my breath.

"Schnapps, maybe?" Emma asked.

"Objector's choice," Sophie said, her lips turning up into a little smile as she tilted her head and looked in my direction. *Yeah, she heard me.* "What should we drink?"

"Whiskey," I said, wondering what her usual drink of choice was. Because when she was dressed as a bride, I would've pegged her as a cosmo drinker, perhaps someone who enjoyed a nice chardonnay. But this Twinkie-tossing, wild-eyed girl was a bit of a mystery. "Unless you're dialing back to something lighter."

"Not at all," she said, pulling the elastic from her hair and shaking out the half-bun. "But tequila punches too hard."

"Have a shot with us, Objector," Emma said, or rather, squealed. "The pizza's already on the way."

"First of all, you *have* to stop calling me that."

"Why?" Sophie asked, putting her hands on her hips and screwing her eyebrows together. "What's your real name again?"

"Max," I said.

"Max," she repeated, raising her eyes to the ceiling as if it held an opinion on my name. "I mean, that's a fine name and all, but The Objector is next level."

"It makes me sound like an off-brand superhero."

She snorted a little laugh, and I noticed her freckles when she crinkled her nose. "Like a lawyer who got stuck in radio-active waste, right?"

"Exactly," I agreed.

"Which whiskey, Objector?" Emma asked, gesturing toward the bar. "You're drinking with us, right?"

"Thank you, but I can't—"

"Of *course* he isn't," Sophie said, rolling her eyes and climbing onto one of the two barstools. "He is a man, and it's their job to disappoint us. Please pour me a shot, Em."

"Didn't you just call me your hero?" I asked, sliding my hands into my pockets as she ignored me and reached for the shot glass. "Like two minutes ago?"

"Your actions *were* heroic and I'm very grateful," she said, circling a perfectly manicured fingernail over the top of the tiny glass and turning her back to me. "But I said what I said. Emma, my love, will you pour my whiskey shooter, please?"

Something about the all-knowing way she said it and her absolute dismissal of me made me shrug out of my jacket, toss it on the sofa, and grab the stool beside her.

"Make that two, please."

Photo by Jackson Okun

LYNN PAINTER lives in Omaha, Nebraska, with her husband and pack of wild kids. She is a community columnist for the *Omaha World-Herald*, as well as a regular blogger for their parenting section. When she isn't reading or writing, she can be found eating her feelings and shotgunning cans of Red Bull.

VISIT THE AUTHOR ONLINE

LynnPainter.com

LynnPainterBooks

LAPainterBooks

LAPainter

Ready to find
your next great read?

Let us help.

Visit prh.com/nextread